WHAT IT

SEEMS

ALSO BY EMILY BLEEKER

Wreckage

When I'm Gone

Working Fire

The Waiting Room

WHAT IT SEEMS

SEEMS

A NOVEL

EMILY BLEEKER

LAKE UNION

PUBLISHING

Text copyright © 2020 by Emily Bleeker
All rights reserved.

Published by Lake Union Publishing, Seattle

www.apub.com

Amazon, the Amazon logo, and Lake Union Publishing are trademarks of Amazon.com, Inc., or its affiliates.

ISBN-13: 9781542043748
ISBN-10: 1542043743

Cover design by Rex Bonomelli

Printed in the United States of America

To my dear friend Kelli: Fate brought us together. Writing brought us closer. Life bonded us forever. You're not getting rid of me anytime soon . . .

CHAPTER 1

I run my hand over my ever-swelling belly. The maternity dress is ill fitting. And it's purple. I feel more like a love-starved singing dinosaur than a grown woman.

We should get a nicer dress, I think, scanning the rack of maternity wear in front of me. It would be useful for days like today when Mother wants to work Nordstrom Rack. This purple monstrosity is good enough for Target runs or even an occasional Walgreens, but anything by the Wharf should require additional attention to detail.

The woman at the service desk shifts, and I catch the movement out of the corner of my eye. She's watching me—closely. Much closer than I like. *Mother's rule number one of leaving the house: never get too close.* Which includes avoiding eye contact, especially in the fancy stores. Usually no one looks twice at me, just a young mom-to-be running her fingers over baby clothes or lingering near the maternity bras as casually as possible. But today it's not just the service desk woman; there is someone else rifling through the circular rack of clothing, checking prices and sizes. Another expectant mother walks around the circumference, methodically pulling out a few new maternity dresses, probably to take them to the changing room, though how she thinks she'll be able to tell if the dresses will fit in a few months, I don't know.

"When are you due?" the woman asks, and I jump at the sound of her voice. I glance up briefly so I don't seem like a weirdo. She has long, beautiful blond hair pulled back in a ponytail and shocking blue eye shadow, making her deep aquamarine eyes shine like they're backlit. I want to ask her what it's like to be that beautiful, or at least compliment her eyes, but I can't. The imagined words collect in my mouth, and I swallow them down. If eye contact is restricted, then conversation is forbidden.

But there have to be exceptions, or at least that was the point I kept trying to make Mother understand. It would be weird if a gloomy, silent twenty-year-old sulked her way through the maternity department. I have to say *something*.

Rule number two of leaving the house: keep it simple.

"The end of June," I answer with as little hesitation as possible, getting another glimpse of the woman's lovely eyes. "And you?" I ask in return, trying to mimic other conversations I've observed. I mean, I don't meet a lot of pregnant women in real life, but I've done enough research online to know what I'm talking about. Or at least I think I have. I pick up another dress without looking at it and put it over my arm to try on, hoping this isn't the worst mistake of my life. If Mother knew, she'd kill me. The pile on my arm is heavy, and I have to shift my belly to one side to get comfortable again.

"Lucky. This little one is cooking till October. My mother-in-law says it's bad luck to even be shopping yet, but what can I say? The rubber band trick with my jeans isn't working anymore. I need real maternity clothes." She pats the tiny swell above her waistband that could just as easily be the result of a large lunch rather than a growing human. "I'm new in the area. It would be nice to know some other moms. My name is Kelly." She puts out her hand.

I stare at it, my heart beating like it does when I scrub the kitchen floor. It would be so easy. I could shake her hand, tell her my name, make a friend, connect with another human being. It sounds invigorating and terrifying at the same time. What am I trying to do, break *all* the rules? I mean, this is the main rule, the one that trumps all others, and I'm just gonna break it? It echoes in my head, and it's Mother's voice I hear.

Rule number three: tell the truth as often as possible.

What the heck do I have to lose? I mean, I don't want to be rude, right? I juggle the clothes in my hands and readjust the bag strap before touching my fingertips to Kelly's palm, unsure of how to shake hands convincingly. "Tara."

My cheeks burn, and I'm sure she can see the embarrassment splashed across my face. If Mother came out of the dressing room, if she saw me right now, it would mean punishment.

Usually I'm pretty good at dodging Mother's punishments. I'm not a silly little girl anymore. It used to be penance in the closet for a week, or at least it seemed like a week; it was hard to tell when it came to darkness. I went through "rebellious phases" like any kid, or at least that's what Mother called them. It was easy to get too lazy, too prideful, too arrogant. I was so stupid back then, pushing against Mother's rules, thinking this time I could change them and then . . . bam. Mother always knew the right way to inflict pain; usually it was without laying a single hand on me. Dolls had been burned. Sheets of handwritten stories torn to shreds. I almost preferred it when she used to spank me. But ever since the computer was put in my room, I've been the perfect angel. Even when I want to yell that I'm an adult, or when I want to remind her that no one is perfect, or that one day I'd been throwing up all night and felt too sick to get out of bed, put on the fake belly, and do a store run—I hold my tongue. I can't lose the computer.

"Nice to meet you, but I . . . I have to go." I pull my hand away and put it under the clothes on my arm, jerking my head in the direction of the changing rooms. "Mother . . . I mean . . . my mom is waiting for me."

The woman squints and takes an aggressive step toward me, her once beautiful eyes turning dark and fierce. Her voice is suddenly low and urgent.

"They know you're shoplifting. They saw you put the perfume in your bag, and they called the police. I was supposed to keep you occupied, but . . . you seem like a nice girl."

No. Alarm bells clang around inside my head. *Caught. Caught. Caught. Caught.* It's the worst thing that can ever happen. If I am caught . . . It's the worst infraction possible.

Dang it. A cold sweat breaks out at my temples when I put it all together. Kelly isn't another shopper; she's a loss prevention officer. Mother warned me about those, said they carried hidden Tasers. She said they didn't understand how hard it was to get by as a single mom in this world. Said they were heartless, evil, cunning.

My mouth is suddenly dry. I open it, try to talk, try to think of some kind of excuse, but nothing comes. Mother is gonna be furious. Kelly continues in an insistent, hushed whisper.

"Just put the bottles back and leave. No one will stop you." She pauses, a flash of concern breaking out on her hardened face with its pierced lips; maybe she stifles a sigh. "You've got your baby to think of."

I nod, glancing down at my belly. Mother said strangers were dangerous. Mother said they were unkind. Mother said everyone wanted to hurt me. Mother said women like Kelly would put me in jail for the rest of my life.

I don't look up. Each hanger hits the bar with a clink as I put the items back on the rack, making me think of the sound of prison gates closing. My hands are empty except for the ragged reusable Walgreens tote I've been carrying under the curtain of clothes. It's almost like I'm watching from another part of the room as I place the bag on the floor, the weight of hundreds of dollars of stolen perfume dropping as soon as I let go of the handle.

"They're all in there," I manage to mumble, placing a hand over my belly protectively. The bag is clean. It has no identifying information, no wallet or name written inside. Gosh, I don't even *have* ID if they do arrest me. So, yeah, I give up the bag and its contents gladly in exchange for freedom, even if it means facing Mother's anger.

"That's a good choice," the loss prevention officer says, looking me over one last time, no longer seeming sympathetic.

"Yes, ma'am." I can't stop rubbing my belly, maybe out of habit but also out of fear and discomfort. I don't want to go to prison. Mother says she'll never help if I get arrested, says I'd deserve it 'cause I can be careless. She says that if I ever get caught, she'll burn all my stuff, remove every piece of evidence that I ever existed. Says she'll make "Tara" disappear.

"Go find your mother," Kelly orders, picking up the bag of stolen goods. "And you tell her never to come back here again."

She takes a few steps away from me like she's giving me room to pass by. But it feels like a trap. Instead, I take two steps back and then spin on the ball of my foot. A million eyes, human and electronic, are watching, but I can't let anyone see the panic crawling up my back and gathering in my shoulders. We have to get out—now.

Mother is supposed to be in the changing room in the Women's section, waiting for my haul. I glance at my dollar-store digital watch—I'm fifteen minutes late. I'm never late for Mother anymore. To Mother, late is a synonym for failure or proof that I don't love her enough.

It makes me so mad, 'cause why else am I doing this? I'm not some criminal. I don't pilfer perfume and other stuff to sell it on eBay for a couple of bucks for myself. I do all of this because I love Mother. I owe her everything. She took me in after my mom got arrested. She adopted me when my birth parents didn't want me back.

But even when what she wants me to do is technically illegal, I can't seem to get rid of it—this craving to please. I hate it. So when Mother gives me an order, I ignore my conscience and shove perfume into bags and stuff athletic wear up my dress, and she slips sunglasses into my purse, and then I sell it all online. It's the family business.

Finally at the dressing rooms, out of breath, heart pounding, I rush through the open doorway. Turning the corner, I catch my image in the three-sided mirror all the fancier department stores put at the end of their dressing rooms. Mother forbids mirrors at home, which I don't get 'cause I'm not even close to beautiful. I don't need a mirror to tell me that, but my reflection reminds me that my mental image of myself is accurate.

My face is covered in red blotches, a few raised to whiteheads. With my bulging belly and my greasy, stringy hair, it's clear—Mother is right. I have no place to go. No one would want me.

"Mother," I whisper, happy to look away from the gross stranger in the mirror. Usually Mother picks the third stall from the back on the left-hand side. She'll wait there with her own haul of stolen goods, and then we'll smuggle them out, maybe even buying one or two items to throw off the store employees.

But today is different. I lean over, nearly crawling on the floor, looking for Mother's sensible walking shoes under the changing-room doors. She got them a few weeks ago from a Target where she took off her old, tattered Nikes, put on the new shoes, placed the other pair in the box, and, without blinking, returned the box to the shelf and then walked out the sliding glass doors.

"Mother!"

"Back here, sweetie!" she calls, her voice the singsongy "I love you" tone she uses only when other people are around. It is fake, so fake. I'm sure anyone listening will hear the artificial sweetness that coats each word, but if I'm being honest—I like it. It reminds me of a time when my parents seemed to love me. Those gauzy, ancient memories that I'm pretty sure are nearly all fantasy have faded to near nothingness over time, but there are still moments when I let myself pretend I'm one of the lucky ones.

"Coming, Mother," I call back. I quickly tap on the dressing-room door, and it swings wide, Mother behind it. Her face tells the opposite story of her voice. There's no love or care there, only fury. Her tightly permed silvery-white hair bounces at the ends but is weighed down from products to the roots. The deep creases on her face hang low, along with her frown, her icy-blue eyes pale with anger.

"Get in here, you fool," she says under her breath. No one else is in the changing room, but it doesn't matter; Mother never says her hurtful words loudly, even at home. When I was little, my parents would some-times yell at each other late at night when I was supposed to be sleep-ing. I'd curl up in a ball under the covers and pray that we could have a happy family with no yelling. But when Mother took me in at eight, I learned that quiet doesn't mean calm and silent doesn't mean safe.

"I'm sorry, Mother. I'm sorry I—"

"Lift up your dress," she orders, not even listening to a word.

"No, we can't, we have to go." I cover my belly.

"Go?" Mother's hands freeze, filled with boxed jewelry sets. She looks at me like she's seeing me fully for the first time. "Wait. Where is your bag?"

"I . . ." I don't even know how to form the words. Tears are coming, but I can't cry. That would be the worst thing—to cry. "We have to go."

"You got caught, didn't you?" she asks, taking a step back and put-ting the boxes on the simple wooden bench behind her. With her back turned, it's hard to tell what's going on in Mother's mind. I want to say that it's not my fault or find a nice way to explain away my failure, but there isn't time. Not if we're going to get out of the store before the police show up.

"They've called the police, but Kelly says we can go if we don't take anything and never come back."

"Kelly?" Mother stalks around, the piles of clothing beside her shuddering with the sudden movement. "You talked to someone? Oh,

Tara." She shakes her head and reaches for her belt buckle. That belt . . . she hasn't used the belt in years.

"She talked to *me*, I swear. I was in Maternity, and she was being nice because of . . . you know." I gesture to my swollen midsection.

"Stop acting like you're some kind of mother. You don't know what it means to be a mother. You are just a child, playacting. Lift up your dress, Tara." Mother steps closer; the smell of cigarette smoke and coffee billows across my cheek in a familiar breeze that always makes me gag.

I have to obey. The flowy rayon fabric is silky in my fingers as I lift the dress one inch at a time until my abdomen is exposed. A large prosthesis curves out from my body. A zipper sits on one side of the contraption. Mother used to wear the belly, but she's too old and started to draw attention with her age and the protruding midsection, so now it's my turn. For some reason it always makes me sad that the baby I pretend to caress and carry is fictional. I have no idea what it's like to really be pregnant. Not now. Not ever, if Mother has anything to do with it.

Mother grabs a few handfuls of stolen goods—necklaces, earrings, wallets, and gloves—and shoves them into the zippered opening. Usually I walk into a changing room five months pregnant and walk out ready to pop, but today Mother doesn't push the belly to its limit. In two minutes flat she's filled the cavern and zipped it back up before I drop my dress into place.

"That will have to do." She sighs, shaping the fake belly expertly with the sides of her hands. "Come on. Go." She points to the changing-room door. There are still plenty of items on the bench behind her. Hopefully Kelly will take the full dressing room and my empty hands as evidence of reform.

On the way out of the store, Mother slips her arm through mine and holds on tight like an elderly grandmother who needs support to keep from falling. If only I was as talented at acting as Mother is. But I'm sure misery is written all over my splotchy, mortified face. Before foster care, all I ever wanted to do was play with friends and ride my bike. But after Mom and Dad went away, after I lost my baby brother and sister to some unknown relative who didn't want me, it was like all the sunlight had gone out of the world. I have no joy out here. The only true happiness I have ever felt is inside the walls of my bedroom after Mother has gone to sleep.

"Put your hand on your belly, dear," Mother stage directs through gritted teeth. And I do what Mother tells me to do, just like every other day of my life. Never mind that Mother will punish me when we get home for breaking so many of the rules, or that if we get caught, I am the only one concealing stolen merchandise, or that some logical voice that still exists inside my head tells me that I should get help and leave—I won't. How could I ever leave my Mother?

CHAPTER 2

Twelve years earlier

My head hurts, and something is wrapped around my arms and legs, making them burn. I'd look, but I don't want to open my eyes. The room is really dark; I can tell even through closed eyelids. Maybe the night-light is broken. I've always had one, the plug-in kind with a switch to turn it on and off, and one of those little light bulbs that screws right in. I've always told Daddy that I'm not really scared of the dark; I just need some light so I can go to the bathroom without knocking over the glass of water Mama always gives me at bedtime.

Mama doesn't like it when I make a mess, especially now that the twins are around. They cry so much more than I ever thought possible. All night long they fuss, whine, and whimper for no reason. Mrs. Stark gave me the stink eye in Language Arts the other day when I fell asleep during silent reading.

Most nights I shove my head under a pillow and wait for Mama or Daddy to get a bottle in the babies' mouths or change their diapers or something. Tonight is different—there is the pain in my head, but tonight it's also . . . silent. It's almost nice. It used to be like this all the time, but I've gotten used to the twins' squeals and the way Mom and Dad freak out when one of the squirmy little lumps needs something.

This room smells different too. It's a stale smell, like when we visit Mamaw's house in Atlanta. Her house is always so hot. We go in the summer, and the only room in the whole house with air-conditioning is her room. Mamaw didn't get her dusting done in her bedroom the last time we visited so no one was allowed in, no matter how many hours we'd been in a car and even with Mama's giant tummy. We all sat in her fancy front room that day, and my legs made slurping sounds every time I tried to get comfortable on the plastic coverings over her furniture.

But this isn't Mamaw's house. I try to remember, but it's fuzzy, and my head hurts so much. Last night, when it was very dark and I was still tired and the babies were crying, I slipped out of bed and tiptoed into the front room. Mama was there. I think she was crying.

"Mama, I can't sleep." I wanted her to tuck me into bed like old times. When I was little, she'd plop me in bed and sweep my bangs off my forehead. Then she'd sing in this cracky, wobbly voice that helped me go to sleep when Daddy was at work. But that didn't happen when I snuck out of my room last night. She had one baby in a bouncy seat and the other cradled in her arm, nursing, tears making Mama's face shine.

"Go back to sleep," Mama ordered. Her voice was so hard, angry, like she hated me.

"But I can't," I whined. "The babies are too loud."

"Sweetie." She huffed and then kept going. "I can't do anything about the noise. Your dad is at work already, and I'm doing the best I can . . . you . . . you . . ." Tears filled Mama's eyes, and a sob stopped her sentence in its tracks. The baby in the bouncy seat, Cory maybe, continued to cry, and my ears hurt from the high-pitched wailing.

"Can I have a snack?" My stomach grumbled. Mama said no dinner last night because I got sassy about setting the table. But she feeds the babies when they're hungry; she could feed me, right? But Mama's face didn't get soft or worried. It turned red, and she wrapped her fingers in the baby's nightclothes while taking a deep breath.

"GO . . . TO . . . BED!" Mama screamed in a new, scary voice, one I'd never heard, that startled Clara, the baby at her chest, enough to make her stop eating and stare as though she actually understood.

Mama's order shook the framed family photo above the couch. It hadn't been updated with the new portrait yet, just Mama, Daddy, and their little girl—me. The way it used to be. The way I wanted it to be. That smiling mommy in the picture didn't cry while holding babies. She didn't scream either. That mommy loved me.

Without moving an inch, I stood there, staring up at Mama, my bottom lip trembling, lonelier than I'd ever been in my whole life.

"I . . . I'm sorry, Mama . . . I was just hungry . . ."

But Mama didn't hear me. She was busy getting Clara to eat and pushing a pacifier in Cory's mouth . . . and that's the last full memory I have. I blink and grit my teeth, determined to recover more of the story, but the rest is almost as dark and shadowy as the room I'm in.

The pain in my head won't leave, and suddenly a stranger is beside me on what I think is a bed. Cool, calloused hands touch my arms and face. It's a like a knife in my skull. I want to open my eyes, see if Mama and Daddy are here too, 'cause it's not Mama or Daddy sitting on my bed. It's someone else—humming a song I've never heard before.

My eyelids are so thick I don't know how to force them open. I struggle against their weight, determined to get some answers. Scared. So scared. I concentrate so, so hard, and they finally crinkle up. I can feel every wrinkle and crease, and I immediately want to close them again—but I don't because I'm afraid of the darkness that awaits me there.

When I try to turn my head just the tiniest bit, the pain spreads through my skull and down my neck like the squirrels in my backyard, scrambling up the great oak tree to find acorns for winter. The hurt makes blackness tickle at the edges of my vision, and the room dims another notch.

"Oh, dear one, don't try to open your eyes. Rest." The stranger's voice, no longer singing, now coos tenderly right by my side. A breeze on my cheek and the slight dip in the mattress lets me know she's there—whoever *she* is. There's a staleness to her, like she bathed in smoke this morning or bought all her clothes from the crowded racks at the thrift store my mom takes me to sometimes for playclothes. My throat closes up. I might throw up right here in the bed, unable to move.

"I wanna go home," I tell her. My voice is tiny and breakable. This is not home or Mamaw's. "I wanna go *home*," I repeat, a little clearer, wetness gathering in my eyes. I want my own bed, babies crying and all that. I want Mama to make me feel better. I want Daddy to make me laugh.

"Little one, you don't remember, do you?" the woman says, her breath an even grosser version of her body odor. A nasty taste burns at the back of my throat.

I search my memories. The babies crying, Mama crying, Mama yelling . . . my room . . . There is something else there on the edges of it all. Angry that Mama ignored me, hurt that the babies were so much more important to her . . . I decided to teach my parents a lesson. Only a few more images come through: Mama's face twisted, the stubborn stomping of my feet in my rain boots, the air making me shiver, streetlights, my bike, car, hard crack against the blacktop. Darkness.

"I tried to run away," I say, the images finally coming together into a story.

"Yes, dear," the voice confirms.

"But . . . but I fell down?" That is as far as the hazy memory takes me. Bike, car, pavement, darkness, people talking around me, bright lights, sharp pains in my arms, and a kind voice singing, always singing.

"You didn't fall, sweetie." Her fingers prod at the bandages along my forehead. "You were on your bike," the woman hints, still just out of my sight line.

"I ran away." I remember a little more. Speeding down the dimly lit sidewalks of my neighborhood, the predawn chill stinging at my cheeks. I *was* running away from . . . home . . . from Mama . . . from the babies . . . from everything. But I wasn't just running. Something was chasing me.

"Yes, dear. Yes. And then do you remember what happened? With your mother's car?"

Things are too fuzzy. The farther I ride my bike in my half dream/half memory, the more uncertain the memories become. The feelings are there more than the actual series of events. First anger, fury, then a deep sense of revenge. Finally, fear, terror, pain, and then in the end there is nothing. Blank as the screen when the TV is turned off.

"I don't remember."

"That's probably for the best . . ." The stranger's hand wraps around mine, pressing the bandages against my raw skin. "We can discuss it when you're better."

I whimper. I don't like the hand or the way the lady talks like she knows anything about me or my life. I'm trapped in her grip, which gets stronger with every passing moment, or maybe I'm running out of energy. But I want to see her, this woman behind the voice. A teacher? A nurse? I try to turn to my side, but pain runs up my spine and through my skull and screams at me to stop. But I won't. Not yet. Not till I see.

"Don't try to move, dear one. You should rest." There's a crinkle and rustle, and when my cheek finally reaches the cool, stiff sheets, the woman has turned away. All I can see through the darkness is a skinny lady, her hair light blond, almost white like a witch's. She is frightening but also frail looking, like the grass in the front yard last summer when it didn't rain for weeks and weeks, and my Fourth of July sparkler set off a small fire when I dropped it.

"Who are you?" I whisper, words still rubbing oddly in my throat and tumbling out of my mouth. The woman turns back from her task, something tubelike cradled in her free hand.

"You can call me Miss Lila." Her sweet but crooked smile reveals a yellowed row of dentures. Wrinkles ripple across her face like waves, and the light blue of her eyes is a clear colorlessness in the darkness. She's old, not Mamaw old, but principal old or teacher old.

Miss Lila turns to face me fully this time. She holds up the thin tube with a long needle at the end, like the ones the doctor used when he gave the twins shots at their three-month appointment. I don't want a shot. No one said anything about shots. I wiggle and then pull my hand away from Miss Lila. But it's useless. The needle plunges through my skin and deep into my flesh, like it's made of Play-Doh.

"Oh!" I gasp. The needle slips out of my arm.

Miss Lila leans in to give me a kiss on my forehead. I would pull away from her stringy hair and her strange smell, but a heady warmth spreads over me, and the edges of my world get droopy.

"Go to sleep, little one," she coos like Mama used to before the babies. Mama. All the old flashes of jealousy melt away, and all I long for is the safety of home.

"Miss Lila?" I force my mouth to say her name, not sure if I'm remembering it right. "Can I see my mommy?"

"Oh no, sweetie. I'm sorry, that's just not possible," Miss Lila says matter-of-factly, like I'm silly to even ask. She leaves the bed, taking the syringe with her, and settles back into an ancient-looking wooden chair.

"Why not?" My bottom lip trembles as a longing covers me like a blanket. Words are getting harder. Sleep is pulling me deep into an echoing cave.

"Because, dear one"—Miss Lila's voice bounces around me—"your mother was the one who did this to you."

CHAPTER 3

Present day

"No dinner for you. I'll decide your punishment by morning," Mother says with perfect calm as she closes the door to my bedroom. She'd been silent on the way home from Nordstrom Rack; the only sound in the empty cargo van was the clank of Mother's dentures clicking in and out of place over and over again. That quiet sound of fury frightens me as deeply as the rattle of a rattlesnake's tail.

"Yes, Mother," I whisper, head bowed, never daring to make eye contact when Mother is angry. The lock on my door scrapes shut from the hallway. That sound, that metal contraption that keeps me locked inside, is also a comforting sound of safety. When I'm locked in, I'm in my own world. When I'm locked in, I'm free.

As I settle into the faded peach comforter, my mind spins with the possibilities that tomorrow holds. Punishment. Mother calls it the refiner's fire. I close and open my hands. The tight white scars there still hurt on occasion. A reminder, she says, of the lessons I learned as a child. I'm usually able to avoid punishment. I've learned how to please Mother over the past twelve years. A happy Mother means a happy life.

My stomach growls. I'd better get used to it. No food—that's a given during punishment.

"Twelve years," I whisper, eyeing the row of dolls on my bed, their plastic, glass, or porcelain faces and faded half smiles. "Angela, can you believe it's been twelve years?" I lean over and place a strand of her red hair behind her glass ear, and then, as though it were part of my own body, I rest my hand on my fake belly, pretending that Angela is a sister or friend who is also trapped in the weird world I'm stuck living in. "Oh, I know you hate it when I wear this thing, but you know Mother."

I laugh and roll my eyes, jumping off the bed and tearing off the loose dress that's four sizes too big and hangs like a tent over my fake pregnancy. Yanking the straps off my shoulders, I let them drop down my arms, and the whole dense, smelly contraption that fits a lot like a one-piece bathing suit falls to the ground with a soft thunk. Stepping out one socked foot at a time, I kick it off. I'll have to hang it nicely before morning, but for now it sits in an off-colored fleshy lump on the floor. Now free, I drop onto the bed in my thin tank top and stretchy shorts, both damp with perspiration.

"Oh, it's so good to see you all." I sigh. The thought of morning is scary, but looking at my line of girls and one boy on the bed, it's like I'm with family. I scooch back until I'm propped up in line with the prettily placed dolls, hands on my flat, empty stomach.

I doubt I'll ever know what it's like to have a baby in there. Mother has warned me about the dangers and shame of pregnancy, but I still have a few memories of my baby brother and sister—my birth parents wanted them. They were loved and held and kissed by family and friends. We even had a party when they were born. But I was only a child, so maybe I didn't notice the rest.

They were three months old when my birth mom became overwhelmed by the burden of caring for the twins and me. Mother said she'd stopped feeding me and that I weighed only thirty pounds when I was placed in her care at eight years old. And when I tried to run away . . . I rub a lumpy spot on the back of my head where I hit the pavement twelve years ago. Mother said my birth mom claimed it was an accident, that she didn't see me crossing the street, that she was just so tired from the babies, but the police didn't believe her. In the end it was my birth father who signed me away when it became clear he'd be responsible for three children on his own.

I turn over on my bed with a huff, pressing my slim stomach into the mattress. I don't like to think about that day, and what's worse is I can't even remember most of it because of my head injury, only bits and pieces. Mother says it's best to forget, and I've found the only way to keep that loss from hurting unbearably is to avoid thinking of my "before" family. I slide my finger under the cotton rim, where Angela's stuffed body meets her fragile neck, and touch the silver band hidden there. My bracelet, the only thing I still claim as my own from when I was a child in that house.

I found it crumpled under my body, clasp broken, when I woke up after my shot that first day at Mother's and tucked it under my mattress. Even back then I think I knew I had to hide some things from Mother, for my own good. For hers too. Now Angela hides it inside her hollow neck and head. Mother still doesn't know. It's a secret shared with bits of fabric, glass, and stuffing.

"So, I almost got caught today," I say, in an audible but quiet whisper, too soft to be heard through the doors or thin walls. Saying the words out in the open feels good, like just proclaiming that fact makes it less likely to happen again. I prop my head up on my fist and eye the smallest doll at the very end of the row. She has a blue bow and short, curly brown hair.

"Shh, Carly, I don't need I told you so's. Mother picks the stores, not me. You know that." I swoop up the little-boy doll with a bow tie and a bowl cut. "I know, Jessie. I worry too." Jessie's doll body is stiff when I kiss the part in his hair and return him to his place in line.

"Yeah, she's pretty mad. I don't know what's going to happen now. Don't be scared, sweetie, I'll protect you." I tug on the one remaining braid of the blond doll with a hat on her head, trying not to remember what Mother did to Shelly the last time she got really angry.

Sometimes I realize how crazy it must look, the way I talk to my dolls. I don't do it in front of Mother, but she must hear me through the walls, because she likes to tell me I've lost my mind, and for a while I wondered if I had. But it's not like I really believe they're alive—I know I'm pretending. I know Angela isn't really talking to me and that Shelly didn't actually cry when Mother cut off her hair. They're make-believe—but they're also the only family I have anymore.

Besides, I've watched people on YouTube who make money playing with toys and recording the videos. Sure, I skip the videotaping part, but it's no different, right?

"Hey, boys and girls, stop. Stop fighting." While lost in my thoughts, I pretend a cacophony of worried chatter has broken out among the dolls. With glowering eyebrows and clenched teeth, I put on my best Mother voice and scold the little figures lined up before me.

"Come on, you know Mother loves me," I tell them firmly. "I'll make this okay. She won't hurt any of you, I promise. I'll make sure of it."

Mother loves me. Those words never feel right coming out of my mouth, but I still say them over and over again. Mother loves me. She keeps me safe in the house—because she loves me. She fixes my flaws—because she loves me. She steals and lies—because she loves me. But even when I say it or think it, I know that the only time I feel real love is with Angela, Carly, Sam, Shelly, and Jessie. And I'm pretty sure that's imaginary too.

"Who's ready for dinner?" I ask, ready to put all those feelings about Mother and the fear of what's coming in a mental box. I'm home with my family; now it's time to breathe. One good thing about Mother's silent anger is that I get a little more freedom and quiet than when she has me working twelve-hour days on eBay.

As I lower myself to my knees by the side of the bed, I am careful to keep my movements silent. Reaching far under the mattress, I search for the crinkle of plastic. Mother doesn't allow food after eight o'clock, but I'm always hungry. Always. And tonight, put to bed without dinner, my hunger is doubled. My body is long and slender, and the only sign that I'm a girl instead of a teenage boy is the annoying swell of my breasts that never goes away no matter how thin I get.

"Who's been playing around with our dinner? Carly? I see that smirk. Did you move the baggie?" I ask with a playful glare at the slightly askew, brown-haired doll that often plays the part of troublemaker in my stories. I try again, but obviously Carly hasn't moved the baggie of snacks. If it's gone, there's really only one other real possibility of who moved it. The thought of being discovered after keeping this secret for so long makes my stomach jolt like I've had a cup of burnt coffee from Mother's coffeemaker. I reset my position, wondering if my angle is off.

"Dang it, where is it?" I wonder out loud, not even pretending that Angela scolds me for my crass language.

Mother couldn't know, right? If she did, I'd already have been punished. Then again, she's hard to predict. Sometimes after a big haul from a store, she'll pull me into her arms, comb my hair, and tell me stories about when I was a little girl, first placed in her home as a foster child. Though I can hardly remember that time, I love the stories. When Mother is kind, I almost love her.

But then things can change so quickly. This is the most confusing part of my life—how fast it changes. One minute I'm Mother's little angel, and the next she's locking me in my room with no food, or breaking my favorite toy to teach me a lesson, or telling me in a calm, gentle voice all the ways I've failed her as a daughter. Those are the bad memories.

I dig in deeper between the mattress and the box spring. I have to find the bag of food. It *has* to be there. If it's gone . . . there is no second half of that sentence. If Mother already knows I'm hiding food, then tomorrow's discipline will be even worse than I've calculated.

"Here it is!" My fingers brush the crinkle of plastic. The bag of food. My heart rate drops instantly.

The bag, full of granola bars, boxes of raisins, and a few of the generic fruit snacks Mother got from the clearance shelf during her last grocery run, falls into my lap. I snuck the fruit snacks out of the garbage can after Mother called them candy, and even though they're getting stale and make my teeth ache, they're one of the highlights of my day.

"Hold your horses, Sam. I know you're hungry. It's coming," I say, my words slightly muffled by the Ziploc bag clenched in my teeth while I readjust the mattress. I'm starving. Mother requires fasting before a big trip to the city in order to "gain favor with God" and to help remind me that without the goods He provides, we'd be nothing. Yeah, even the dolls laughed at that one.

"Oh, you guys," I gently nag. The kids are all jumbled in a pile, knocked down from when I lifted the mattress. I carefully break off five small pieces of the granola bar with my fingertips and place them on the silver wrapper in front of the lifeless group.

"Cheers!" I exclaim, like I always do, invoking a flash of a memory where my birth parents said that to each other while holding fancy glasses full of bubbly golden liquid.

My share of the snack is gone in a few short, stale bites. When the game is clearly over, I gather up the dolls' pretend meal, dumping the crumbs onto my palm. It's tempting to toss the bits of granola and chocolate into my mouth to curb the still-raging hunger inside me, but instead I squint up at the sliver of light shining in through the long, rectangular window at the end of my room.

It's just high enough that I can't reach it without climbing. The small photo studio where I take pictures for our eBay shop is perfectly positioned to provide just enough lift to get me to the window's ledge, though I'm careful to avoid the photography equipment on the table. The camera is the nicest thing we've ever stolen, and I'm still impressed Mother convinced the guy at Best Buy not only to unlock the case but to leave it unlocked. Not to mention sneaking that sucker out with all the store security. But now that piece of equipment feels like a part of my body when I use it. It took a few months to get the hang of the foreign technology, but after practice and reading the instruction manual dozens of times, I have some of the most artistic pictures of stolen home goods on eBay.

It's not hard to get on the table. Once there, I rise up on my tiptoes and reach to the corner window, the latch broken for the past four years, but even with that I can only open it a crack. Using the fingertips of my empty hand, I push the window open wide enough that the late-spring night wind blows in. I love that smell; it's the smell of freedom. It's a smell I both long for and fear.

On the ledge outside the window is a short piece of a branch that's fallen off the maple tree shading the west side of the house. But the branch isn't there by chance. I left it there so I could let Sampson in.

Sampson, a tiny common sparrow that somehow found his way in through my cracked window during a particularly cold night in the fall, is the only living friend in my life other than Mother. At first, he was flighty and fickle and only visited if I put out an offering or sometimes when it was very cold outside, but I've taken my time in gaining his trust, and now I consider him a member of my family. I have to be careful, only putting out the crumbs at night, only letting him in my room till before sunrise. He's my little pet now, quite tame, and I like to pretend he loves me as much as I love him. Mother can't know. She doesn't like it when I love anything other than her.

"There you go, Sampson," I whisper into the empty air outside the window as I dust off the crumbs onto the sill. It takes time for my friend to come, and often he is spooked away if I'm waiting too close to the window. I scurry backward and hop down from the table, my bare feet silent on the wood floor.

Invigorated by the food and the night air, I feel a twinge of happiness in my core as I look around my room. It's been such a hard, scary day, but here with my dolls and Sampson, I'm home. This is my whole life: the faded peach comforter, the flowered vines that fill the wallpaper, the five pairs of lifeless eyes that gaze back at me like old friends. Unlike the rest of the house, which is clean but neatly packed with boxes of stolen goods and bags of empty cans waiting to be taken to the dump to be recycled at $1.60 per pound, my room has escaped the creeping grip of Mother's obsession. It is mostly mine.

Only one thing is missing. For a long time the window was my only source of entertainment and portal into the outside world. It was enough for much of my childhood. Mother insisted I be educated, so I had homeschool workbooks to keep me entertained by day, and Mother's sleepy juice would put me out each night. But then Mother decided two things—first, that it was cheaper to finish my schooling online with stolen access codes, and second, learning how to sell shoplifted goods on eBay was the primary goal of my education. On the desk across from my bed is my saving grace and favorite item in the house—an old but fully functional desktop computer.

"What do you say, kids? Should we check our channels?" I conspire with the dolls and imagine Angela nodding. Mother has been silent since she turned the lock, and if tonight is like all the other nights I've been locked in my room for "punishment," she's zonked out already. Judging by the empty prescription bottles I've found in the garbage with her name on them, I assume she takes a sleeping pill when she's worked up. I'm not certain, but I imagine she swallows them down with a few swigs of Wild Turkey, the only alcoholic beverage Mother keeps in the house, to take the edge off. I have no solid proof, but there has to be a reason she's out for a good twelve hours on these nights.

"I know, I know . . ." *It's risky.* I finish the sentence in my head. It *is* risky, but even with an unknown punishment hanging over my head, I don't care as much as I should.

Sitting, I jiggle the mouse, and the screen flicks to life. My heart flips inside my chest, just as shaky as the arrow on the screen. There's only one icon—the internet browser. It's through this dusty, clunky gray portal that I took my school classes and religious instruction and run Mother's business.

All sites that could have "adult content" are blocked, and Mother warned me years ago that she can watch anything I've done on the computer when she's not around. But I've learned a few tricks to keep myself safe. The library has plenty of resources, and as long as I get my copies made, she doesn't consider that I might be reading when we go there. It took a few weeks of research to find out how to locate and remove the keystroke recorder and then search for other programs that might be lurking in the background. I've found that there's little I can't learn how to do with a bit of research. It helps that Mother only knows the basics of technology and relies on me to run the online parts of the business at her bidding.

I have everything I need on this computer. And since turning it on five years ago, even with the parental controls, I've seen more of the outside world than I could ever have hoped in the years leading up to its acquisition.

Scooching up closer to the screen, I listen carefully to the sounds in the house. There's a breeze through the crack in the window, the rhythmic slap of the screen door shifting in the wind, the whine of the neighbor's dog chained outside overnight, and the tick of the grandfather clock in the hallway. But no Mother.

It's time.

I may not be able to walk out the front door, or even my bedroom door. I may have acne on my face and scars on my hands, and it may be true that my only impressive skills are the ten different ways I know how to sneak merchandise out of a store without getting caught, but every time I turn on this computer and log in to YouTube, I feel normal.

CHAPTER 4

"Today we're going to make a bucket of slime," Alyssa Feely whispers to the handheld camera she positions above her as she walks into a kitchen with tall white cabinets and glistening granite counters. "And then we're going to pour it on Daddy's head while he's in the pool." She says the last sentence to four-year-old Ryland, whose curly head of blond hair bounces with each giggle.

"Now, Kelsey"—the camera shifts to a smiling ten-year-old with a bright purple streak in her jet-black hair—"you gotta go play with Daddy in the pool so he has no idea what we're doing."

"I'm on it!" She runs out a pair of French doors in a neon swimsuit.

"And Connor, you aren't getting out of this! I need your muscles." The camera twists once again to a teenager with dark hair sitting on the couch typing on a phone. He doesn't flinch. "Come on, this stuff is heavy!" Ryland giggles again in the background.

"I'll help you, Mommy!"

"I know, baby! I know. But we need Connor's muscles too!"

Connor sighs and puts down his phone on the couch. Then he bounces up from his seat and runs across the family room.

"What do you mean? Ryland has the best muscles around!" He scoops up Ryland and bench-presses him above his head.

"Well, looks like it's just me and my boys." The camera settles into a stand pointed at the kitchen island, and Alyssa comes around to the front, where she talks through each item on the counter in an exaggerated whisper.

I sit back in my chair with Angela grasped under my arm and clutched against my chest. I press the earbuds into my ears as far as I can. They crackle every time I shift in my seat, not to mention that I never have the guts to turn the video's volume up past a dash or two on the computer. I'll have to swipe some new earbuds soon. It's been on my to-do list for a long time. Even though I can easily sneak a pair from just about any of the pharmacies or gas stations we hit, stealing something I want for myself makes me feel guilty.

There are six YouTube families I like to check in with at least once a week, but the Feely family is my favorite. The way the mom and dad look at each other like they're still in love, and how Connor babies Ryland, and the way Kelsey is her daddy's princess and her mom's best friend. With the Feelys, I've been to Disney World. I've experienced Alyssa's pregnancy, ultrasound, baby shower, labor, and delivery of Ryland. I know through the Feelys what it's like to be a sister and a daughter, and in some ways I know what I'd want if I ever got away from Mother and got married.

"Daddy is going to love this." Alyssa Feely laughs as she uses her manicured hands to mix a giant plastic container full of glue and food coloring. I am dying to make slime. Even if I can't make it, I just want to know what it feels like. It seems like it would feel like laughter: soft and pliable but also slippery and unruly.

Mother would never allow that sort of mess in her house. It makes sense; she's always hated laughter of any kind.

This is a video from three months ago, but it's still one of my personal favorites. I scroll through the videos on the menu to the right, half watching the slime firm up as they add the magical liquid that causes the whole pastel mess to solidify. In this case, it's bigger than the blob in the black-and-white movie clip they edit into the final prank video. At minute 14:32, Alyssa and Connor carry the full container outside and dump it on Stan while he's sitting on one of the reclined chairs laid out by the pool. But instead of waiting around for the laughter and tickle fight after the prank, my hand freezes with the mouse in my palm. Finally, the new video for the day pops up on the sidebar.

It's later than usual, but the Feelys talk openly about how packed their evening schedule is and how some days they have to edit videos late into the night in order to get one out every day. But the feeling of seeing a new video uploading is like nothing else in my life. It's the way I imagine it would feel if I ever got to see my brother and sister again, or my friend with the braids who lived down the street, from second grade. But not my mom and dad. They abandoned me. I can't imagine ever wanting to see them again, and if I did, it wouldn't be this feeling, this exploding-confetti-on-Christmas-morning feeling. This swimming-in-a-hot-tub-full-of-waterlogged-Orbeez feeling. This slime-between-the-fingers feeling.

The title on the new video is intriguing. Instead of detailing some moment in the Feelys' extraordinary normal life, it reads in bold letters, *DO YOU WANT TO BE OUR INTERN?*

I let my feet drop to the floor with a louder thump than I'd intended. Angela's red hair sticks to my arm as I lean forward.

"Intern?" I whisper to myself, forgetting the game of pretending Angela and the other dolls are listening. I'm not entirely sure what the word means in this context, but it does sound like an invitation. I click on the video. It's only three minutes, much shorter than usual for the AllTheFeels channel. The only other time a video has come in this short was after their dog Sammy died and the kids were too upset to talk about it on camera. Oh, and the one time they had to evacuate their house suddenly because the wildfires were moving toward their subdivision. In fact, the shortest videos are about bad things. No. *Intern* couldn't mean something bad, could it?

I rush to click on the video. I turn up the volume a notch or two after their eclectic standard opening, when the whole Feely family comes into focus, scrunched together on the couch. This isn't good. The family never just sits, ever. Every single face looks so serious, like they're ready for business.

Stan Feely sits in the middle of the long leather sectional, his wife, Alyssa, beside him, their hands entwined. Kelsey snuggles up to his empty side, his arm casually flung behind her. Connor sits next to Alyssa with Ryland bouncing up and down, the only movement on the screen. It has to be bad news.

I slide up to the edge of the irritating molded-plastic seat, the metal bolt under my right thigh scratching me the way it always does if I'm not careful. But today I barely feel it.

Stan speaks first.

"Welcome to AllTheFeels. I know, things look a little different today. We aren't going to be doing a fun video, this one is a little more serious." Stan's voice is steady and regulated in a way that's unfamiliar to me. He's usually the goofy one, a kid at heart, playful and creative. Alyssa says he's like a puppy dog; he likes to wrestle and snuggle with his family, the king of the surprise tackle hug. This is a different Stan altogether. The lights in the house are dim, and it's clearly nighttime in the video.

"It's been a fun few years in our house. We had our little Ryland. We've gone from a few thousand subscribers to over two million Feelers who subscribe to our channel. It's been quite a ride, and we can't complain, can we, sweetie?" He squeezes Alyssa's hand; her eyes look glassy and tired, like she's been woken up from a deep sleep to make the video. But when her husband addresses her, she smiles, and the darkness evaporates like someone has flicked on a light switch.

"Yeah, babe. We are SO, so lucky." She leans over and kisses his cheek. He pauses like he thinks she might take up where he left off, but though the smile remains, the light in her eyes fades nearly immediately.

"But, if you'd like to continue to enjoy daily videos on our AllTheFeels channel, we need your help. We've had some . . . medical complications." Stan hesitates, his grin faltering for only a fraction of a second but enough that I notice. "Now, we aren't asking for money or donations of any kind, but we *are* looking to expand our family by one member." He looks over at Connor this time, and he seems to pick up on the cue to speak. I wonder if they've practiced this part.

"Yeah, we're looking for one of you Feelers to intern with us for the next three months. If you're interested, you must be over eighteen, enrolled at an in-state college, be well-acquainted with our channel and fan base, have computer skills, and, most importantly, possess a fierce desire to learn."

Stan reaches around behind his wife and ruffles Connor's hair like he's a puppy that's learned to sit and stay.

"If you're interested, please follow the link below." Connor points to the area under the video like he can see the words typed there. "Fill out and submit the online application. Interviews will be held next week at the Four Seasons in Los Angeles and then in two weeks at the Ritz-Carlton Hotel in San Francisco."

Kelsey bounces in her spot, clearly aware it's her turn to talk. "We can't wait to meet you!"

"Yeah!" Ryland shouts and pumps his fist at the camera, snuggle-worthy as always. I wish I could give him a hug or put him on my shoulders like Connor always does. I wiggle the tips of my bare toes as the end credits fly past. The worry I fought at the beginning of the video is gone, now replaced by a tingling potential. *Part of their family.* I move close to the screen and pause the video before it can go on to the next one in the lineup.

One of the Feelys. The idea is intoxicating. My parents didn't want me. Mother wants me, but is this destined to be my life forever? I know that's what she wants, for me to live with her forever. To shoplift and sell stolen goods online. To live behind a locked door. Mother says she needs me, but . . . what if I could have a real family?

The frozen, smiling faces of the Feely family call to me. I could be one of them. I already *am* one of them, they just don't know it. There is no one better for this job than me, even if I don't fit all their requirements. Even if I'm not as smart or pretty or creative as the other candidates. I *get* this family. If I could bring myself to talk to Stan and Alyssa—they'd have to see it.

I rarely think about leaving Mother, mostly because anytime I focus on the details it's all too much to process. Sure, I've had those dreams of freedom, but I put them away as soon as they bubble up. But maybe . . . maybe this is my way out. I wouldn't be alone. I wouldn't be destitute and vulnerable. I'd have a real family. I jiggle the mouse and hold the arrow over the glowing blue link. One click—it seems so simple. My finger floats over the right-click button.

"Do it," I whisper to myself. "Do it. Just do it." My heart pounds in my chest, and the sweat that was drying under my armpits and around my hairline starts to bead up again. My knees shake like the floor is about to give out. "Click the button. Click it." With my eyes squeezed shut and my body quivering, I let my finger drop until I hear a click. When I get the guts to look again, the screen changes slowly as the new website loads and the computer makes a sound like it's thinking. As the application form appears bit by bit, I put my hands on the keyboard, ready to type. Somehow, the decision has already been made.

I don't have to go to the interview, I reason with myself as I read over the first few basic questions. *I don't have to leave Mother. I don't have to change my life. It's just a fun fantasy.* Of course it's a fantasy; there's no way I can get Mother to risk another trip to the city after today's disaster, but that doesn't stop me from filling out the form.

The questions should be simple, but even the most basic ones end up being quite complicated. *Name.* I look at my doll—Angela Sampson. The name flows off my fingertips like I was born with it.

Birthday. Well, there's no use in lying about that one. I type in the birthday I celebrate with Mother every year. Okay. It's getting easier. With a slow determination, I pick through the keyboard with my pointer finger and fill out each portion of the application with truth or a careful twist of the truth. Less than an hour later, all I have left is the essay section. I haven't set foot inside of a school since I was removed from my birth parents' house twelve years ago. Sure, I've finished Mother's required homeschool programs, but in my mind I'm still basically an eight-year-old little girl who wants to put hearts above my *i*'s and draw illustrations for all my stories.

The question: *Here at AllTheFeels we want every voice to be heard in our creative process, including yours. If you were to be selected as an intern for the show, what's one constructive criticism you'd be willing to explore with our team? Sell us on you. How are you unique?*

Unique. Well, I don't feel unique in any way. Not any major way, at least. I'm one of the most average (if not below average) people who ever existed. In fact, I imagine that if I'm ever introduced to the Feelys, at first they'd likely ignore me like an old piece of furniture. But there's one advantage I'm sure I have over every other applicant. I love the Feelys like they are my own family. I want nothing more than to see them succeed. It is like nothing I've ever experienced, this desire for something outside of my body to thrive. I mean, two million subscribers is nothing to scoff at, but they're not even in the top ten of family vloggers. My mind might not hold the state capitals or the periodic table of elements, but it does hold a wealth of knowledge on this family and is bursting with ideas of my own.

Each of the Feely kids is fascinating to me—I could watch Connor and Kelsey all day doing all the normal things they do in their lives. I want to know them better—and I bet a lot of their followers do too. If the kids could have their own channels that funnel through the AllTheFeels page, the Feelys could triple their views. Maybe even showcase Ryland with some of his own videos—a day-in-the-life kind of thing.

My favorite idea is a giant challenge that would include a crossover with other YouTube families. It would have to be something well planned out and prepackaged for the other channels to plug in to their recording schedule, but would become almost a game of tag or a tournament-style competition that could not only benefit the Feelys' bottom line but create partnership opportunities. I think about this stuff way too much. I may not be in college, but when I'm working long hours for Mother or I can't sleep because of nightmares, I dream up these ridiculous scenarios that probably wouldn't work but sound amazing in my mind.

One letter at a time, I type it out slowly. Every detail. Every ounce of devotion. I write until the form tells me I have exceeded the word limit, and even then I go back to make sure I included all the good parts. They may never see my face because, come on, how am I going to get to the Ritz-Carlton? Mother would never, ever give me permission. I could sneak out, but I tried that once and . . . Mother says only bad little girls leave their homes, and even though it sounds silly, the guilt is still there. I mean, the whole reason my birth family abandoned me is because I ran away. But this letter—at least the Feelys will see it. They'll know my ideas and understand my emotion. If I can't get out, then at least I'll know I tried.

With a nervous flutter in my belly, I hit "Send" on the document and sit back with satisfaction. I don't break the rules often, but when I do, it feels good. Scary, but good. And this time it feels amazing. Maybe Alyssa is reading my application right now on her fancy phone. Maybe she'll call Connor over to point out a particularly clever idea. Then Stan will ask them what they're so excited about, and they'll be talking about me. I smile.

"Well, Angela, this turned out to be a lovely day after all." I search around by my side for the red-haired doll, wanting to share my brave moment with someone I care about. But Angela isn't there.

"Angie—where did you go?" I grumble, trying to sound like a loving but disgruntled mother. I graze her hard, fuzzy head but with enough force that she tips off her precarious resting place on the side of the chair and lands on the floor with a deafening thump. The feeling in the room transforms from an electric buzz of exhilaration to a weighted dread that shifts everything into slow motion. Each beat of my heart is slow and distinct, and the space between them is enough to bring clarity to the glowing computer screen and the granola-bar crumbs on the ledge and the pregnancy belly in a pile on the floor—all capital offenses in Mother's world. It takes three full heartbeats for the world to speed up again.

With the expertise of a CIA agent, I use all of my library-obtained knowledge to open the browser history and delete it. Then I clear the cookies and sign-in history before powering off the computer. As soon as the final warning chimes in my earbuds, I yank them out of the jack and stow them back in their hiding place.

With the earbuds removed, I can hear Mother shuffling around in her room. I imagine her angrily getting out of bed but still taking time to put on slippers with the methodical precision that controls every aspect of her life. Double-checking the drawers on the desk, I adjust the keyboard, flip off the power switch on the side of the computer, and reinstall the keystroke logger she hid between the keyboard and the computer tower. The tower is still warm, and if Mother decides to touch it, she'll know I've been online. If she finds anything, if she finds that application, there will be consequences.

With careful movements, I dance my way across the floor, skipping the squeaky section near the foot of my bed and the worn spot where I place my feet every morning when I start my day. I shove the pregnancy belly under the bed with my foot, hoping the darkness will deter her from inspecting too closely. With the tiniest of squeaks, I settle into the indentation I've left in the ancient mattress over the past twelve years, the familiar smell of dust and stale sweat the closest thing to home I can remember since being removed from my parents' house.

I clutch under my arms, and a trickle of sweat races down my cheekbone. The telltale sound of Mother standing outside my door makes me freeze. The window is open. A little chirp from the sill sends a chill of terror through my veins. Sampson. If I'm sleeping and the room is still, maybe she won't notice.

I relax my eyelids and force myself to breathe deeply, imagining what I'd sound like if I were asleep. Once, Stan Feely had taken an online course to learn hypnosis, and he tried to get Alyssa to fall under his powers. It didn't work, but I still liked it, wondering if he'd accidentally hypnotized *me* through the monitor. With a deep, cleansing breath, I imagine Stan's voice. It's low and comforting, and my mind slows and my body relaxes almost instantly. Even when the lock scratches open on the bedroom door, and a slat of light falls on my face, and Mother's raspy breathing fills the silent room—I lie still, letting my memory of Stan's voice fill and calm me like I imagine any good father would.

She stands over me, and her smell is as familiar as Angela's. With shaking fingers, she brushes a strand of hair from my cheek, and I focus on the memory of Stan's words in my mind. The floorboard I'm always careful to avoid squeaks under her retreating footsteps, and I wait for the sound of the door and the lock, but instead there's a little squeak from the window. No.

"What in the world?" Mother says, under her breath, and instead of leaving, she rushes across the room to the open window. I wonder if I should sit up or say something to distract her or to save little Sampson, but I don't know what I *can* do.

"Shoo, shoo!" she orders. "Disgusting," she mutters, breezing past me without further interaction.

The door closes unceremoniously, the dead bolt returning to the position I love the most—locked. That was a close one for all of us. I don't sleep; I can't. It's too hard when I can't stop wondering if my happiness is worth risking the safety of the few things I have left that I love.

CHAPTER 5

I caress my hefty rubber belly. It's empty, no loot inside, so I look about five months pregnant, barely noticeable beneath the frumpy beige-and-white maternity dress that must be from, at the earliest, 1983. Mother sits beside me, eyes glued to the highway, grumbling the un-curse words that bring as much tension to my eyes and shoulders as the forbidden ones she insists evoke the devil. Today Mother's disguise is the one I hate the most—a scarf around her head like she's covering up baldness from cancer treatments. She adds to the gross, manipulative display by wearing an oversize Y-ME T-shirt with a pink ribbon splashed across it.

Mother only wears this getup when she works alone. People avoid me as a single, unwed mother, clearly too young to be pregnant and on her own. The same holds true for Mother when she wears the cancer uniform. Onlookers sidestep us like they are scared it could happen to them. But together the two of us are an oddity that brings too much attention.

Mother might be crazy, but she's also crazy smart. It didn't take me long to learn this fact as a child, after my injuries from the accident started to heal and the full extent of Mother's rules became clear.

"Why did I let you talk me into this?" Mother asks between gritted teeth, the tension boiling over into anger like it always does. Pretty much any emotion Mother has eventually translates into anger.

"Uh . . ." I hesitate. I have to find the exact right way to answer without seeming too eager. It has taken over a week of punishment, apologies, and my own version of manipulation to get to this day. The interview.

I had to create an email from a fake account asking for a pair of Gucci boots similar to a pair we auctioned a few weeks ago that Mother had lifted from Neiman Marcus. I requested my size and suggested a delivery date that could only be fulfilled within a small window. Mother's feet are much bigger than mine and would ruin the boots if she even figured out how to get them on. Plus, she'd just been in that shoe department a few weeks ago. There was a very strong chance that she'd be recognized if she went back again. But the "buyer" was willing to pay above what we got for our highest bid in the last auction, so I knew Mother would take notice. It was a long shot. In my mind, if it all came together and got me to the interview, then I'd know that this was the right decision. So far I'm on a well-groomed path right into the Feelys' lives, even if it's just for a fleeting moment.

The tightness between my shoulders now creeps toward my throat. "I know, it's a terrible idea. But the money is so good, and I want to make up for the huge mess I made at Nordstrom Rack. I . . . I want to prove myself to you. I still feel so terrible about it." I sound so fake. She's going to catch on if I'm not careful.

"You *should* feel terrible about it. It was a disaster, and we're living off rice and beans because of you. You know how hard it is for a single mom out there right now. You *know* it, Tara. But you don't care, do you?"

"I'm sorry, Mother." It is the sentence I say more than any other. And a part of me does feel sorry, ashamed. But another part, a part that's been growing since watching the Feelys—doesn't. "That's why I want to make it up to you. I know you always want me to be more productive. I'm going to do it for you now, Mother. I'm going to make you proud."

There is an overeagerness in my own voice, and I force myself to lean back in my seat and stare at the line of cars on the exit ramp in front of me like my heart won't break if Mother does a U-turn and takes us back home this minute. She clacks her dentures and scratches up under the faded pink scarf with a neatly trimmed and slightly yellowed nail.

"I swear if you mess this up . . . ," Mother mutters under her breath, putting on the right-turn signal that makes my heart jump with hope. I hold as still as possible. Any move or wrong word can ruin this plan. The tension in the van is thick, like the space between us is filled with gradually firming gelatin. Usually that feeling, the she-could-snap-at-any-moment feeling, makes me shut down. It's like a mind-control drug that cracks me into line like a dog with a shock collar. But today, I let it solidify. Today I might get to meet the Feelys.

I shift only my eyes to check the clock: three thirty p.m. It's taken longer than expected to get downtown. My target is six blocks from a narrow unmetered backstreet Mother usually parks on, and from what I've seen on Google Maps, the hotel is another mile north. It's going to be tight, but—I can't even focus on the risks.

Dang it, I never ignore the risks. My life is one constant risk-assessment experiment, but in this moment the only thing I want is to see the family I wish was my own. It may only be long enough for them to laugh at my pieced-together résumé and the handwritten business plan I stowed in the pregnancy suit before leaving my room this morning.

In the acceptance email I got from the Feelys a few days after turning in my application, the form letter explained that the interviews are an open call for all invited applicants but close at five p.m. I'm on the list, but that's it. If I don't show up, they'll forget about Angela Sampson forever. If I want to see the family, I have to rush.

Mother puts the van in park, unlatches her seat belt, and adjusts her scarf in the mirror, all traces of hair expertly hidden.

"Your job is going to be the big payout today." She yanks the keys out of the ignition and then turns her eyes on me, the wrinkles around them looking deeper every day. I struggle to inhale, the fear and euphoria combining into an intoxicating yet noxious gas that could either take me under or make me float like helium. "You go to Neimans. Take your time, but don't be fancy, don't overpack with loot. All we need is the boots. I'll hit the mall, and we can meet back here in two hours." She holds up two wrinkled fingers and gives me that look, the one that keeps me in line like I'm wearing a leash. "Two hours, Tara. I mean it."

Mother cocks her head, actually looking at me for the first time that day. Maybe for the first time in many days. She reaches out and flattens a flyaway that has escaped my carefully crafted ponytail from the morning. I'm not allowed to use mirrors; Mother considers them the "authors of vanity," but at the right angle I can use the darkened computer screen instead. Today I took extra time and care to make sure I was at least neat and clean. I've never been beautiful. It's easy to see after watching makeup tutorial after makeup tutorial. My skin is mottled with scars and active acne pustules. But even if all those blemishes were magically removed with some kind of real-life Photoshop, my eyes are narrow and dark, and my teeth, though straight enough on the top, are crowded in on the bottom and keep me from smiling widely.

"You are my girl, you know that, right?" Mother says, her eyes softening and growing moist. She puts her dry hand against my face and traces a thumb down my cheekbone. "Be careful. I need you."

Guilt washes over me. Mother is controlling and hurtful. Some days I want to claw my way out of my locked room and run far away and not worry that I'll starve on the streets. But how can I leave the woman who took me in when my own mom hurt me? A woman who sacrifices and literally risks everything in order to put food in my mouth? A rush of trepidation quickens my pulse, and I consider telling her everything, every last detail, every minor betrayal and major infraction. How can

I even think about crossing that invisible line and meeting the people who live a full life on the other side of the screen?

"Yes, Mother," I whisper, tears threatening to give me away. Then Mother's caress changes, and she grabs my cheeks, her fingertips pressing against my jaw, pulling me toward her. The strain is unbearable, and threatens to force my jaw right out of its socket. I lean forward, my face just inches from hers, her smoky, stale breath filling my nostrils and mouth, hitting my tongue in a warm, nasty wave.

"If you get yourself caught again, you better run. And if the police get you, don't you dare say my name, you understand?"

"I . . . understand," I respond timidly, but she doesn't let go.

Her rapid breath bathes my face, and I try to take in as little air as possible. I close my mouth and swallow as her grip grows more intense, her short nails cutting my skin. With a grunt of disgust, she shoves my face away, and I lean against the cool glass of the van window, panting.

"Be back here by six," she says, and I nod against the window. Without another word, she's gone. The driver's-side door slams, and I'm alone. I could just go to Neimans, stroll around the store, get the boots, and be back to the van in twenty minutes. Or . . . or I could really do it. I could go to the Ritz-Carlton and meet Stan and Alyssa, Connor and Kelsey, and little Ryland. For so long I've let my fear of Mother keep me in line, and most of the time I don't mind her rules, I really don't. But today is different.

I sniff and rub the sore spots on my jaw, hoping they won't be too obvious to the passersby on the street. I'll start walking, just walking—nothing is wrong with walking, right? As I open my door and let my feet hit the ground hard, there's a flutter of excitement instead of fear. I like that feeling. I like it a lot.

CHAPTER 6

The Ritz-Carlton looks like a palace, towering white columns like the ones I saw from the chapter on Greek mythology when Mother still kept track of my homeschooling, a ramp leading into the front doors. People, fancy people of all shapes, colors, and ages, seem to float in and out of the breathtaking structure. It makes sense that the Feely family would be inside of this dreamy place. The Ritz-Carlton, the Feely family, and me—three things I thought I'd never find in a sentence together.

It's getting a little cool outside, and my arms fill with goose bumps, but under my clothes sweat builds up behind my fake belly and on my calves inside the Gucci boots covered by my dress. I rest my hand on my abdomen instinctually, a move Mother taught me years earlier when she used to wear the suit.

"Mothers like to feel their babies at all times," she'd say, rubbing the belly with a half smile. When Mother wore the suit, she used to tell me about the little girl she carried once a long time ago. But when I started asking too many questions about what happened to the child from her story, Mother clammed up and acted like she didn't know what I was talking about. Now that I wear the suit, Mother talks less about her birth daughter and more about how much safer it is for me to look pregnant. It keeps men from lusting after me. I hate that word—*lusting*. It makes me feel gross.

For a long time I would hide behind Mother's leg or skirt when a man passed by. I used to avoid videos with fathers or brothers, so afraid of what they might be like. But then I watched one of the Feely videos where Stan was learning to braid his daughter's hair. He brushed her hair with extreme gentleness, cringing when Kelsey did and working hard to separate each strand, his large hands fumbling to weave them together into a sad braid. He was nothing like the red-eyed lust monsters Mother had warned me about.

I lean forward so the bulky skirt billows out with each step toward the front doors of the hotel, making it nearly impossible to tell that I might be pregnant under this tent of a dress. When I got the belly—I don't know, it felt like a protection. Wearing the heavy suit, I could look up from my feet and come out from behind the fabric curtain barrier of Mother's dress.

Ugh. I drop my hand in revulsion. What am I doing? I don't want the Feelys to assume I'm some unwed mother. What would they think of me? Mother says women who have babies out of wedlock are low women, disgraceful. I have to find a bathroom as soon as I get inside and take this thing off.

I push through the front doors, keeping my eyes down so I don't see the judgment on the doorman's face or from the fancy people who actually belong in this beautiful place of marble and mirrors. The two-thousand-dollar boots hiding beneath the fabric of my dress make a light tapping that echoes in the stone entry but is quickly drowned out by the background sound of voices chattering away in the bustling lobby and the distant ding of the trolley out front.

I should've guessed from all the windows and pillars, but this place is huge. I have no idea where I'm going and don't have the guts to ask any of the populace sitting in the lobby. The email said something about a conference room, but the only sign my frantic scan turns up points straight ahead to the lobby and a desk where two hotel employees stand in uniform behind computers.

"Oh darn." I let out a frustrated grunt and then bite my lip. *Darn* is not a word I'd dare say in front of Mother. Mother is not here. I can say and do whatever I want. Normally, I'd freak out at the idea of talking to strangers, but today . . . today I want to just because I can. I walk boldly toward the desk, wobbling on the low heels of boots I've never worn before, and navigate my way through a maze of ropes that feels like a test that was created to weed out the less intelligent guests. A well-groomed woman with short blond hair stands behind the counter.

"Next, please," she says, as though there's a line out the door instead of just me. I'm ridiculously relieved it's a woman looking back at me.

"Hi, uh, I'm here for the interviews for the Feely family. I . . . I thought there would be signs or something. I'm late." It's nearly five o'clock, and I'm cursing my decision to go to Neiman Marcus first.

The uniformed woman wears a nametag that reads *Linda*.

"What is your name?" she asks, taking a long, slow look at me. I cross my arms, which reminds me that I still look pregnant. I have to get this belly off ASAP.

"Uh, Angela. Angela Sampson." I think fast, trying to remember the fake name I used for my application a few weeks earlier. She shuffles through a pile of file folders on her desk. With a click at her headset and a mumbled phrase I can't really understand, she looks up with a forced smile on her face. She holds out a blue folder, which I take, and then waves to a man who just walked out of a door in the back wall behind the desk.

"Chris, could you take Angela to the Feelys' suite, please?" she says in a hushed whisper, like it's a state secret. I take a peek inside the folder, feeling like I'm intruding on a personal conversation. On one side is some formal-looking paperwork asking for names and addresses and phone numbers that I can't exactly give. On the other side is a full-color packet of information with pictures of the Feely family, some of which I recognize from their website and YouTube channel. I want to curl up on one of the comfy couches in the foyer of this great big building and dive right in, take in each image, devour each bit of information. But when the large man with a blue sport coat and an earpiece pressed into his ear touches my elbow, all thoughts of the printout fly out of my head.

"This way, miss." He gently presses against my skin and bone, guiding me away from the granite counter where Linda is already back at work on whatever held her attention on the computer screen. The man, Chris, is taller than me by a whole head and a half. His arms bulge under his coat, and it pulls across his shoulders in a way that makes me feel tiny and breakable.

He points to the elevator doors with a bob of his head. I've rarely been on an elevator and find them unnerving. It's not the close quarters; I don't really mind the walls pressing in or doors closing or even the movement of being lifted off the ground with the help of some gears and wires. No, I hate being in there with other people, and the idea of entering the elevator with this man sends streams of sweat down my abdomen, under the latex belly. The prosthetic belly. I almost forgot. When the doors ding open, I jump backward.

"I . . . I have to go to the bathroom," I say, glancing up and down the hall for the women's room sign. I could slip out of the belly, stash it in the bathroom . . . somewhere. I don't know. I try to figure out other hiding possibilities.

"There is a bathroom in the suite," Chris says, pointing to the open doors with a flat hand, a man of few words, apparently. I rub the belly again, not sure what to do. Am I really going to meet the Feely family looking like what Mother would call "a little whore"? The doors start to close in front of me, and Chris stops them. I'm sure it's a sensor, but there's some nervous part inside of me that wonders if he even needed the electrical help.

"Miss?" he asks, his face still and chiseled, waiting for me. I can run, or I can go with him. I imagine both scenarios, one with me sprinting away from this giant man, his thick fingers and frozen face, and not stopping until I get back to the van. The other with me walking into the interview with my handwritten essay and seemingly pregnant body and meeting the family. The first future seems safest, but the second—to see Stan Feely's slow smile when he looks at his wife. To hear Alyssa's delicate laugh and take notes on her effortless gracefulness. Maybe, if I'm lucky, one of the kids will be there, like little Ryland or Kelsey. Oh gosh, what if Connor is there? What if he says hi to me or I get to tell him about the ideas I have for his own channel?

A few other hotel patrons get on the elevator, and now three sets of questioning eyes are looking back at me. My face burns with so many people staring at me, right at me, and I'm struck with an animalistic desire to run. I rub my cheek where Mother's nails dug into it earlier. It's not sore or anything, but it's a reminder of what's waiting for me outside this building, back at the van. It may be freedom from this moment of discomfort and panic, but it's not safety. It's Mother.

"Sorry," I say and dash onto the elevator before I have a chance to back out.

Once inside, Chris grunts something and pushes a button. I don't see which one, and the man and woman in the elevator with us stand silently holding the handles of their rolling suitcases, one clicking the button on the top over and over till I want to scream. But I don't. I'm going to meet the Feelys. This is real life.

CHAPTER 7

Sweat has left a distinct outline of my fingers on the glossy cover of my interview folder. I wipe at it with a clump of toilet paper, preparing to make the best first impression possible. Just through a wall and door are the Feelys. It's too late to turn back now, so I'd better be as ready as I can.

Thankfully, Chris is gone, probably back at the front desk. His oversize presence stole my voice and made my joints freeze up at even the briefest touch, which made every shuffled step and word spoken just disastrous. When we reached the Feelys' suite, Chris gave a firm, aggressive knock that made me flinch and hold my stupid pregnancy prop. I stared at my feet, wondering who would come to the door. Stan, Alyssa, Connor . . . but when it opened, a stranger stood on the other side. He seemed angry; *brooding* might be the term an author like Emily Brontë would use to describe him. When I read *Wuthering Heights*, a book Mother would never have allowed in my hands, I thought it was supposed to be a romance, but when I closed the cover of the stolen library paperback, I could only think about how awful those families were. Maybe families were just terrible.

But that was before I found AllTheFeels. This man had dark hair, piercing blue eyes with circles underneath, and an abrupt way of speaking that didn't fit into the fluffy, cotton-candy version of the world the Feelys lived in.

Chris left me with the guy, and I almost missed him as soon as he was gone. He may have been enormous and mute in an unreadable way, but Chris also seemed to be there to help me. This new, dark, brooding man was a judger. I saw it immediately as he ran his gaze over my midsection and then up to the mess my hair must be, and I was instantly glad I couldn't read his thoughts.

"You're late. There are still several other people in front of you, so you might be out of luck. Résumé?" he asked with his hand out, as though he wasn't delivering devastating news.

A cluster of young, attractive, and carefully dressed twentysomethings sat and stood in a varied pattern in a sitting area I could see just over his shoulder. One, two, three . . . six . . . six other applicants still here. They all looked so stylish, even the guy wearing a pair of baggy jeans and a ball cap bobbing his head to something coming through his EarPods.

I might not get in. If that happens, then I did all this for nothing. My ankles wobbled inside the sweaty leather boots. The brooding man still had his hand out, waiting for my application, but the handwritten pages of my résumé were inside my prosthetic pouch. I paused, grimaced, and held my belly, remembering some of Mother's tricks of the trade.

"Oh, can I use the bathroom?" I asked without answering his question. I made my eyes vulnerable and needy, which wasn't even too much of a stretch in that moment. He sighed and pointed to a closed door a few feet away.

"Why not?" he said with enough irritation to make me blush.

"Thank you," I said, and ducked into the bathroom with the blue folder still in my hands. I've been hiding out in here ever since. Once I retrieved my notes and résumé out from under my dress, I stopped in front of the mirror, and I can't seem to walk away even as I've listened to several other potentials say polite farewells to the gloomy man at the door.

I have to get out there, or I'll lose any chance at meeting the Feelys, but my image has me transfixed. My skin flames red at my cheeks; the sore, raised bumps that ache as I fall asleep are even uglier than I imagined. My hair is tidy but greasy in the tight ponytail, and when I smile my teeth look yellowed, especially after getting a glimpse of the bleached whiteness of the woman's teeth at the front desk.

I'm tempted to take this contraption off and stash it somewhere in the bathroom, but my rattled mind can't seem to figure out how to sneak back in and put it back on, not to mention the fact that I've already used my "situation" to escape to the bathroom in the first place. And these boots—I heft my leg up onto the closed toilet seat and unzip one boot down the back, thinking I'll shove them inside of my pouch, but stop midzip. That would make me look hugely pregnant, and who would want to hire me then?

Frustrated, I yank the zipper closed and work to flatten the latex belly as much as possible with my hands. With only my Keds inside, the cavity collapses to a minuscule bump under the folds of my maternity dress.

Maybe they won't even notice, I think, practicing small steps to hide the boots that are the only reason I'm able to be here today.

I scratch at my teeth with my fingernails and splash some water on my face and then smile again. Better. Mother says beauty is a curse and that I'm lucky to not be troubled with it. But today I wish I had that burden.

I dry my hands, collect my belongings, and take a deep, cleansing breath. *Dear Lord, bless me with strength.* I start to pray but then stop. Would God listen to a rebellious daughter like me? Probably not.

When I step out of the bathroom, the clipboard man is waiting for me. There are only two remaining candidates on the couches now, a girl wearing heels with a pair of skinny jeans and another girl with a laptop on her legs. I instinctively know I'm going to be the final interviewee after a day of smart, attractive, accomplished young people. I should just leave.

The bathroom door closes behind me, and I walk on my toes to keep the heels of my boots from thumping on the thin carpet, but I only get a few steps toward the exit when I'm intercepted.

"Uh, everything okay?" He glances at my bump like the baby is gonna explode out at any second; clearly my efforts at looking normal have not had the effect I hoped for.

"Uh, yeah . . . you know how it is," I answer awkwardly, referencing my midsection. I might as well use the excuses as long as I'm stuck looking pregnant.

It seems like he hasn't caught on to my escape plan and gestures toward the sitting area. "This way," he grunts, and moves forward.

"Wait." I stop and plant my feet.

He looks at me, his cold eyes flashing with irritation. "We really are severely behind schedule."

"Uh, I'm sorry, but . . ." I glance behind me at the door that leads to the hallway, biting my lip and holding my folder against my chest.

"You *are* here for the interview, right?" He sighs, tiring of dealing with me. "I was planning on getting you checked in, unless you want to leave, 'cause I'm sure that would be fine too."

The pretty young women in the adjacent room are watching us now. The fancy one looks like she's laughing at me, and the studious one is sizing mc up like I might actually be competition. I can imagine their thoughts: *What a weirdo. Who does she think she is? Why won't she just shut up and sit down?*

"Here." I hand over the stack of printer paper covered in my hand-writing, the women's attention substantial and painful. If I'm compliant, quiet, I can fade into the background where I like to be.

"What is that?" he asks, eyeing the papers like they carry a disease.

"My résumé. You . . . you asked for it before." My cheeks are hot and I could cry.

"Oh." He takes the papers and places them under his clipboard. "Your name?"

I swallow. I should've taken the time to get a sip of water in the bathroom. Nerves make my mouth dry and hands shake. The fancy girl is only semi-watching me like I'm some sort of entertainment she's going to blog about later, but the studious girl must not be worried about my potential, already back to typing loudly on her keyboard.

"Angela. Angela Sampson," I say quietly, knowing it's a lie.

He checks over his list and then looks up with a slant in his already suspicious eyes that makes my ears ring. Does he know something?

"Wait, YOU are Angela?"

I wilt under his uncomfortable assessment. Why is he asking like that? The name is fake. It can't be the name. Unless they did a background check or something. Could they do that with just a name? I flip through all the possible ways I could've been exposed, but the clipboard guy doesn't seem angry or even accusatory. He seems—impressed.

"So, you're the one who wrote the essay, huh? I never would've guessed." He looks me over, slowly this time, like I do sometimes when I'm reading a word I've never seen before and can't figure it out in a sentence. He looks almost amused, but I haven't told a joke.

"You read it?" My face is hot. Both girls must've heard the same curious excitement in the guy's voice. The laptop girl is now looking like she might cry, and the one with the high heels is staring off into space with her arms crossed tightly. I'm just trying to recall what I wrote on the application that could be of any interest to this guy.

"Oh yeah, I read it." He holds up my résumé and the pages filled with a few ideas for the Feelys that I'd written up when they asked for a proposal. He flipped through the eight pages, a slight smirk never leaving his face. "So you have computer skills and are proficient at Excel, but you handwrite your résumé? Huh."

I'm ready to melt into the floor. I guess I never thought anyone would read the documents I submitted other than the Feelys. I rush to make up an excuse.

"My . . . my printer was broken," I stutter out. He nods emphatically almost like he's making fun of me.

"Henry!" A familiar voice penetrates the door in the side wall just as he's about to ask another question. It's Alyssa Feely. I feel like crying and laughing at the same time. They're here, on the other side of that wall. I can't believe this is real.

The clipboard guy is not nearly as impressed with the call. He curses under his breath and checks something on his paper, abandoning his line of questioning, and returns to treating me with the same irritated indifference as everyone else in the room. I'm not complaining. The fewer questions the better.

"Okay, we will pass this on to the family. You can find a seat." He points to the couches. Without waiting for me to move, he checks his clipboard and calls out, "Forrest?" The laptop girl hastily gathers her belongings and pushes past me like I'm a piece of furniture rather than a human, a toothy smile plastered on her face. Henry, if that's his name, guides her to the door, which turns out to be a series of two doors, the one on the opposite side already open. Then they poof, disappear into another world, a world where the Feely family lives. A world I hope to get a tiny peek into today.

As soon as we're alone, the high-heel girl across from me puts both feet on the ground and leans forward, watching me. I avoid eye contact by checking my watch. It's already fifteen minutes past five. I have to leave in the next ten minutes if I'm going to make it back to Mother in time. Anything longer than that, and I'll have to run. I'm not supposed to run. I'm supposed to blend in, play my role. Dashing through the streets is not fit for the persona I've taken on as a part of Mother's plans.

"Are you for real?" the girl demands. I'm still distracted by the glowing numbers on my wristwatch ticking down to consequences that are both predictable and completely unpredictable at the same time.

"Me?" I answer, barely paying attention. If each interview takes five minutes, like they said they would in my email, and there's only a little bit of small talk during transitions . . . I start to work the numbers in my mind.

"Yeah, you. Are you for real, or is this some kind of act to get their attention? Like a character?"

She expects me to say something, but what? I rarely talk to people other than Mother, and even then it's usually only the superficial niceties that I've been well trained to volley casually but carefully. This question is wholly unexpected and harder to answer than my timing issues.

I'm pretending to be someone I'm not, that's for sure, but I don't think that's what she means. I've seen some of those vloggers, the ones who act obnoxious or wear funny makeup to get followers. Is that what she's assuming? That this is an act? I can't think of any answer that would make sense to this pretty brunette who looks like she spends more on her nails every month than Mother does on food.

"I mean, I can see your boots." She points at my feet peeking out under the curtain of my maternity dress. "Those things are a couple grand at least. And that guy knew you. Do you have a channel or something?"

The boots. I tug the fabric down and cross my ankles under me so the soft leather is totally hidden. The girl doesn't wait for a response.

"You know what, forget it," she says, standing up and tossing a monstrous leather satchel over her shoulder, checking her phone. "My boyfriend's been waiting for me for like half an hour, and he's getting pissed. If they're all excited about a stunt like this, I'm not interested. No one over five watches them anyway."

She stomps out, taking giant strides that make her legs look even longer than they did when she was sitting down. I think she tries to slam the door as she exits the hotel suite dramatically, but the hinges slow it from making anything louder than a click. The invisible grip of Mother tightens around my arms and chest in response to her anger.

I can't understand what she saw in the two minutes we populated the same room that would cause someone so beautiful and polished to run away. Mother says the world doesn't understand us—that they're evil and vain and that there's no kindness out here. There are two columns in my brain, one that keeps track of when Mother's wisdoms are right and one that tallies when she is wrong. I add a check to the "Mother is right" side.

Henry and the other applicant emerge from the other room, and I look at my watch. Without another interview between me and the Feelys, I might make it back before six. I sit up straighter, a warm tightness crawling up my neck. It's my turn.

Henry and the laptop girl have a short, hushed conversation by the door. I hear something like "Check your email for updates." When he turns his attention back toward where I'm sitting, I make certain that my feet are covered and that I don't draw any attention to the empty seat across from me.

"Uh, did she leave?" He points with a pen at the girl's vacant spot. I nod, hoping he won't ask me for more information. Stan calls out from the other room, and Henry's features twist into a brief ripple of annoyance.

"Be right there!" he shouts back, and then looks at me. "So, are you coming or what?"

"Yeah, I'm ready," I say, absolutely terrified and not sure if I even believe myself anymore.

CHAPTER 8

We walk through the doors and into the adjoining suite. A U of couches is arranged by the windows to my left, nearly identical to the set in the waiting area. There's a bedroom doorway directly across the room from me and then a small kitchen to my right. Seated on the maroon cushions are a man and woman, very familiar but also strangers.

It's the Feelys for sure, Alyssa and Stan, but they don't look exactly like the vibrant YouTube stars I've come to know and love. Alyssa stares at her phone, thumbing through the screen, zombielike. Stan has earbuds in place, eyes closed, head leaning against the back of the loveseat. A black camera sits on a tripod with a large microphone attached on the top, pointed directly at a chair in the corner. This must be my spot. Fear stands on my shoulders, and I feel like I'm being pulled backward by a rope.

"I don't want to be on camera," I say, stumbling back far enough that I bump into Henry. He grabs my upper arms and holds me away from him. His hands are strong and unexpected. I don't know that a man has ever touched me this freely, and the sheer power in his fingertips sends a thrill through me, my stomach flopping.

Alyssa's head pops up, and despite the dark circles and uncharacteristic ponytail, when her lightning-blue eyes meet with mine, I feel like she knows me somehow. I see myself how I fear she sees me: the pregnant belly, the odd-fitting maternity dress, the neat but still obvious ball of grease I've just seen in the bathroom mirror.

"Hey, honey, no worries." She smiles, warm and comforting. "It's just for us so we can remember who said what. You won't be on the channel." She gestures for me to come toward her. Henry gives me a little nudge and lets me go. Without the pressure of his hands on me, I feel like I'm floating in an odd, weightless dream.

"Stan." She pats her husband's leg. He shoves her hand away at first, which makes something funny run up my spine, but Alyssa doesn't seem fazed. "Stan," she says again, firmly, patting again. He starts and looks up, yanking out his earbuds.

"Huh?"

"Our last applicant is here," she says sweetly, and the cloud of confusion and irritation is replaced with a giant smile that follows Alyssa's gaze to where I stand. If he finds me repugnant, it doesn't show.

"Hey! Great to see you," he says, and I want to believe he means it. He waves at me and points to the same chair Alyssa invited me into moments ago.

"This is *Angela*," Henry says with an emphasis, like my name is code for something. He clips a mic on my collar, and I try not to recoil when he brushes my skin. He places the box the mic is connected to on the armrest behind me and backs away.

"Oh, this is Angela, is it?" Alyssa perks up and sits on the edge of her seat and adjusts her dark-framed glasses I've never seen before. Like he's received a silent message from his wife, Stan stands and extends a hand.

Though I'm familiar with the practice, I've never shaken a man's hand before. Trembling, I touch his palm, ignoring the masculine calluses that scratch at my fingertips. I can't look at his face, so I focus on the floor and then sit in the corner chair. Maybe his eyebrow lifted in that mischievous way it always does on the channel when he's being playful with his family.

"Go ahead and get settled," Alyssa croons, and I wonder if I should shake her hand too but end up chickening out. I can smell her from my spot in the corner; she smells of coconut and vanilla. I bet her hands are soft.

"Henry." Alyssa gestures to the camera. When he takes his position behind it, and the red light comes on, the questions start. My mouth is dry, and I wish I could ask for water. This feels far more like I'd imagine a job interview going than I'd expected. I thought I'd see the family. Get the warm fuzzies and get out. But now I'm here with a camera watching me and two familiar strangers asking questions. Alyssa starts.

"Please state your name, for the camera."

"Angela Sampson." The fake name rolls off my tongue.

"You are from . . ." Alyssa looks at the résumé I brought and squints at my handwriting. "Oh, I see you're from around here."

I'm starting to regret the list of lies I wrote down. I just cross my hands over my belly and tuck my feet back under the chair, nodding like everything she's saying is accurate. *If I don't talk, I can't get caught.* Mother's number-five rule when out in public. Alyssa runs through a few more basic questions, and I answer with the essential sounds and responses. Then Stan, who's been sitting silently listening until now, leans forward and interjects.

"Hey, enough small talk. From my notes I see that we were pretty impressed by your essay and some of the thoughts you shared when you filled out the application. You seem to know your YouTube family vlogs pretty well. Do you have a channel?"

"Uh, no, I . . ." Words fail me at first. Stan, who's always felt like my father figure stand-in through the computer screen, now has eyes that cut through me.

"Wow, you are just a shy one, aren't you?" He slaps his knee and looks at Alyssa with an air of disappointment, like it's exhausting trying to talk to me. "We should let her go, babe. She looks like she's in pain."

"No." I almost yell it. I'm not sure why. I do want to leave, and I *am* exhausted, but I don't want to be kicked out. I've worked too hard to get here.

Stan's eyebrows shoot up, and he stifles a chuckle. Alyssa slaps at his leg like she's shushing his behavior, but it doesn't seem out of line to me. I am ridiculous. He's right.

"I'm sorry. I . . . I'm so embarrassed. I've been watching your channel forever. I never thought I would get to meet you. I . . ."

"Oh, honey." Alyssa oozes sweetness as she refocuses her attention on me. I hope she can't tell how close I am to crying. "Well, are you even interested in the job? I mean, you know it's unpaid, and you look like you've got your hands full right now."

She takes an extra-long look at my pregnant midsection. She noticed. Dang it. Before I can answer, Henry pipes up from his position behind the camera. I forgot he was still in the room.

"Alyssa, you can't ask her about medical conditions during the interview." He sounds irritated.

"Oh, goodness. I'm sorry, sweetie." She reaches out and taps my knee, and I feel terrible. Just terrible.

"Probably shouldn't call her 'sweetie' either, Alyssa." Henry can't seem to keep his opinions out of the dialogue. I don't care if she calls me sweetie. In fact, I like it.

"It's okay, I don't mind," I interject, but no one seems to hear me.

"All right, I got it from here, Henry." Stan hushes the young, bossy interloper with a firm hand in the air. Then he turns to me and puts on the dad face I'm so used to. With Alyssa's "sweetie" and Stan's cocked head and partially scrunched right eye, the pounding in my ears drops off and a flutter starts up in my chest. This is the Feelys, the real Feelys.

"Hey there, Angela. Most of the people we've seen today either want to grab some screen time with us, or they have their own YouTube ventures they'd like to hype through AllTheFeels, but you"—he pauses and squints the other eye as though he's trying to see me through a clouded glass—"you don't want to be filmed and don't have a channel of your own, so what brings you here today? You're clearly smart—your firm understanding of our market and competing channels was impressive—so why does a summer internship even appeal to you?"

I take a deep breath. I can't make a fool of myself. I let myself pretend, just like I do with my dolls and Sampson. I pretend I'm wearing a nice dress, and that my hair is clean and brilliant and shines when the light hits it, like Kelsey's hair. I pretend I actually went to the schools I said I did on my application, and that my understanding of social media came from some in-depth research and study and not from watching hours and hours of videos because they're my only way to connect with humans outside of Mother. I'm good at pretending. Instantly, my spine straightens and my hands stop trembling. I am not Mother's daughter now. I am Angela Sampson. I belong here.

"Mr. and Mrs. Feely," I start out, timid. "I'm here because I believe in your channel. I find your channel as fun and exciting as Five and Dime and Candie's Candies." I list two of my other favorite family vlogs that have even bigger followings than the Feelys. "But it also makes me feel happy and inspired, like the Flying Forstons and Taylor's Helping Hands." I see Alyssa nod and write something down. I continue, getting a little bolder. "AllTheFeels is my favorite channel." I pause. Even Stan is smiling now. But I'm not finished. "Personally, I worry it isn't enough. I don't want to speak out of turn, but when I watch your content, it's all the same thing over and over, and so much of it I've already seen somewhere else. Do you guys even watch other channels?"

My question sounds rude when I hear it out loud. Flustered, I try to think through a way to take it all back, but Stan clears his throat and speaks dispassionately.

"Uh, of course we do. We watch lots of other channels."

"Oh good!" I blurt, relieved he's not angry. "Good. Then you know that the Candies have done that twenty-four-hour challenge you just dropped in twelve different videos. And the Forstons did the nose-piercing prank and ear-piercing prank Kelsey just did, like, ten months ago?" I've talked to the dolls about my thoughts on my shows so often it feels rehearsed. This time it's different, though. It's fun talking to someone about this stuff who can talk back. I wait eagerly for their answer.

Alyssa is leaning forward, and Stan bites his bottom lip, looking over my head to either the camera or Henry, then back at me.

"We don't copy other vlogs, if that's what you're saying," Stan says defensively.

"Oh no, that's not what I'm saying. Everyone does a lot of the same things online. From what I can tell, it's about the timing and the views . . ." I rush to fix my error, but Stan doesn't stop.

"Did they send you here? The Forstons? Are they pranking us?" Stan looks around, amused and a bit concerned.

I take in a deep breath, not sure what to say to that kind of reaction.

"No! No . . . I'm not from anywhere. I mean . . ."

"Are you sure? 'Cause Ted said he was going to get me back for that poker game. And this would be hilarious." Stan is already laughing like I've seen him do countless times on their channel when he calls out a prank before the reveal. But I can tell Alyssa knows I'm for real—well, at least my interview is real.

"No, Stan, stop," Alyssa interrupts, talking like she knows me. She looks calm, and fascinated, like she's watching some event she's never seen before. "You've done your research, haven't you?"

My mouth is still parched. I swallow a few times.

"I . . . I guess I watch a lot of YouTube," I say, shrugging.

"A lot of people watch YouTube, but I think you watch it in a different way. You know what I'm saying, Stan?"

"Maybe?" he says, sounding unsure, but Alyssa has something on her mind, though I think she's at least 30 percent sure I'm still a big joke.

"No, no, I really think so. I think she watches YouTube but not aimlessly like most viewers." She looks at me like I'm a puzzle she's finally figured out. "I don't think you even know you do it, but you're watching AllTheFeels like an analyst for *our* channel."

"I don't know about that . . ." I barely get the sentence out, and I'm sure the camera microphone would never be able to pick it up. Alyssa is back in interview mode.

"So, Angela." She checks her notebook and then speaks again. "If you were part of our family, what would you bring to our team?"

Family. Oh, how I'd love to be part of their family. Even for a few months—it sounds like heaven. I'd give up so much to have a taste of it in real life. And even if it's all a fantasy, I still want them to want me. Alyssa is staring at me, pen in between her clenched hands.

"I think you need, um, someone to watch the other families' videos? And I think that person could talk to your commenters more? Maybe Kelsey and Connor—I don't know if you saw this idea in my essay, but I thought maybe they could have their own channels?" Each suggestion sounds like a question, but I clear my throat and continue through several moments of hesitation. "I don't think it would take much to get you guys to the next level. I mean, your family is *so* amazing, you know? If more people could see it . . ."

The last words fall out of my mouth slowly. The room is eerily silent, like the video when Kelsey forgot her line in a play on opening night. Is it weird how much I care about them? I know I'm not normal; I play with dolls and pretend to be pregnant to steal stuff and live with my mother. Mother.

Oh my god. Mother.

I glance at my watch. I've missed my on-time window, and even if I leave right now and run—I'm going to be late. I rip off the mic and drop it on my seat, forgetting to adjust my movements to look pregnant.

"I'm sorry, I . . . I have to go. I'm so sorry I wasted your time."

"Wait." Alyssa stands up and tries to stop me, but she's still connected to her mic, which is wrapped up under her shirt. I might be small, but I'm fast. I slip out of her grasp. Nothing else matters at this moment other than Mother. Mother. Mother.

Henry blocks the door that leads to the room I entered through. His hands are up in front of him like he's begging me to calm down.

"Hey, hey, hold on. Hold on."

"I gotta go," I say, my fear of Mother trumping my fear of men. I push him out of the way and rush through the door.

"Henry, walk her out," Stan's voice orders from the other room, and Henry bolts after me, but he's too late. I'm at the exit to the hall.

"Hey, stop for one sec," he pants, snagging the door as I try to close it behind me.

"I don't have time. I shouldn't have come."

"Why not? You did great." He sounds nice now, instead of the stormy brooding man I met when I walked in. The complete attitude change is jarring. "Listen, I've seen far, far too many interviews today, and I can tell they really liked you. Don't you want to leave your phone number? It's not on your résumé."

The elevator is four doors down and just across the hall. It's my escape hatch, my portal back to reality. But what am I escaping to? From one nightmare into another?

"You seem nervous," he says from an interested but safe distance, following me as I dash down the hall. "What are you so scared of?"

"My moth . . . my family is waiting for me. I can't stay . . ." I slap at the button on the wall and then step back to watch the numbers crawl up one at a time.

In that moment—he looks at me like he hasn't before. His thawing eyes meet mine, and for a second I feel like I should just tell him everything. But then he sniffs, lingers on my hairline and blazing red cheeks, and I know he can't really see me, no one can.

"Is it your boyfriend?" he asks.

"Boyfriend?" I blurt out, the word feeling strange in my mouth and making me forget for the briefest moment about the elevator and escape.

"I didn't see a ring, so I assumed . . ."

"Oh," I say, finally understanding. The baby—he's asking about the fake baby's father. "No, it's not like that. I'm just running late." The elevator dings, and I step back to let a family of four trickle out. It's my chance. I sprint inside and press the *L* button for the lobby.

Thankfully, Henry doesn't come after me, though I can hear him saying something pleasant as the doors close, like "Thank you for coming, and they will be in touch," but he stays on the other side.

Alone, I lean back against the glass, wood, and metal walls, the latex suit baking me alive, but I don't care. Now that I'm out of that room and away from frustratingly intense Henry, it hits. Euphoria.

Pressing my trembling fingertips against my lips, I try to repress my smile, but it won't go away. I did it. Even through the close calls and all my mistakes, I did it. Alyssa's smile. Stan's eyebrows. They liked me. For the first time since I can remember, I feel like I belong.

CHAPTER 9

I feel stuffed—no, I *am* stuffed. With every step toward the van, I am uncomfortably aware of the awkwardly concealed boots inside their hiding place, where I stashed them before leaving the Ritz so they didn't get ruined in my run. It's late, and I know Mother will be angry. She has no way of knowing of my visit to the Ritz, but that doesn't mean I'm safe. I'm late, and even if she doesn't know it—I disobeyed.

I pass a parked police car and my heart races. Between Mother and law enforcement, I'm going to get a permanent palpitation. The pregnancy suit helps me look innocent, but it also makes people want to protect me. Usually it's grandmotherly women or a middle-aged man holding a door or asking if I need directions, but in the evening, especially in a big city, I've found that police officers become very attentive.

When I turn the corner onto the unmetered street where Mother and I parked before I went on my surrcal adventure, my stomach drops. It's gone. The white cargo van that's Mother's pride and joy is no longer lodged against the curb of this somewhat shady side street. This has never happened before. My head spins, and I stumble against gravity as the downward slope of the street pulls me forward. What am I supposed to do now?

"Miss, can I help you?" A deep, masculine voice echoes down the street and hits my back like someone has tapped on my shoulder. He sounds friendly, but then again, wouldn't that be the best way to trap a woman? To sound friendly? I know enough about disguises to understand that they're not always as obvious as a wig or baggy dress.

I straighten my backbone and take a loud breath in through my nose. Whatever is coming up behind me, good or evil, I need to look strong. Hands over the bulge of stolen cargo, I turn and smile. *Be Alyssa,* I tell myself, remembering her easy smile and assuring, motherly ways.

With a flip of my ponytail, I turn around and face the man coming up behind me, but it's not a maniac in a hoodie—it's a police officer. I don't think I could be more scared if he was stark naked holding a butcher knife.

"Hello . . ." I hesitate and clear my throat. "Hello, officer."

"Are you okay?" he asks, hands on his hips.

I bob my head and keep on my "Alyssa" smile.

"Oh, I'm fine." I don't know what to say or do. If Mother sees me with him . . .

"It'll start getting dark soon." He states the obvious. I keep smiling, hoping it doesn't look as fake as it feels, searching for an excuse.

"I . . . I walked a little faster than I thought and got here before my . . . um . . . husband. He'll be here any second." I hide my bare left hand.

"You're meeting here? In this alley?" he asks, gesturing at the dark space between the two-story apartment buildings, with a touch of something like suspicion.

"No, um, down by the stop sign." I point fifty feet away to the closest intersection. He takes it all in—me, the sign, the alley, and the streetlight above him that blinks on in the twilight.

"Okay, if you're sure you're all right." He takes a casual step back, and with every inch expanding between us my smile widens.

"Yeah, of course."

I don't know how I'm doing it, but I'm doing it, pretending to be someone else like I did with the Feelys. And this police officer believes me. Mother told me men are to be feared, yet today I met men who were helpful. She told me the police want to hurt me, but this one wants to protect me. She told me being pregnant without a wedding ring made me a slut, but the Feelys didn't treat me that way. She also told me she was the only person who cared about me, but she drove away and left me to fend for myself because I was a few minutes late. My head spins with so many conflicting thoughts as the officer continues his exit.

"I'll be just up the street if you need anything, okay, ma'am?"

"Thank you so much," I say, hoping I don't sound too pathetic. I like being called ma'am, and it makes me stand a little straighter.

"Have a good night." He touches his forehead; he's now at the top of the sloping side street, and I wave back. But as soon as he turns the corner, my smile drops. I have no idea what to do. I'm alone, truly alone, for the first time, maybe ever. I've done my highly structured jobs without Mother, made copies at the library and even gone into a store to actually buy things while she was waiting in the van—but I always knew where home base was.

The street is void of life as the sun disappears behind the two-story buildings on either side. Fire escapes climb the brick walls like wrought-iron decorations, and I wish my life offered such carefully laid-out escape plans. How often have I dreamed of a moment of freedom like this? But now that the specter of Mother's white van is no longer in front of me, I'm at a loss.

Head tilted up, counting the gaps between apartments and wondering how often they test those ladders, I twist slowly, the tent dress catching in the breeze and billowing out like I'm a princess in an animated movie. But it's only a brief moment of fantasy that falls away as I take my eyes off the sky and remember the empty alley.

I don't know how to get home. I have no money. I have no sense of direction or navigation. My stomach is beyond empty, and though I normally might be able to sneak a granola bar or bottle of juice from the convenience store on the corner, I'm too awkwardly full to pull it off now.

I wrap my arms around my chest and rub the rash of goose bumps on my exposed skin. If I was really a lost, lonely pregnant woman, I'd ask the officer for help, but . . . I have no husband or home to go to. Ugh, my back is starting to ache from the weight in my belly, and I just want to take it all off. I shuffle my way back to the wall and lean against it, the cold stone freezing my skin through the thin fabric of my dress. As I sink to the ground, the unfinished edges of brick and mortar scratch my back. I'm grateful for the pain—it takes away the anxiety for a moment, but as soon as the sting evaporates, the fear returns. I never thought freedom would be this frightening.

Knees angled out to accommodate the prosthesis, I pull my dress around my legs like a blanket. I don't spend a lot of time outside, beyond walking to and from the van during work trips Mother takes me on. I could go back to the Feelys, but how could I explain showing up again? They must've interviewed a bunch of far more educated and polished potential interns. Even if they liked me—that doesn't mean they'd want me.

At a mental dead end, I hug myself tightly, the most alone I've ever been. Even after my birth parents gave me up, at least I had Mother. At least I had a home.

A face flashes across my memory. Mom . . . my real mom. Her dark eyes beamed at me while we raked leaves in the yard. She made me feel so special, loved. That house with blue siding and windows flanked with white shutters, small but also the biggest thing in my life. For a split second, I'm homesick for my first home. For a family I thought loved me, before my birth mother hurt my head so badly my brain still gets fuzzy, before I realized my birth father didn't protect me, before I was placed with Mother because no one wanted to take care of me after it all fell apart. Do they still exist out there in the world? Maybe things would be different if I could just remember . . .

No. I crush my shoulder blades into the wall till the sharp edges cut into my flesh. There are some memories I can't find in the filing system of my damaged brain, but there are others I don't want to access. The good things hurt too much. I have to lock them away and never let them out.

It's better to focus on the pain when I think about my family. I need to think about the way my head ached for a month after being placed with Mother and the thick scabs that covered my palms and forearms like scales. Even through the hazy twilight of pain and medicine, I can't forget that my birth mother hurt me and then my birth father gave me away, and I've never, ever looked back. Mother never received one letter or a request for a status update or visitation. Nothing. Why would they help me now?

"Get up." Two feet in a familiar pair of bulky white gym shoes stop next to me.

"Mother!" I gasp, my gaze flying up to her stern, unemotional face, her white curls gelled back and halfway up into a clip at the crown of her skull, the scarf from earlier missing. I was so lost in my thoughts that I didn't hear her approach.

"Get up," she repeats, kicking at my calf with her foot, not hard enough to sting but not soft either. I struggle to my feet, and the low heel of one of the boots stabs at my abdomen through the latex lining. My ears ring, and I want to do everything right, everything, but underneath the scrambling I can breathe again.

"You're back." I lurch forward to hug her, but the deadness in Mother's eyes stops me. I clutch my hands in front of me and make my body as still as possible and stare at my feet. "I'm sorry."

Mother sighs, and it's like a thousand razor blades cutting into my skin.

"Get in the van," she says. I don't know where it is, but I start walking in the direction she nudges me. My feet peek out from under my dress in a regular and comforting rhythm. I don't know where I'm going, but I don't dare lift my head. She'll make sure I get there. That's the simplicity of my life with Mother—I never have to make the hard decisions. I listen and follow. It's an act of submission that comes as more of a reflex than a choice.

The van is at the top of the hill, and I get inside compliantly. When the door creaks shut, I stare out the window so I can watch the city transform from eclectic buildings pressed together in a way that looks random to me into a uniform darkness punctuated by yellow lights from inside. This far away it isn't as important what happens in each structure; it's more about their beauty and permanence. The farther away I get, the more beautiful the whole picture becomes.

In the past I would spend the ride apologizing, but Mother is already devoted to her punitive silence, and so I act sorry rather than saying it. She's furious, and I'm frightened. I'll beg for forgiveness as I grovel at her feet tonight, detailing all my failures as a daughter. I'll gladly take all the blame and plead for mercy. But it won't be a full confession. I'll keep the rest of my sins as my own secret. I'll tell my dolls, I'll tell Sampson; I'll remember every smile, every strand of hair, every word, and every last terrifyingly fabulous touch. But Mother can never know.

CHAPTER 10

It's dark in here, but I got used to the darkness after the first day. By whatever today is, I'm so hungry and dehydrated that I'm only semi-aware of my surroundings. I know Mother must be asleep because the lights in the kitchen that shine under the closet door during the day are gone. I sigh and slink down the wall onto the floor. That's the difference between morning and night—sitting up or lying down. That's it. And depending on how much longer Mother leaves me in here, I don't know if sitting up will still be possible tomorrow.

In the morning I'll get a small bottle of water, a bucket I no longer need, and my vitamins. Always my vitamins. I know in Mother's mind these efforts at caregiving mean she's doing something to nurture me, but really all it does is prolong my suffering. I've never wanted to take my own life, but when my stomach is hollowed out with hunger and I can barely open my eyes, I pray to be released. If Mother won't let me free, then maybe God will.

The haze is a blessing, really. The stomach pains have stopped, and I have no desire to move from the spot I'm curled into in the corner of the quiet closet. I haven't been locked inside here in years. I fit better when I was a child, and in the corners—behind the curtain of mothball-scented coats and ancient dresses that remind me that Mother is good at blending in and hiding who she really is—are secret scratchings. I don't add to them anymore, but when my legs cramp and my stomach rubs against itself, I run my fingers over a simple family of stick figures—two tall, one medium, and two tiny.

Back when I used the pin from an old brooch to make them, I thought my birth parents would find me and realize the mistake they'd made signing away their parental rights. But it's not that long-lost family that brings me comfort now, it's the memory of what hope feels like. It's the same feeling I had when I saw the admiration in the Feelys' eyes and when Henry begged me not to leave.

In those confusing early months when I was first removed from my home and placed with Mother, I thought it was impossible to live without the hope of a reunion. Now hope is the one emotion I avoid at all costs. It's like a cancer that sprouts inside of me with just one seed and grows and grows and grows until it takes over my whole life.

I gave up hoping for my birth family a long time ago, but now a new genus of hope is growing inside of me whether I want to let it root there or not. And in the three-by-three closet I've been in for more days and nights than I can comprehend, it has become my lifeline. My hand drops to the pine planks underneath me. I search my fuzzy brain for those beautiful, glowing memories of the interview I've been sustaining myself on, Stan's laugh and Alyssa's interest in my thoughts. But the weaker I get, the more I lose control of my thoughts. The edge of a soft white garment tickles at my face as I start to drift out of consciousness.

◆ ◆ ◆

"Miss Lila . . . this isn't my birthday," little me insisted, following her around, a fistful of helium balloons bouncing behind her.

"I told you a thousand times, darling, this is your *new* birthday. You get presents and balloons and streamers. What more could a little girl want?"

I glanced around the kitchen. It was tidy as always, counters clear of clutter, dust, and crumbs religiously maintained, but today there was a beautiful chaos in that room, strips of gauzy paper draped on every wall, clusters of balloons in the four corners, and a table filled with all my favorite foods—pancakes with Mrs. Butterworth's syrup, watermelon cut in squares, multicolored Skittles nearly overflowing in one of the glass cereal bowls I was never allowed to touch.

"No, it's fun, but . . ." It wasn't my birthday. At almost nine, birthdays felt very unique, like no one else had ever had my birthday and no one else ever would. I could remember a few from before my parents abandoned me, and as far as I could recall, there hadn't been balloons or fanfare, no real party. I had some memories of brightly colored wrapping paper and adding eggs to a boxed cake mix. So this celebration made me feel like a princess . . . but not really.

Miss Lila sighed heavily and turned slowly to face me. The bubbling excitement that had consumed her then-lightly creased cheeks and heavily lined eyes since her declaration of "Happy birthday" early that morning all drained out in an instant.

"But what?" she asked flatly, her eyes narrowing.

"Will we still celebrate my real birthday?" I squeaked out, trying to make it okay that it was four months from my birthday.

Miss Lila hesitated, looked around the room and then back at me. I knew by now what anger looked like on Miss Lila, like the half-frozen surface on the ice trays when they hadn't been in the freezer long enough—still but also a sloshing liquid underneath the thin barrier.

"This *is* your real birthday. Your old one is null and void now that you're my daughter," she explained stiffly, a forced smile back on her face, less effervescent than before. I didn't understand all the words she was saying back then or the full meaning behind them, but I also knew not to break the ice. After all, this was more joy and beauty than I'd known since being dropped into foster care.

Stop being so selfish, I ordered myself.

Stifling all other questions, I helped Miss Lila finish decorating the kitchen. She had this pattern of making things exciting and an adventure when she got her way. I worked very hard to make sure Miss Lila always got her way, at least when it came to me and our life together.

With the kitchen dripping in decorations and the anticipation of our eclectic dinner overwhelming me, we sat down to eat. I'd never seen such a thing: pancakes, syrup, candy, and a bottle of fruit punch to swallow it all down. For half an hour I gorged myself at Miss Lila's bidding, pretending I was a princess or had magic powers to make wishes come true.

Chin sticky with syrup and sugar, I sat back, my stomach stretched to its limit. I started when Mother turned off the overhead lights. The room was dark, and a little thrill of fear gurgled in my belly along with the sugar and carbonation.

"Miss Lila?" I whispered, anxiety rising inside me. Just as I was about to call out again, this time with more force, Mother came in the room, her giant smile exposing her tar-stained dentures, carrying a lit cake. It was beautifully decorated with chocolate frosting, sprinkles, and scrawling letters that read *Happy Birthday, Tara!*

"Tara?" I whispered, meeting Miss Lila's eyes through the smoke hovering over the cake, flames reflecting in their glassy blueness. "Who's Tara?"

"Why, it's *you*, dear," Miss Lila said matter-of-factly. Her white-blond hair frizzed around her face and almost appeared on fire too.

"No, my name is Angela," I said, boldly this time, forgetting to protect the thin ice of Miss Lila's ego. I didn't understand adoption, but I knew my name. You don't just forget your name. My name was Angela. I'd forgotten a lot of other things, but I remembered that. I stood up.

"What did you say to me?" Miss Lila growled, as though I had said a string of curse words.

"My name is Angela," I said, slower, more determined this time, planting my feet squarely on the floor. My stomach rolled again, but I held strong, staring right into Miss Lila's eyes as she rushed toward me, a flaming cake between us.

"Don't you *ever* say that name again, do you hear me?" Her voice pitched up, and her stinky, smoky coffee breath swept over my face and nose, making the nausea rise even higher.

"Angela," I repeated, something otherworldly overtaking me, giving me courage that seemed misplaced even to my nearly nine-year-old mind. But I'd lost so much already: my home, my parents, my baby brother and sister. How could I be expected to give up not only my birthday but my very own name? With a stomp of my foot, I said it over and over again. "Angela, Angela, ANGELA!"

"You selfish little girl," Miss Lila spat, the cake shaking so hard in her hands that the flames flickered. "No wonder your parents didn't want you. I only want you because the government pays me to want you."

Tears blurred my vision, and I couldn't see anything but a fluid sheet of shimmering light. My name was Angela. I thought of my special bracelet, hidden inside one of my dolls to keep it safe. When I was a very little girl, my birth father used to say that if I got lost, at least I'd know my name. I had never felt more lost. It was my name. No one could change my name, right?

"My name is . . ." Before I could say "Angela" again, Miss Lila let out a high-pitched wail, and the flames leaped from her hands and flew toward my face. The smell of chocolate and burnt hair registered before Miss Lila's frantic movements. It didn't hurt at first; it was more scary than painful, the flames framing my face and spreading around my head in a crown, my long hair simmering, a duller glow than when the fire was on my birthday cake. But then the heat hit, and I slapped at the flames, screaming in a pitch I'd never heard before.

Miss Lila was too busy tearing apart the room to notice the fire spreading across my hair and hands. All around me in surreal slow motion, streamers floated down from the walls and hit the floor silently.

I stumbled backward, tripping over the long two-sizes-too-big dress Miss Lila had given me for my birthday celebration.

"Help! Help me!" I screamed, frantic, falling to my knees. "Help me!!!"

The white fabric of my dress, buttoned at my wrists, suddenly burst into bright yellow flames and started to crawl up my arms. The fire, it was hungry, out of control, consuming me inch by inch.

"Mother, please . . ."

Out of nowhere, a deluge of fruit punch came down over my head, and the flames sizzled into oblivion. The relief was immediate, the cool, sugary liquid taming the fire and the pain momentarily, slipping into my mouth and down my white dress, staining it red. Mother stood in front of me, the room coming into focus as the smoke and soot from the fire on my body cleared. The room was in shambles, the cake smashed on the floor, the decorations littering every surface. Miss Lila was out of breath, puffing smoke like a dragon that had just finished destroying a village. She tsked and knelt down in front of me; I was screaming, my arms and hands in intense, boiling pain.

"Look at you," she said, gently assessing the damage to my hair and the burns on my face. She worked her hands down my shoulders and arms, rolling up the sleeves of the old-fashioned dress, checking the first-degree burns under the cotton fabric and then the angry, red second-degree burns on my palms. She sighed, sounding almost compassionate. Dropping her hands, Miss Lila looked into my eyes, frowning. "You ruined your dress."

The magic relief of the fruit punch was wearing off, my face and hands red-hot like they were still on fire, and my hair . . . my hair was so light, like it had evaporated from my head. I wanted to cry against the agony, I wanted comfort, love, understanding . . . I wanted a mother. I looked at the woman I had always called Miss Lila, desperate.

"Help me . . . please."

"What is your name?" Miss Lila asked as she sat back on her heels and pressed her lips together, her cold eyes creasing at the corners like she was calculating a long list of numbers. That's when they came, the tears. I couldn't hold them back any longer. They fell down my face, the salt stinging my burns as they raced toward my chin.

She spoke carefully, her words measured. "I want to help you, but I only help good little girls. Answer me." She snapped her fingers in front of my face. "What is your name?"

"Tara," I sobbed, holding up my damaged hands, engulfed in invisible fire. "I'm your good girl. I'm your Tara."

Miss Lila nodded. "And I am your mother." She gasped like she'd just seen my injuries for the first time. "Oh, my poor dear. I'll make you an ice bath, and then we can clean up this mess." Miss Lila straightened my dress around my shoulders and rubbed them sweetly. "After all, it is your birthday, isn't it?"

CHAPTER 11

It must be morning again. The light from under the door wakes me, and I untangle my fingers from the hem of my white birthday dress that still hangs, singed, in the closet as though the scars on my hands aren't a strong enough reminder of what happens when I cross Mother.

Usually she doesn't leave me in here this long. Usually she gives me a crust of bread and water a few times a day and lets me out to use the bathroom. I don't even need to use the bathroom anymore; there's nothing inside of me. I stare at the door. It's flimsy enough, hollow, made of pressed wood with a thin veneer on the top that's stained to look like wood. I've often wondered if I could kick through that door. Maybe not right now when I'm so weak, but why didn't I even try when I was strong? I hate myself. If only I was stronger, I would've stayed with the Feelys. I would've walked out the front door the minute I turned eighteen. I would've told someone about the closet or the sleepy juice or all the impossible rules. I would've done . . . something in all of these years. Instead, technically a grown woman, I might die on the floor of a closet because I was too afraid to cross my Mother. I'm so disgustingly frail, in more ways than one.

Mother is coming. I try to sit up, but my arms give out as I push off the floor, and I give up almost immediately. The strong version of myself would sprint for the door when it opened, overpower Mother, run out the front of the house and to safety. I almost chuckle. Sure, I like to dream about it all, but I've never been able to stand up to her, not to her face. I have the little ways I show my rebellion, hiding food and sneaking out to see the Feelys, but I don't know how to say no when she's standing in front of me.

The door opens, and the light is so blinding I have to cover my eyes against it. Mother's white gym shoes shuffle against the wood floor.

"Good morning, darling." Her voice is sweet and dripping with syrup. It's always like this—after the punishment comes the nice Mother. Sometimes it almost feels worth it to be locked in a closet or kept from food just to get a few days of nice Mother. I don't know if she ever feels bad about what she's done to me, or if the kindness is a calculated mind game to manipulate me into the sort of daughter she wants, but whatever the motive, it's as predictable as the sunrise. This thought used to keep me going, knowing that I'd see the "sun" again, but I'm starting to realize that the sun rises in the frozen tundra just as often as it does over a tropical ocean.

"Good morning," I croak out, my throat scratchy and dry. I can't remember the last time she brought me water. Has it been a whole day?

"Well, what are you still doing sleeping, you lazy bones?" she teases, and it's my job to pretend like nothing has happened.

"I'm a little thirsty," I rasp, lowering my arm and squinting at the light. Mother comes into focus, the light silhouetting her like an angel visiting from heaven, her white hair catching the sunlight in a broad, bright halo.

"I have everything you could ever want, dear one," she croons, and I want to believe her. Stumbling, I find my way to my feet, and her strong, calloused hands slip under my armpits and pull me up to standing like I'm a little child again. When my face is inches from hers and the unappealing but familiar smell of tobacco and coffee gags me, she wraps an arm around my waist and welcomes me back into the house. The table is set and filled with food: scrambled eggs, bacon, cubes of watermelon, piles of grapes, and a bowl of fried potatoes. When I settle into my chair, I have to restrain myself from chugging the glass of orange juice next to my plate or inhaling the meal in front of me after starving for so long. Too much too fast won't restore me; it will make me seriously ill. Mother seems to think that she's making up for lost time, but I've come to understand that I can never trust an inconsistent feast.

I nibble around the corners of my plate and sip at the thick, acidic drink by my hand. When Mother walks away for a moment to retrieve a basket of biscuits she's forgotten, I shovel a third of my plate back into the bowls the items belong in and then pour myself a glass of water from the pitcher on the table. The chilled, colorless liquid does more to revive me than all the calories in the world.

"I've missed you," she says from the stove. Hearing loving words from Mother is so out of place in my world that the novelty is both exhilarating and paralyzing.

"I missed you too," I parrot, never sure what she wants to hear. She returns to the table with a platter of biscuits and eyes my plate approvingly.

"I'm glad to see you got your appetite back," she says, like sitting and starving in a closet was my idea. Now that my eyes have adjusted to the light and I can see her up close, I can make out a dusting of flour on the yellowed floral apron she always wears when the cooking mania takes over. "I know I haven't had time to cook a lot lately, so I thought I'd make up for that."

"Yeah, um, thank you." I know this is a hint to grab one of the biscuits on the platter, so I do and take a sizable bite.

"Your grandma Jean used to make these biscuits. We always had them with honey and butter, but they are just as good on their own, don't you think?"

"Yeah." My word is lost in a jumble of crumbs and flakes, my mouth still too dry to dissolve the bread fully. I know I should be grateful, but my stomach is overloaded, and I'm barely keeping it down.

"Tara, you look like you're finished." She pauses and assesses my plate and then my face and then my hands clasped across my aching stomach. I'm afraid to break this spell. I usually try to convince myself that "nice Mother" is the new normal. That this time she's really changed and the world is different and fair and bright. I tell myself that forgiveness is important and that family is everything and . . . Then I catch a glimpse of my nearly skeletal white wrist sitting next to her fleshy and sun-speckled arm. How have I gotten here?

"Yes, Mother," I force out, almost robotically. Somehow Mother doesn't catch on to it. Instead she starts gathering the food that will now be our meals for the next week at least. I'm confused; usually she'd make me do the cleanup.

"You should go to your room." She waves me away. I wonder if she knows she's gone too far with the punishment this time. I glance up at her, that stupid glimmer of hope still flickering inside of me. She points to my closed door. "You have a lot of work to catch up on. I'll clean this all up, and you can get started. I couldn't figure out how to connect the camera to the computer. I'm sure you can get that figured out in no time, right, hon?"

Ah, yes, the work. That's why I'm out here and why she's treating me like a princess. I push away from the table, my head swimming a bit. I don't mind work; in fact, after the darkness and boredom I crave it. And the computer—I can hardly let myself imagine what might be waiting for me there.

"Okay," I say, too sick and weak to think of more of an answer.

"I left all the goods in your room. Pictures and posting today. You can do the envelopes tomorrow. Let me know if you have any questions." Mother stands with her back to me, hands in soapy water. She's put all the utensils in a pile on the table—the dirtied forks, serving spoons, and even the giant butcher knife she used to cube the watermelon.

That knife, with its faded wooden handle and sharper than I'd ever expect, has always frightened me. It seems too large for any non-nefarious purpose. But today, today my fingers itch for it. For a brief second I imagine what it would be like to pull it into the palm of my hand, the wood scratching against my skin. How it would make a soft metallic whisper as I slid it out of the pile. There's an anger inside of me that's rising; I wish I wasn't the coward who smiles and says "yes, Mother" for every damn task.

My nails dig into the cloth covering, and as my fingers walk across the table, I gather the fabric, inch by inch, under my hand. Each movement brings the pile of utensils closer to me. Each tug makes me long for the power of that blade. Mother drones on in the background, and it all seems so easy. Why haven't I thought of it sooner? I could just get rid of her. No more stealing. No more starving. No more terror and locked doors and humiliation. Just as the handle of the knife grazes my knuckle, Mother turns to face me, hands filled with billowing white suds that curl around her wrists like the frizz on her head. I freeze, sure she will notice my homicidal intent. But she doesn't.

"Well, what are you waiting for?" she says, like it's not the first time she's asked. I let go of the cloth and smooth it carefully.

"Yes, Mother," I say, the passive girl inside of me replacing the momentary warrior. Who am I kidding? I'll never be able to do it. My worst fear in life, worse than the hunger or the pain of punishment, is ending up like her. Killing Mother would make me Mother.

I take the pile of silver and bring it to the sink. The water plops, and warm suds splash onto my wrists when I drop everything into the tub. Not bothering to wipe the bubbles from my arm, I head for the bedroom, leaving a small trail of water behind me. She might notice. She might get angry. But what else can she do to me? She's broken me. I am hers—forever.

CHAPTER 12

The sun set hours ago, and I'm still working. I stretch my arms across my body and twist my back, enjoying the freedom to move. I don't even mind all the work Mother has piled up. Now that she's sleeping soundly in the next room, I have my window open, my dolls all spruced up, my earbuds in, listening to YouTube while I post picture after picture on eBay. Sampson hasn't come for a visit, but I have a feast prepared for him on the windowsill, and I can't wait to see him bounce around with excitement as he gobbles up every last crumb.

For now, I'm consumed with work and YouTube. The Feelys have a video up about the interviews. Thankfully I don't appear on screen, but I do get a good look at a few of the smiling, beautiful, eager faces who obviously signed the waiver. I must've been the oddball of the day, someone they'll tell stories about for months to come. Oh well, at least they didn't make a video all about me, 'cause they could've. They really could've.

I haven't felt so happy in a long time. Sure, it came with some pains, but the dreamy visit to the Ritz was worth it. All the embarrassment seems to fade into the background when I remember walking those halls. I can pretend I was wearing a pair of skinny jeans and a cute blazer over a fluffy top, that I had perfect white teeth and skin that made my eyes look boldly dark instead of empty. I allow myself those false memories, a present to my frail body and tired mind.

The Feelys have been busy since our meeting. Several videos based on their trip to the city and interesting adventures they've been on. Their videos have a new edge to them, more like a window into their daily life and less like a reboxed version of someone else's channel. I can't get enough. I devour each video until I'm no longer working but just watching.

Each of the Feely kids was given a camera and asked to film their day. When I see the world through Connor's and Kelsey's lens, I find myself wishing I too could spend endless hours playing dolls or painting the mural in the garage. When Ryland lays his camera on the table for twenty minutes of dinner, edited down to about two minutes of screen time, I want to hug him for letting me feel like I've had dinner with the Feely family. They pass their food to the right. They say a quick prayer before eating. Ryland negotiates eating four peas, two chicken nuggets, and five spoonfuls of mac 'n' cheese before asking to be excused. It's beautiful. When he snuggles into bed that night, Alyssa sings a soft lullaby I've never heard before about rainbows and dreams, and it feels like she's singing it to me.

Every one of the ten videos has more likes and views than the one before it. Their subscribers have jumped by tens of thousands, and views are up by nearly a million. A million. What magic is happening here?

There's one more video. It's brand-new—today. Alyssa and Stan are in the thumbnail, and the title is—*Where are you, Angela?* What in the world? It has to be a coincidence. Triple-checking my earbuds, I click on my name like it's a personal invitation. The new window pops up, and I immediately enlarge to full screen, not even pretending to work anymore.

It's just Stan and Alyssa sitting on the leather couch in their rear family room. Usually they're surrounded by kids and movement and laughter, but today it's only the two adults sitting in the middle of the couch, separate but tilting in toward each other where the cushions leave a cavern between them. Their faces are not the animated ones I've come to expect through the screen; they're the more serious, realistic faces of the two humans I met a few weeks ago. Alyssa speaks first.

"We're sorry for the change in our regularly scheduled content, but today we need to do something a little different."

Stan takes over without hesitation, which lets me know they either practiced this or are reading off prompts. "As you know, we've been looking for an intern to join our production and family and have been overwhelmed by the interest in our search. After a long application and interview process, one candidate stood out above the rest."

Alyssa takes over. "Yes, she walked into our lives with a humility and passion that both won us over and made us want to know this amazing individual better. But here's the problem, and why we're reaching out to our YouTube community."

My heart is pounding. I mean, I don't know for sure they're talking about me, but . . . somehow I know they are. How did they see so much in me in that fumbling, humiliating interview?

"Somehow our little Cinderella of an intern left before we could get her phone number. But we know she watches our channel regularly, so we want to send out one last message before we'll be forced to move on." Stan finishes and sits back, letting Alyssa take the spotlight. He's staring into the camera like he's looking through the computer and into my heart, soul, and mind.

"Angela." Alyssa says my name, and I flinch. I should've picked a name with no connection to my present or past. If somehow Mother ever saw . . . but how would she? Can't consider it now. I refocus and listen closely.

"Angela, we want you to come be a part of the Feely family."

That sentence, it's like a dream come true. They want *me*. Not just to work for them but to be part of their family. No more Mother? No more stealing? No more starving and closet, and I wouldn't even have to think about using a knife against Mother, or any other homicidal ideations. Maybe the Feelys should've adopted me after my birth parents signed me away.

"Check your email, dear," Alyssa says, with a gentle scold, already sounding like she's my mom trying to keep in touch while I'm at college. "We're waiting on the edge of our seat to hear from you."

"You have until Sunday night to get back to us. Then we'll move on." Stan has an edge of urgency to his reminder, and I can tell he means it.

"Talk soon, Angela. You're priceless."

Alyssa's closing words shake me to the core. This is what she says to her children, each and every one, as they walk out the front door and to school each morning. "Don't you forget," she says, the remembered voice echoing in my mind, "you're priceless, and don't let anyone tell you otherwise."

A calming warmth starts where my heart is and then spreads, first through my chest and into my shoulders and neck, head, ears, arms, fingers, toes. They want me. They love me. They think I'm worth something.

I can't get into my inbox fast enough. I fumble over the keys and end up typing strange URLs before I can get the right address in and click Gmail.

It's been weeks since I've been in here, and a few pieces of junk mail fill my screen in rapid succession like a centipede. But then it's there. Alyssa@AllTheFeels.com. One, two, three, four emails spaced a few days apart, starting just a few hours after our initial interview. It's a different email address from the one that sent me the scheduling information. I'm not sure what this change means, but I'm eager to open the emails.

When I click on the earliest message, it plops onto the screen, fully formed. *Angela* and *We liked* and *hope to hear from you soon* . . . The bits and pieces my brain can snatch up start to form a positive picture in my head, and, breathing shallowly, I force myself to start at the beginning.

May 13

Angela,

Thank you for meeting with us today. We liked what you had to bring to the table but are still working to make our final decision. In the meantime, we were hoping to get some contact information from you, references, school contact, etc. We hope to hear from you soon.

AllTheFeels,
Alyssa

May 20

Dear Angela,

Hello from Santa Barbara! After careful consideration, we've made our final decision on our intern for this summer. We'd love to talk to you on the phone. Is there a way to contact you directly? Please email ASAP, or give me a call.

AllTheFeels,
Alyssa
234-555-2344

It feels a bit like I'm on one of their prank videos and Stan is going to jump out from behind a plant with a camera, laughing. I eagerly advance to the next email.

May 22

Angela,

I hope we have the correct email address. I've reached out to you several times now about the summer intern position you interviewed for. I know in my last email I wasn't very clear on our intentions, but we would like to offer you that position, pending a background check, etc. I don't seem to have any further contact information for you.

We need to hear back from you by May 26, or else we will need to, reluctantly, go another way.

Talk soon,
Alyssa
234-555-2344

Then the last one was from today, just an hour or two ago.

May 26

Angela,

If you saw our video, I hope you're reading this right now. We've implemented some of your ideas, including the kid-focused mini-channels, and just today we accepted a deal with the Forstons for a charity challenge in August. We've seen a huge boost in views and follows in just these few weeks and would love to make you a part of our team, but we're unsure how to proceed.

Henry mentioned that you told him there have been some struggles at home. I'm sure this is a chaotic time, and if you need to pass on this opportunity, we understand. But the mom in me can't help but offer some additional assistance. Henry would kill me if he knew I was getting so personal, but my sister got pregnant in high school, and my parents kicked her out. Her life got really hard after that, and I see a lot of potential in you, Angela.

As you know, this was intended to be an unpaid internship, but we've discussed it, and if you're willing to spend your summer with us, we'd love to pay you a small salary. There are summer housing options on campus at Westmont College, and Henry says he can help you there if you need it. And we can help you with transportation. I know this is crazy—believe me, I keep hearing it—but hiring an intern was my idea, and I want you.

Sunday is our deadline. If I don't hear from you by then, Henry and Stan want to move on, and I really can't stop them.

Hoping to see you again soon,
Alyssa

PS—Henry's ready to help. You can email him at Henry@AllTheFeels.com or call him at 234-555-2637.

I slump back into my chair, the exhaustion of the day in my bones. I should be happy. They picked me out of all the applicants, and from the videos I just watched, there were hundreds of written applications and dozens of in-person interviews. And out of all those probably very normal people, they settled on weird little Angela Sampson.

But the initial thrill of acceptance plummets into despair almost immediately. They want me but . . . Mother. I might not be in the closet anymore, but I'm still trapped. With the cool, calculating movements of a machine, I close out of my Gmail account, erase my history, put away my earbuds, reattach the keystroke logger, and press the off button. It hurts too much being this close. I have to get away.

I dive onto my bed and talk to my friends. "Hey, pretties! I've missed you guys." I give Jessie a side-glance. "And handsome. I didn't forget you, Jessie. Come here, Angela."

I grab the little red-haired doll and run my finger under her lace collar and into the small hole between the fabric and the glass joint of her neck, relieved when the cool steel of my old ID bracelet chills my skin. With a quick glance over her dress and hair, I check for any signs of Mother's revenge. A clump of hair, a crack in the glass of her face. Of all my dolls, I was pretty sure she wouldn't hurt Angela. She loves this doll almost as much as I do, for some reason. But I check for damage just in case.

I used to have eleven dolls; three of them were my favorites: Francine, Sally, and Nora. They were beautiful, and unlike my other, more common plastic and cheap glass dolls, those three pretties were made of pure white porcelain with painted eyes. I'd brush their hair for hours, practice hairdos that I could never do on myself. They were my treasures.

Then Mother started making me steal. First, a necklace in my pocket at T.J. Maxx. I could hardly stop crying in my bed that night. I may not have had the best parents or all of my memories, but one I couldn't get out of my head was when my birth mom taught me not to steal, the day I rebelliously walked out of 7-Eleven still clutching a candy bar I'd been begging for. I had decided I'd just hide it. No one would know. I'd even planned how I'd get rid of the evidence by burying the wrapper in the backyard. But it didn't take long for my birth mom to hear the crinkling in the back seat of the car and investigate. When she saw the unwrapped chocolate hidden under my thigh, she looked me in the eyes and said, "Angela, that is stealing. We don't steal."

I had to go back inside and tell the guy behind the counter what I'd done. He chuckled at the tears in my eyes and let me keep the candy bar without paying, but my birth mom made me pay him back anyway. I'd never felt so ashamed in my life, walking up to the smiling man who gave us free Slurpees on really hot days and never made me remember to have pennies for taxes.

After the first shoplifting trip with Mother, I couldn't stop thinking about how upset my birth mom would be if she could see who I'd turned out to be, which just brought more tears. I cried into the night, and when even the light from the moon had faded into black, I was still sobbing, brokenhearted. Who had I become?

I barely noticed the lock on the door scratch open. Mother walked in with the grape sleepy juice clutched in her hand and sat on the edge of my bed, pouring the purple liquid into a measuring spoon without saying a word.

I hated that syrupy liquid and the way the fluid took me to a gauzy dreamland where I sometimes saw my birth parents before the babies, before the big hurt. And that night, Mother was angry. She shoved the spoon in my mouth.

"Stop this crying immediately," Mother scolded, always a brick wall when I could've used a bag of feathers. "I thought we were past this childish boo-hooing. Here." Mother filled the spoon again and went to push it into my closed mouth, but before the metal could drag against my already sore lip, I opened my mouth wide like the baby sparrows I watched in their nest just outside the window. *Please swallow. Please.* I tried to muscle past the gag reflex, but the liquid seemed to just double in volume the longer it was in my mouth.

"Swallow," Mother ordered, echoing the voice in my head. She put her hand over my mouth, pinching my nose. I couldn't breathe. Mouth full, lungs empty, it was like drowning on dry land. With a desperate gulp, the medicine pushed past the gag reflex and slipped down my throat finally. But Mother didn't seem to notice that my mouth was empty. She kept her hands in place.

"Mmmm!" I vocalized, shaking my head back and forth. "Mmmmmmmm!" The scream in my throat scratched and rumbled inside with no discernable escape.

"My heavens." Mother lifted her hands and looked at them like they were covered in slime. "I was trying to help. No wonder your parents didn't want you anymore. What a difficult child."

She wiped the imperceptible coating off onto her pant legs and looked at me with the same scrunched face of disgust. It didn't take long for the sleepy juice to start its magic, and I dozed off into the dream world I both craved and feared. But when I awoke the next morning, still groggy from the late-night dosing, something was different. Off. Usually my girls—my Francine, Sally, and Nora—were tucked in tight by my side. But that morning they were gone. A week later I found a baggie of shattered white ceramic in Angela's outstretched arms. I never cried about stealing again.

After I lost those fragile beauties, Mother went after Terry, Mary, and Lucy. So now I check so closely that I lose track of time—under each dress, around each seam, hairline, and piece of plastic. When I get to Shelly, I stare at them, stunned. Relieved. Mother hasn't hurt even one.

"Well, we got lucky this time, huh, kids?" And for a moment it feels almost okay that I'm stuck here. I've got enough, and I have freedom within these walls after Mother locks the doors. I live a full life back here with my little friends, the Feelys, Sampson, and my photography.

It may not be everything; I might not see the whole night sky at one time or know what it's like to have a boy look at me like he loves me. I don't remember what it's like to eat when I want or what grass feels like with no shoes on. And despite watching a million slime videos, I've never made it. I've never even felt it. But that's okay, because this is enough—right? If I just keep doing my best to keep Mother happy, I can have these pockets of peace, and it would be greedy to want more. It would be selfish.

"You're all my family," I whisper to Carly, Jessie, Shelly, and Sam, and caress Angela's hair, pretending to tuck it behind her ear. "I will always protect you."

I'm suddenly aware of how exhausted I am. In the darkness, I tug at the covers, the energy from the earlier carbs and adrenaline now wearing off. The bed smells like sleep, and I'm ready to drift off.

"Good night, pretties. I love you, Angela, Jessie, Carly, Shelly, and Sam." Yes. I'm sure of it. They're enough for me. Oh, my dolls and my little visitor. How could I forget? I'm still surprised he hasn't come. "Good night, Sampson!" I whisper toward the window, feeling loved.

I plop my head on my pillow, stretching out, wriggling my body deeper and deeper into the concave mattress. Sleep approaches fast, and I'm already thinking through tomorrow. I'll delete my Gmail account so I'm not tempted to look anymore. It's easier this way. I might need to stop watching the Feelys for a while too, just until this pain of almost and what if passes.

The to-do list grows as I turn onto my side. Lost in my plans, I slip my hands under my pillow, like I normally do while drifting off to sleep, when I touch something wet and soft. I yank my hands out reflexively and hold them up. A dark liquid coats my fingers, and I touch them together just to be sure I'm not hallucinating. Whatever it is, it's sticky and thick, and it makes my skin crawl.

On my knees, I flip the pillow so that it stands up against the headboard. The underside has a small, dark stain that has soaked into the fabric, and there's a matching dark mass on the mattress underneath.

"Oh my gosh." I gasp, a deep, unnerving shiver vibrating through my bones and into my very being. I cover my mouth, forgetting the strange substance on my fingers till it's on my face. I never, ever turn on my lights past bedtime, but tonight I stumble off the bed and toward the wall, heart flopping, sure yet unsure of what I'm about to find. With a quick flick, the room fills with light, and I see it—the red on my hands, my bed, my pillow, and in the middle of it all, a small ball of feathers.

Sampson.

I scream.

CHAPTER 13

"Good morning, Tara! We have some delicious leftovers from yesterday. I hope you got your work done so we can enjoy our day." Mother's voice is grating, and I can't answer. I couldn't sleep in the bed last night, so I curled up under the computer desk, knees to my chest just like in the closet, and I rocked. I rocked and rocked and rocked, that image burned into my mind. But it didn't leave, and it hasn't left. And I'm still sitting there, stunned.

"Tara?" There's a touch of frenzy in Mother's voice when she sees the bed empty and the bloody scene I didn't have the heart to remove. My dolls are all tumbled over onto their faces like they're bowing down in mourning for our loss. "Tara?" Her voice pitches up.

I cover my ears and bury my face in my knees. I can't look at her. She's hurt me so many times, torn me down and humiliated me, but this time is different. She's broken something inside of me. And like those dolls she broke when I was a ten-year-old, and Sampson's broken little body, nothing can put those pieces back together.

"Tara," she scolds almost playfully, "there you are. What are you doing under that table?"

I don't answer, even though I know I should. I just got out of punishment; I should be afraid of going back, but that must be what's broken—I'm not afraid of her. I'm angry. Anger is not an emotion I'm used to letting myself feel, but it's boiling and bubbling inside of me, uncontrolled, and the only way I can hold it in is to clench my legs tight and make myself into a ball. Otherwise, I *will* explode.

"Oh, what, are you upset about that little bird thing? Listen, it got into the house through a window *you* left open, by the way. And I was just trying to get it out, and . . . well, you saw. I meant to clean it up before you came back in, but . . . I was so busy trying to run the business without you and making your special meal."

She stands by my toes, and I can feel her there. I hold my breath, keeping every part of her away from me, including her smell. I rock again, mostly to keep myself from losing it. Mother just speaks louder.

"Fine, you want to throw a little fit, go ahead. That bird is disgusting and dirty. I'll toss it in the bin." I'm sure she's touching Sampson, and part of me wants to scream "NO!" but at the same time, I don't think I could ever touch him again. "There, all done." She claps her hands like she's wiping germs away and then pauses.

"Tara, I'm not kidding. Get up now." Mother's voice turns into a growl, and I know I'm pushing my limits, but that feels good. "Tara," she warns, and I can feel her essence in front of the desk again. "Get off your ass and get out here, you lazy little whore. It's your own damn fault that vermin died. If you hadn't been feeding it, this never would've happened. You killed that little nuisance when you lured it in here with your crumbs."

Mother despises vulgarities, and I know that I've really crossed a line when she lets them spill into her language. Usually this would be enough to send me scrambling out and begging for forgiveness at her feet, but not today. I let my hands drop and my body uncurl.

"I did not kill Sampson."

She laughs. "Is that what you call it? What a ridiculous name. You will never grow up, will you, child? You *will* clean this mess. With bleach." Her feet, clad in the same bulky white gym shoes she always wears, barricade my way out. This is how Mother works. She tells me to come out but also keeps me from leaving, standing in my way, muttering about needing several gallons of the sterilizing liquid.

The broken bits floating around inside of me poke at my feet and legs, and without much planning or forethought, I kick her shins through her acid-washed jeans, as hard as I can.

"What the . . . ?" Mother yells, too stunned to be angry just yet, but also knocked off guard just enough that I can scramble out from under the table. She's bent over, grasping at her legs, and I stand, crouched, ready for anything. She flips her curtain of permed nearly white hair and sets her icy-cold stare on me.

"Oh, that was a mistake. A BIG mistake," she growls, and it's like I'm watching her grow in front of me. She rises to full height and stands with no fear, staring me down. "What a disgusting child, treating your mother this way."

"You are not my mother," I spit. I'm trembling now, just noticing the dried blood on my hands and how it cracks on my face when I talk.

Her hand lands a hard crack against my face before I even notice she's moving. The force knocks me off my feet, backward into the photography table. My skull lands against the corner with a sickening crack.

Daggers of light splinter through my field of vision before I hit the ground. Not a sound leaves my lips, just a soft thump like when we toss heavy boxes into the back of the van. And then a gray dimness, rolling in slowly.

"Damn it." Mother sighs and taps my foot with her own and then crouches over me. "Tara," she yells in my face, her breath sour and her clothes smelling of stale smoke. "Tara." She taps my cheeks, touches my neck, and lifts my eyelids. I couldn't respond if I wanted to. "Damn it," she whispers again.

Without another word and without attempting to help me, she leaves the room, slamming the door hard. I think she takes the wastebasket with Sampson's mangled body, but I can't know for sure. I lie as still as possible and listen. Mother usually takes some time to regroup before she comes back to dole out punishment, but I've never kicked her before. I've never really fought back before. She could be headed back in here with a knife or some way to tie me up and put me in the darkness.

But she doesn't return, and there's no slamming of cupboards or drawers and no menacing shattering of glass or crunching of plastic. Instead, there's the familiar squeak of the back door and the roar of the van. With tires squealing, she peels out and, as far as I can tell, is gone. I take a deep breath for the first time in a long time. She thinks I'm passed out. She thinks I'm so hurt I might be dying. Maybe she's going for help. Or maybe she's finding a way to finish me. A place to hide my body.

"Wake up," I tell myself out loud. "Wake up!" I can't let the darkness take me down, or when she gets back, I could end up like Sampson. I have to hide. I flip onto all fours, and my head spins; I think I might throw up. I dry heave, and I'm sure I *would* throw up if I'd eaten anything more than breakfast yesterday. But I don't have time for any of this. I've got to move faster. There are so few places to hide in this room, and I've tried them all, but when it comes down to it, when she comes back, it buys me very little time, and then I'm stuck.

"But where can I go?" I ask my doll friends. They don't answer. They never answer. Today I wish they would. Angela is lying facedown, right next to the bloodstain on the bed.

I crawl across the floor on all fours, my head pounding like it did when I first woke up in this room twelve years ago. As I fight to get up on the bed, the room spins, and I want to give up. I'm still weak from starving in the closet and my night of no sleep. It would be so easy to just give in and drift off into a dark bliss. But when I turn over my little Angela, there's a dried thumbprint of blood on her forehead. The walls have dark, rusty slashes where my fingers grasped for the light switch last night. And just as clearly as if Angela whispered it in my ear, I hear it, something I've known is the truth but that I'd been avoiding for a long time.

You will die here.

There's a trickle of something warm down the back of my neck. I touch it, and I don't even need to look at my fingers to know it's blood. My brain, shaken and blurry as it is, begins to formulate a plan. I wipe the blood on the bedspread, not caring that Mother will already be furious at the mess she caused but will find some way to blame on me. With shaking hands, I take Angela in my lap, facing her outward like when I do her hair.

"Shh, I know. I know," I whisper, imagining the worried chatter of my friends rising into a crescendo of thoughts, concerns, and emotions. *Break the window. Contact the police. Tell the Feelys. Check the door . . .*

The ideas swirl in a fierce tumult that's impossible to tear apart into one workable idea. *Break the window. Contact the police. Tell the Feelys. Check the door. Break the window. Contact the police. Tell the Feelys. Check the door . . .*

Then, the last idea repeats again and again, replacing all the others. *Check the door. Check the door. Check the door.*

Did I hear it, the scratch and click of that dead bolt that has been the sound of safety and freedom within these walls for so many years? In her fury and frenzy, with me passed out on the floor, did she really forget?

Check the door.

Sitting Angela on the bed, I stumble the few steps to the door, and I know even before I put my hand on the brass knob. The steel bar I can usually see bridging the space between the frame and the door is gone. I touch the gap with trembling fingers caked in dry, rust-colored blood. One more voice pounds through my thoughts, but it doesn't belong to a doll; this one sounds a lot like me, and it's screaming.

RUN!

CHAPTER 14

The kitchen is empty and clean—just like Mother always leaves it, except for the flicker of the fluorescent lights. Lights left on mean money wasted, and Mother doesn't waste money. My door unlocked, lights on—Mother didn't just leave, she fled.

I have no possible idea where she's gone or how long till she'll be back, so after dressing in the false belly and filling it with a few small items, and with Angela crowded inside, I lunge for the rear door, hoping for a second miracle. The knob doesn't even budge. I jiggle the door and ram it once with my shoulder, but that only makes my head spin faster.

I scan the kitchen. When I was little, I'd seen Mother put the key up on hooks inside the cabinet to the right of the door. Tall enough to reach now. *What did that specific key look like?*

But as soon as I touch the handle, I know something is off—the door is too light.

Inside, the hooks are gone, and so are the keys. No. They have to be here somewhere. I slap open every cupboard one at a time, switching to the next when I don't hear the jangle of metal against metal. I stop looking only to grab a fistful of bills from Mother's change jar and shove them into the plastic grocery bag I've been filling with things that didn't fit in the belly.

The drawers are empty of anything useful, filled with silverware or pencils or boxes of generic-brand saran wrap. Then I see it—the knife. The giant butcher knife I'd imagined using against Mother yesterday morning is nestled between a rubber spatula and a plastic serving spoon. It slides toward me on the ivy-patterned contact paper lining the drawer.

Desperate, I grab it, not sure exactly what I'm doing but remembering Stan using a butter knife to open a door at their house when Ryland accidentally locked himself inside. I position the tip of the knife where I think the latch should be. The blade shaves off paint and chips the wood at the doorframe, but I keep at it, twisting and stabbing and hitting metal. Finally, the flat side of the blade slips into the lock and unlatches it with a satisfying click. Never has such a single sound meant so much.

The door swings open, and the back staircase, the grayed wood of the planks peeking through the peeling green paint, welcomes me like a bridge to a new world. I sling my plastic bag of paltry belongings and cash over my elbow, knife still clutched in the other hand.

Run, the voice in my mind urges once again, aggravated this time. It hasn't stopped chanting since I realized Mother left the dead bolt open in my bedroom. It's urging me forward, prodding me from all directions. *Run. Run. Run.*

The sky is dark, and a clean, electric smell washes over me, sending shivers through my entire being. I glance at the broken door—I can't go back. I might be in terrible trouble. I might even die—but at least I understand those risks.

I turn back to the stairs. At the bottom of those warped steps, there are so many questions, far more complicated than the instinct to run. What if the Feelys don't want me? What if people are as terrible as Mother warned? What if I'm alone forever? What if I can't take care of myself? What if . . .

A raindrop hits my face and falls down my cheek like I'm crying. The fat droplets come slowly at first, plopping against my skin and the porch and my hair. I lift my face as some heavenly dam opens and the silvery drops multiply by a thousand. I don't close my eyes as the streams of water drive down on me, flooding my hair, face, ears, neck, shoulders, the fabric of my dress, and the simple canvas of my shoes. I laugh, and sweet rainwater seeps in through the corners of my mouth. I've never felt the rain before.

The butcher knife falls from my hand onto the porch with a clank—and I run.

My head is pressed against the front window of the library, fogging it up with every breath. Rain clings to the glass and catches the streetlights, making them swirl like a kaleidoscope. My dress is nearly dry now, after my labored run in the rain hours ago.

With what little energy I had left, I'd navigated through the unfamiliar back alleys of my neighborhood, my head spinning from the fall in my bedroom. The bleeding had stopped, but the pain throbbed with each rush of blood from my heart to my head, making it even harder to find my way.

It took me two hours to get to the library. First, I went to the computers and sent off an email to Alyssa, making up a story about leaving my boyfriend and needing help, before closing out of my email, not knowing her response.

Then I hid upstairs—there's the kids' area where there are toys and computers and games based on books and stories I've never had the chance to read. Kids played in hushed voices while parents walked around carrying loads of books. For some reason I felt safer in those bathrooms with the child-sized toilets and flyers for story time. Perched on one of the mini-toilets there, shivering through my soaked clothes, I ate the pancakes I'd tossed in my plastic grocery bag of clothes.

I almost didn't want to look. But, as I swallowed the last bits of pancake, I knew it was time.

I'd never used the computers at the library before today, but I knew they worked. I don't have my own library card, so I waited at a nearby table until I found another opening. I got lucky when a patron got up five minutes after signing in. I slipped into the seat and signed in to my Gmail account again. Right at the top was my answer.

Alyssa@AllTheFeels.com

Where are you?

Angela,

We want to help! Where are you right now? I'll send a car immediately. You don't have to do this alone.

Alyssa

As I wrote a quick response with the address of the library, I had an out-of-body moment. My fingers moved without much thought and clicked "Send" before I could stop myself. A few minutes later, a confirmation swooshed in, and I knew it was finally real. The Feelys were coming, and I was leaving Walnut Creek. The computer timed out a few minutes later, and I've been sitting here at a table by the front window for the past six hours.

I know it's risky coming to a place I've been to with Mother and then sitting in the front window, but she didn't like coming in here for some reason, so she'd make me go inside to use the fax machine or copier. I'd learned how to sneak books out of the library without setting off the sensors. Every year there was a display with the required reading for the local high school, and every year I'm sure I left the librarians puzzled when a whole set would disappear. But, unlike when I shoplifted, I made sure to return those books. I don't like stealing, really I don't. It's just that sometimes I feel like I don't have any other choice.

Anyway, I don't know that Mother could predict my behavior if she wanted to. She doesn't know me, not the real me. She only knows the controlled, submissive Tara she created. But that version of Tara is going to get me in big trouble if I let her. I don't know who I am anymore, but I can't be that frightened child.

The tattered pages of *Wuthering Heights* that used to fill me with awe and fascination now blur in front of me, and I can't focus on the meaning of even one sentence. I shudder with both fear and hope at every car that races by the window. If the library closes before they get here, I don't know what I'll do. I wonder how well they search the building after closing—the bathrooms, the study rooms. I need a backup plan. Like, when the building opens again tomorrow morning, I can go on one of those computers and find a homeless shelter. I shift in my seat. I don't want to go to a homeless shelter.

A blue Nissan slows down in front of the library, and I lean back to hide my face. I've never seen Mother drive anything other than our white cargo van, but I've also never tried to run away before. I swear she can see me, can read my mind, maybe is watching my every move. These are crazy thoughts, but they're there. Blood whooshes in my ears. A teen who had been sitting on a bench, texting, jumps up and slides into the back seat of the blue compact car. Oh gosh, I'm losing it.

A PA system dings on in the background. "The library will be closing in fifteen minutes . . ." A voice drones on about checking out books, and I glance around, counting bodies. Three in line to check out, one more in the computer area shoving books into a backpack, two library employees flirting discreetly in a corner, probably so relieved it's almost nine o'clock. Then there's me. Soon the young pregnant woman with hollow eyes and stringy hair and no place to go will be the center of attention. I hate attention. The room spins, and I can't think of one viable solution to this mess.

A black SUV pulls up, and this time something is different. I can feel it. The person behind the wheel is hidden in the dark interior, and there are no external markings, but there is something familiar and almost homey about the vehicle that makes me straighten my back. This time I'm sure it isn't Mother. The headlights illuminate the slanting rain, and I dart glances instead of staring. The driver's-side door opens and a man jumps out. His movements are loose and limber, like he's dodging linebackers instead of raindrops. It's definitely not Alyssa, he's too young to be Stan, and Connor isn't old enough to make the six-hour drive on his own. It's not one of the Feelys unless . . .

Under an umbrella now, the man reaches the front doors of the library, and I look away so my attention is less obvious. But it doesn't take more than one or two side-glances to have a dual feeling of reprieve and anxiety flood my bloodstream. It's Henry.

Shaking the water off his umbrella, he strides into the modest tiled entry, glancing around like a parent who lost his child in a supermarket. There's worry there, fear, and it's hard to imagine that he's feeling any of those emotions about me. I could wave and draw his attention in my direction, but my hands are like lead, stuck to the tabletop. If I reach out, if I let him take me away from Walnut Creek, I can never come back. There's been pain here, sorrow, grief, but it's also the only home I've known since I was a little girl.

"Hey!" Henry calls out, a little louder than a normal library whisper, which makes all the heads in the checkout line whip in our direction. I stare at my feet. His umbrella clicks shut, and he calls out again, in a whisper this time, "Hey, Angela, right?"

He approaches me, one hand out, like I'm a fragile statue teetering on the edge of the mantel and any sudden move will make me crash if he's not there to catch me. His dark hair has raindrops clinging to subtle curls, and his glasses are fogging up, but that doesn't stop him from landing in front of me.

"Angela?" he asks again.

"Yeah."

"Uh, let's go. Car is running." He sniffs and shakes some more water off the umbrella.

"Okay." I grab the plastic grocery bag that holds the last few items I couldn't fit in my pouch. Henry hesitates, eyebrow raised, but then keeps walking toward the exit. I follow, like a good girl. I'm well practiced at following.

CHAPTER 15

"Do you have any luggage?" Henry asks, holding the umbrella over my head to keep me dry as I lift myself into the giant car. I shake my head, clasping my plastic bag of items to my chest, finding words difficult to piece together. I'd love to walk in the rain again, but I also like this new sensation of someone protecting me.

Henry joins me in the front seat and tosses the umbrella in the back. The seats are leather, and I think they might be heated. The interior of the car is a cocoon of warmth, and the air smells like a hug. There's a deep chill inside of me that I don't notice until the moist heat starts to penetrate my skin from all directions. I keep my belongings clutched to my chest, but my shoulders and back relax against the warmed seat.

"So, you okay?" he asks, looking me over. His cheeks are pink from the chill outside, and his hair is slightly damp despite the umbrella. I'm alone in a car with a man. A young man I barely know. My temples pound, and I stare at my hands. The skin around my nails is peeling, and I want to bite off one of the hangnails, but that'd be disgusting.

I nod.

"Problems with the boyfriend and, uhh, your 'mom' wouldn't help or something?" He puts the word "mom" in air quotes like he doesn't believe my story. I don't even know how to answer him. He thinks I'm a pregnant twentysomething who's running away from my boyfriend when I don't even fully understand how pregnancy really works, much less what it's like having a boyfriend. I can't talk about Mother, that's for sure. The less anyone here knows about my life . . . my *old* life . . . the better.

"Wow, you really don't say much, do you?"

"My mom didn't like Frank," I blurt out and then add, "Frank is my boyfriend." It's so weird saying those words.

Henry sits up a little taller like he's really paying attention now. When I risk a quick glance, he's smirking.

"Of course his name is Frank," Henry scoffs, like he hates my fictitious boyfriend, and it makes my heart flip-flop.

"Is that a weird name?"

"No, but I've only known asshats named Frank, so I'm wondering if your Frank is an asshat too."

I've never heard of that term, *asshat*, and I have to hold back a smile at the mental image it produces.

"Frank doesn't want the . . . the baby." My backstory starts to come together in my mind. "He wants me to put the baby up for adoption, but my mom wants me to keep it, and—"

"What do you want?" he asks, taking a gradual turn onto the 101. I stop, the story line I was working on disappearing from my mind.

"Huh?"

"What do *you* want? I mean, it's your baby and your body. What do *you* want?" His foot is on the gas, and I'm pinned to my seat by acceleration and confusion.

"I don't know." It's safe to look at him now that he's focused on the cars surrounding us on the highway, and I don't think the crinkle in his brow is just from concentration.

"Really? I mean, you must've thought about it in the past . . . however many months." He hesitates, and I remember that moment when he objected to similar questions in the interview.

"I'm five months," I say. I'd thought this math through while waiting at the library. This timeline gives me exactly four months of buffer before they'll expect a baby, just enough cushion. The internship is only ten weeks. I'll figure out my next move before my supposed due date.

"Okay, so in that five months, has anyone, anyone at all, asked you what you want?"

No one, literally no one that I can remember, has ever asked me what I want. I know this is a grand fiction. I know that he wouldn't be asking if I wasn't "pregnant," but still, someone wanting to know my thoughts and needs is electrifying. I blink rapidly, refocusing before he notices. I clear my throat.

"Well, I know I want to work for the Feelys," I say decisively, telling the truth for the first time in our conversation. He seems to shake his head slightly, but I can't really tell for sure.

"You really do like them, huh?"

"Of course. They're amazing." I turn sideways and adjust my belly, getting more comfortable.

He snorts a little and then clamps his mouth closed. I wait for the rest of his response. The road is wet, and the rain is still falling in a light mist. The thrum of the windshield wipers and sparkle of the headlights through the liquid on the glass makes the interior of the SUV feel otherworldly, like I'm on a spaceship and it's taking me to an unknown planet I've been assigned to explore. I swear the headlights carry a fraction of warmth, and I settle back into my seat, and I know I'm smiling.

"I sincerely hope they don't disappoint you," he finally adds, gently.

"Mmmm." My head is swimming and still achy from the fall this morning. The warmth, movement, and a surreal sense of safety are making me dozy. "I don't know how they could ever . . . disappoint . . . me."

My eyelids droop. I don't want to fall asleep—it's rude and strange and leaves me in a vulnerable position with a man I don't really know. But I can't help it. So I place my hands around my belly and latch my fingers together. I highly doubt Henry would ever dare to touch a sleeping woman. He must not notice that I can barely keep my head up because, as I slip into the darkness of sleep, his voice drifts off into the mist, and I think I hear him say, "This will be interesting."

I awake with a start. It's dark, and soft music fills the car. Henry is driving, eyes on the road, and lights of passing cars, fewer than earlier, reflect in his glasses. I can't tell how old he is. At the interview he looked so official with his clipboard and tie, but today he looks younger. His shirt is still a button-up but made of a soft flannel material; a well-worn T-shirt collar is peeking out the top. He readjusts in his seat, and a clean, subtle scent finds its way over to me. I still don't fully trust the man, or any man, but there's something about his face that makes me like to look at him.

Like he can sense that I'm awake, he turns and makes eye contact. A nervous heat crawls up my neck and floods my face, and I'm grateful for the darkness.

"You're awake," he says flatly, the curiosity and friendliness missing from when I first got in the car.

"I'm sorry, I guess I dozed off." I readjust and sit up in my seat. My back is sweating, and the thin, cheap fabric of my dress is wet. I wipe at my face to make sure it's not drenched too.

"We're almost home."

"Home?" Fear takes my breath away, and I think that maybe Henry drove me to Mother's house by mistake. I glance around, nothing is familiar. The streets seem narrower than the ones in Walnut Creek and are definitely brighter, lit by tall arching streetlights that seem to be planted right next to the palm trees dotting the street at regular inter-vals. The clock in the car reads 2:47 a.m. I've been asleep for hours.

"Yeah, we're close. Are you ready for this?" There is a jokingly judg-mental edge to his question.

"Don't you like working for them?" He seems so unhappy, but why?

"It . . . it's complicated." He waves at me like he's washing the topic away. "Alyssa told me to bring you here, since you don't have housing yet . . ." My eyes narrow as he talks. I hadn't really thought through all those details.

"Oh, I don't want to impose . . ." I hadn't planned on arriving at the Feelys' home in the middle of the night. I'm not ready, but that doesn't matter at the moment. I'm a passenger in more ways than one.

We've turned into a subdivision of large homes with yards hidden behind fences and shrubbery; the few quick glances I get of the darkened structures reveal brick arches and three-car garages. I've never seen houses like this up close. How many rooms are inside each one? Are they for one family or two? I'm both overwhelmed and intrigued.

"We're here." We go over a bump at the end of the driveway, and my stomach is in knots. I've seen this house, this driveway. The tan stucco house with a terra-cotta roof and curving stone walk always reminded me of what I thought a castle in some southern island kingdom would look like. I've seen kids play in this yard and a ridiculous and intense game of H-O-R-S-E in this driveway. It's so dark that I can't see the hint of red in the stucco, but there are glowing yellow lights curving up the front walkway, and I feel like Cinderella driving up to the castle, only in my story I was never assigned a fairy godmother and decided to give the ball a shot wearing my rags. I straighten my dress and comb through my hair with my fingers. I can't let them find out who I am. I can't let them realize I'm not good enough.

Henry shuts off the car and gets out, and I shiver, suddenly cold. I don't know if it's from the seats losing their heat or the night air, but once he's gone, I feel it. The passenger door pops open, lighting up the interior of the car, and Henry is there on my side. His hand is out, and it takes me a moment before I realize he wants me to take it. There's something so natural about the gesture that I start to reach out, but my belly shifts and the items inside rustle. I freeze in place. With the light on, my strangeness must be glaringly obvious. I can't have Henry close to me right now. I can't have anyone close to me.

"I got it, thanks." I bat his hand away.

"Whatever," he mutters, and steps back like he's tired of this whole night. And I'm sure he is. He has to hate me by now—gosh, *I* hate me. I yank the grocery bag over my arm with a huff, filled with a profound wave of self-loathing and embarrassment.

How is this my life? We've passed thousands of houses, dozens just in this neighborhood, where people are sleeping in their soft beds and have never had to starve in a closet or steal things to make a living. Henry stands back, still within arm's reach, like he wants to be there just in case I need help. I'd rather fall on my face than fall into his arms. I sit on the edge of my seat, and wait for him to get the hint.

Henry tosses up his hands and walks up the front path without me, which somehow hurts my feelings even though I made him go. Once he takes the turn in the stone walkway and I can't see him anymore, I leap out of the car. The supplies in my belly bag make a loud crunching sound.

I slam the door and straighten my dress. *What have you gotten yourself into, Tara?*

It should be easy enough. I'll just walk up the path to the door. I'll be polite. I'll work hard. I'll keep my head down and stay as quiet as possible. With a deep, shaky breath, my ears ringing, I take a step away from the SUV, my first step into a new freedom.

And I stumble, my head heavy enough to pull me off-balance. I fall on my knees, hard, the rough cement of the driveway tearing at my skin, my hand hitting as a secondary casualty. The sting is instant. The bag bursts, and out spills a clump of granola bars; a discolored bra; one yellowed, wrinkled shirt; several crumpled wads of cash; and my stolen copy of *Wuthering Heights*, which skitters down the drive and onto the grass.

"Oh my god!" I hear from across the yard. Footsteps rush toward me. "Are you okay?"

Henry kneels by my side, touches my back and my arm, so close to feeling the buckle on my back holding the prosthesis in place. I try to push him away, but I'm weak. The blood from my hands smears his sleeve; he doesn't seem to notice, yelling in the direction of the house.

Urgent words swirl around me, and I keep saying the same thing over and over: "I'm okay. I'm okay. I'm okay." But he doesn't listen.

I can't get my feet under me; every time I try, I get tangled in the folds of my skirt and crash again into the concrete. He holds me up with an iron grip under my armpit.

Alyssa is suddenly in front of me in a pair of flowing teal pajama pants and a lacy tank top, her arms out like a mother calling for her baby to walk to her. Stan is by her side, wearing flannel pants and no shirt, a slight belly over what was probably muscle.

"What happened?" Stan asks, sounding horrified. Alyssa finds a spot by my other side, her touch gentle and caring.

"I don't know," Henry says. He sounds scared. "She was just behind me, and I think she fell."

"You *think* she fell?" Stan grumbles as I finally get my feet steady under me. "My god, Henry. Where were you?"

"She was behind me. I . . . I was going inside. She didn't want help, so I . . ."

"Just left her?" Stan presses as we walk past him. Alyssa keeps her gaze on me, and I'm starting to get steady again. Henry's hold almost hurts, and his other hand is drifting to my waist like he's determined to show Stan that he'll keep me from falling again.

"Hey, are you okay?" she asks, probably for the tenth time, but it's the first time it fully hits me.

"Yeah," I say, stiffening. "I can walk now. It's just a few scratches. I'm fine . . . I'm . . ."

"Shh . . . we'll get you inside and cleaned up." She squeezes my arm reassuringly. I lean into her to get away from Henry. He smells so clean, and his heat is making me sweat under my many layers. Alyssa smells good too, like she walked through a sunny field and all the flowers rubbed against her skin, leaving just a hint of their scent behind. But—if I can smell them, they can smell me. I wince.

Alyssa seems to notice my discomfort with Henry, and as we cross the threshold into the Feelys' house, she waves him away, but he doesn't let go. Stan holds the door open and then shuts and locks it, typing in a code on a panel by the front door, angling his body so I can't see the numbers. I can't blame him—I'm a stranger. I wouldn't trust me either.

"Hey, Hen." Alyssa catches Henry's attention when we stop on a large Persian rug. I recognize it from the video where Kelsey spills her slime on the expensive accessory and Alyssa tries several different cleaning supplies to get it out. I look for a stain, trying to ignore the conversation going on over my head. "I've got her."

"Alyssa, let me help."

"I've got her," she says more forcefully.

"Yeah, I think you've done enough," Stan says, breezing past.

"Why don't you at least put on a shirt?" Henry says, and then releases me so suddenly I stagger.

"Boys," Alyssa chides the two men like they're her children. Henry sits in one of the armchairs across from a familiar leather couch in the front room, pouting, and Stan disappears down the hallway that I think leads to the back staircase.

I can't believe I'm here. The vaulted ceilings with three giant wooden beams dividing the space into thirds, where balloons got stuck during Ryland's first birthday and the family had to use Nerf guns to shoot them down. The beautiful ceramic floors that Stan covered in dish soap for the kids to "ice skate" on during the Olympics. The curtains they let the kids pick out on an epic adventure to the fabric store. I sit on the couch in awe that this is real life. Real. Life.

"Sweetie, I'm going to get the first aid kit. You sit here." Alyssa pats the top of my head, not even balking at my greasy hair. I could hug her right now, but she leaves, and I keep my hands on my lap, palms up, blood beading up on my skin. It's starting to sting, and I wiggle my fingers to distract from the many versions of pain I can't seem to escape today.

"I'm sorry," Henry says from across the room.

"It's okay." I try not to look at him.

"It's not okay," he adds, tense, maybe from Stan's accusation. "You're pregnant. The baby . . . is the baby okay?"

He's worried about the nonexistent baby. What a stupid lie I've committed to.

"The baby is fine. It's just a few scratches. It was an accident."

"It was my fault."

"A few scratches never hurt anyone, or at least that's what Mother would always say . . ." My voice trails off. I said her name, and suddenly it feels like she might appear as an apparition.

"Well, I don't know if I agree with your mother. Let's take care of those scratches right now," Alyssa says, reentering the room carrying a hard plastic case with a red cross on it, and then kneels in front of me. "First of all, honey, how is the baby? Did you fall on your stomach at all? If so, we should really take you to the ER."

Alyssa opens the case on the floor and then takes out a pile of square and rectangular packets. One at a time she rips them open and, without taking out the contents, places them on the couch beside me.

"No, no, the baby is fine."

Alyssa puts down another large square packet and then reaches for my stomach like she wants to touch it. She can't touch me, or she'll know. I've come this far; I can't leave the castle now. Not because of a stupid fall and not because I let someone get too close to me. Instinct takes over and, just like with Henry by the car, I slap at her hand.

"Don't!"

My slap makes a cracking noise that I've heard before when Mother would discipline me, and the sound causes me to start. Alyssa pulls her hand back; there is blood on it, but it's likely mine. She's utterly shocked, her face no longer sweet and serene but now with a hurt that leaves lines across her forehead and maybe a glint of tears in her crystal eyes. The pain registers in my hand as the adrenaline of the moment wears off. I've been here not even ten minutes, and already just about every person I've encountered is worse off.

"I'm so sorry, I should've asked," Alyssa says, hardening to me a fraction while using a wipe to clean off the blood on her hand. She gives a forced chuckle. "I remember when I was pregnant I HATED it when strangers would touch my belly. I mean, I always thought, 'I don't know you, and you're touching *my* body?' And look at me, doing the same thing."

"Uh, sorry. In my, um, family we don't really touch much . . ."

"So, is it okay if I help you out? You know, your hands and your knees? Are you okay with that?" Alyssa picks up a wipe and holds it up in front of me, hesitant but also still sincere in her desire to help.

"Yes. Thank you." I lay my hands on the top of my thighs, and Alyssa swabs my palms with a stinging liquid. I want to yank them away, but I grit my teeth and hold still for her sake.

I can't watch as she cleans out the deep scratches that seem to have an unlimited supply of fresh red blood pooling back in after each throbbing wipe. To distract myself from my scratches, the pounding in my head, the fire on my knees, and the hot stickiness of the prosthesis, I take an inventory of the room, tallying all the items I've seen on camera a hundred times, which is enthralling, but then there are the little things I've never seen—like the kids' shoes piled by the door or a stack of papers on the dining room table that usually seems perfectly dusted and arranged.

There are more imperfections than I'd expected—the dust, the papers, the shirtless Stan from earlier, the tension with Henry—and I wait for the flaws to affect me, to disappoint me. But they don't. I know I can never be perfect, but if these people are real, that means that maybe in my defectiveness I can find what they have. Happiness. Success. Family.

Then Henry catches my attention, our eyes linking. He's watching me, and there's a look on his face I don't understand, a bit like interest and a bit like dread, but mostly, it's the expectant stare of someone who knows that something is off, but he doesn't know what. He wants to find out, and he's not going to stop until he knows the truth. My hope bubble doesn't burst but does deflate. He will be my undoing if I let him.

"Should we take a look at your knees?" Alyssa asks, her fingers hovering at the hem of my dress. Stan reenters, this time wearing a shirt. I watch him from the corner of my eye. He's large, larger than he seems on the screen. He's even taller than I remembered, and even if I hadn't seen him bare chested, I would've been able to tell how big he is through the tight cotton of his shirt. He scares me a little. Not in the same way Henry does, like he'll look into my soul and discover my past, but just his pure physical size, and actually the size of his personality too.

"Sorry that dunce didn't do his job. If you have any medical stuff you need help with, let Lyssa know. She knows about all that." He sits down right next to me, and the cushion tips me toward him till we're almost touching. His body heat emanates from his skin and caresses me uncomfortably. I pull my arms in tight to avoid contact. My knees naturally clench together too. Alyssa notices.

"Honey, you're making her uncomfortable."

"She's not uncomfortable, are you . . ." He hesitates, searching for my name. My body is rigid, and my cheeks flush with embarrassment. Here I was feeling all special, and Stan doesn't even know who I am.

"Angela," Henry interjects. He sounds annoyed, but I can't tell if it's at me or his boss. "Her name is Angela."

"Yeah . . . Angela. You're happy to be here, aren't you?" I know from watching Stan Feely on YouTube that he's a hugger. It's actually one of his taglines whenever they do a prank. "Hug it out!" he's known to shout when someone is dripping in slime or shaving cream or after whatever crazy adventure they decided to do that day. Then he'll toss his arms around his prank victim, sharing in the aftermath of his mischievousness. There are even "Hug it out!" T-shirts for sale on the AllTheFeels website. But I don't want to risk one of those big, encompassing hugs. One friendly embrace could ruin everything.

I nod a response to Stan but remain closed off.

"That's what I thought," he says, then stands up and claps his hands together. I nearly tip over once his weight is gone, but I get my body in control and steady myself.

"Well, I for one am ready for bed. Lyssa, you about done here?"

Alyssa has been working on my skinned knees and is securing the last large rectangular bandage. I've been so distracted by my anxiety at Stan's closeness that I hardly picked up on her progress.

"I'm finished." She smooths my skirt over my knees. "Let's get you settled. Rough day, huh?"

"Yeah," I mutter, and she looks at me with soft eyes. She thinks I left my boyfriend, upended my life to get away from a man who had been holding me down. Alyssa Feely is proud of me, and that feels amazing, better than when Mother tells me I was a good girl or I pull off a job perfectly. I need to feel this bubbly thing again. I want to always make her proud. She helps me stand.

"Henry, grab her bags, would you?"

"Oh, I don't have any . . . I don't . . ."

"I've got it," Henry says, covering for me seamlessly. He knows I don't have anything other than the shopping bag I dropped in the front yard. I don't know who this strange addendum to the Feely family is, and I definitely don't know if I can trust him.

"This way, honey." Alyssa leads me by the elbow, and I go. It's so much easier to listen and follow than make decisions. I've made too many decisions today. I'm tired of it. No. I'm just tired.

CHAPTER 16

"Here's your towel, and the bathroom is right there." Alyssa points to a closed door inside a tidy room with a large bed against the back wall just under a picture window. It's one of the most beautiful things I've ever seen. The bed is perfectly made with a shiny purple bedspread that looks brand-new and a curling wrought-iron headboard that makes me picture roses climbing the walls of a hidden garden. There's a faint scent of something delicate that wraps around me. I don't belong here. There's too much beauty in this room—how will I ever sleep?

"I'll have Henry bring up your other things, and you can get some rest. Can I get you anything before I head to bed? A snack? Extra blanket? Pillow for your legs?"

"No," I blurt. The only thing I need is to get some space to think through what happened today and what I'm going to do next.

"Okay then, we can talk job and logistics in the morning." She backs out of the room, leaving the door open a crack. I long for the comforting click of the lock. "Sleep tight," she whispers, walking away.

Open. The door is left open. A high-pitched ringing starts in my ears, and my head spins like I'm going to pass out, a pounding pain pulsating with each whoosh of my pulse. I reach to close it when Stan's loud whisper trickles through the crack in the door, and I can't help but listen.

"She's kinda strange, don't you think?" he says.

"Stop it; she's clearly getting out of a bad situation. Remember what Stacey went through when she left Dan? I think she's brave," Alyssa says, sweetly scolding Stan. "Hold on—we need new towels." A door squeaks in the hall.

"I know. I know. She's some YouTube savant, but still . . . weird." Stan keeps talking, and even with my very limited understanding of subtext, I know he's being sarcastic.

"She's the one, I know she is. The numbers are on a steady climb right now, and I think they'll only go up, and you know I need help. I can't do it all after losing the—"

"Okay, babe. Okay," Stan says in a somewhat patronizing tone, and he must pull her into his arms because her words muffle into nothing. "I trust you, but tomorrow please have her take a shower. We can pretend she doesn't smell, but the kids . . . they're a bunch of loudmouths."

I sniff at my fingers and my arm, drag my hair across my face. I don't smell like the sweet, pure fragrance that fills the room. I knew it. I knew they could smell me.

"Yeah, I know." The closet door squeaks shut. "I've got a plan."

"A plan?" Stan asks, still playing with his wife. Their voices start to fade. "An anti-stink plan?"

My face burns hotter with every word.

"Stan!" Alyssa giggles, and their voices drift as they move a little farther down the hall. I press my ear against the door and hear their laughter mingling as it disappears. They're gone, and I stand on the other side of an open, unlocked door.

The hall light flicks off.

I'm alone in the beautiful room, and I have no idea what to do now. I push the door shut till it clicks, and press in the button on the handle. I take the cool nickel knob into my palm and twist. The lock pops open, and that sickly feeling starts rushing through me again, and the bell inside of my head rings even louder and higher, like a siren. I click it again and then twist the knob, and the button flicks out, unlocked again. Hmm. I lock it one more time and back away, unsteady. I'm free. I should be relieved, overjoyed. But the room is too big and pretty. The door is too thin, and the lock so flimsy. I still don't know if I'm disappointed because it's so easily opened or because a part of me wishes it was locked from the other side.

I should go into the bathroom and scrub my face and hands, or find what makes the room smell the way it does and make myself smell that way too, but the screaming pain in my head grows louder, and my skull pounds like it's pulsing. My bandaged hands and knees thrum in the same rhythm. I tear at my dress and the prosthesis itching and burning on my abdomen, but I can't wrestle out of them. It's all too much. The room spins, the back of my head aches, and my knees give out. I hit the ground with a shock of pain. Then I crumple into a heap on the floor.

Where am I? Sunlight warms the top of my head, but my arms are cold, and the pains in my body start to come through the darkness of sleep. Something tickles my nose and eyebrows. I flinch away. But the tickling doesn't stop. I twitch again and blow air up toward my nose, thinking it's a stray hair. But this time there's a giggle.

My eyes fly open, and a little face is inches from mine, a dirty fingernail hanging in midair ready for another tickle. The room comes into focus. That's right, I'm really here.

I sit up, still on the floor fully dressed. My belly shifts, all the items inside rustling. I need to take this thing off. I've never worn it for so long, and the skin on my shoulders is raw from the straps. The little boy kneels in front of me, his eyebrows raised, little fingers clamped over his smirking lips.

"Ryland." I say the child's name like he's my own little brother. He's more adorable than any one of my dolls. His eyes don't sparkle because they're made of glass; they twinkle because they're filled with mischievousness.

"Hi!" he says simply, not seeming to notice or care that a stranger knows his name. "What's wrong with your face?"

I touch my cheek. It's rough from sleeping on the carpet, and there are deep imprints in my skin. There's a full-length mirror on the back of the bathroom door, and I catch a glimpse of myself there. The carpet impression on my face is barely noticeable, but there's an outbreak of acne across my forehead and cheeks and one enlarged pustule on my nose.

"Just a few polka dots," I say, and try to smile at the little boy. He claps.

"Oh, that sounds fun. I want some." He literally bounces on his toes. Yeah, *adorable* is the right word. "What's your name?"

I can't help but answer. "My name is . . . Angela. Nice to meet you." I offer my hand, remembering to use the made-up name last-minute, totally caught up in our interaction.

"Angela," he says, his *l* lisping into a *w* as he touches my hand and then steps back so he can see all of me. Now I'm the one covering my mouth to keep from laughing.

"Nice to meet you too, Ryland."

"You can call me RyRy if you want. Mommy calls me that," he says, distracted by a small drawer in the mirrored dressing table on the opposite wall. I remember how Alyssa and Connor would call the little baby bundle RyRy and how Stan encouraged him to take his first step by chanting, "RyRy! RyRy!"

"That sounds nice," I say, not adept at talking to a little person. I talk to my dolls, though, and they're little people in a way. I think about poor Angela in my pouch and how I long to see her face, comb her hair, and tell her about the past twenty-four hours. Then a pang of sorrow hits my gut. All my other little friends I left behind. Mother surely won't spare them. Not if she knew it would hurt me.

"You sad, Angela?" Ryland asks, elbow deep in the fully open drawer. It's filled to the brim with tiny, random treasures: a collection of coins, broken sticks, a phone that looks like its battery has been removed, and a clump of rocks and shells.

"I miss my friends," I say, and sit on the end of the bed, peeking in to take inventory of all the objects he's taken the time and effort to hide.

"I have lots of friends," he says, closing the drawer and putting three round, glimmering marbles in his pocket like they're money. "Here." He holds a fourth one out to me, a small, golden marble that looks heavy, but when I take it from his tiny pincer grasp, it's light and smooth as glass. "I'll be your friend, Angela."

The marble is warm and damp from his sweaty palm, but I don't mind. If I'm going to have a friend here, Ryland is probably my safest option. Four-year-olds aren't overly suspicious, and they won't notice if I mess up and say the wrong thing.

"Friends," I agree. Every time he says *Angewa* instead of *Angela*, I get warm inside, and it's hard to not smirk at least a little. "But I don't have anything to give you."

He waves his little hand and scrunches up his eyebrows like he's all business. "It's okay. You can owe me."

"Oh I can, can I?" I laugh out loud this time. This is like talking to my dolls but better. I can't predict what this small human is going to say from moment to moment, and I don't want to. Not knowing is delightful.

"Yeah," he says, and heads for the bathroom door. He disappears through the door. I should probably leave. Friends is one thing, but having him use the toilet in front of me, that's a whole different story. He pops his head back through the crack in the door, staring at me like he's very confused.

"Do you have a baby in your tummy, Angela?"

"I . . ." I'd better get used to answering questions about this fake baby, at least until I figure out what to tell the Feelys about it all. "Yeah."

I nod and do that strangely maternal protective thing, covering my stomach like there's a baby inside and not random objects, including a doll and a few changes of clothing.

"Okay." He shrugs and returns to the bathroom. "Bye, Angela." His little voice echoes out of the room, and I think there's a click of a lock. I push off the bed and stumble over to where he disappeared.

Inside is a white-and-cream-colored bathroom with a sparkling-clean toilet, a bathtub with an elegant, shimmery shower curtain pulled shut, and a double sink parallel with a large, mounted mirror, and then exactly opposite of where I'm standing is a door that matches the one I just went through, except this one is closed fully. A closet? Is Ryland in a closet? No wonder he was able to get in my locked room—he was here all along.

I never thought the Feelys would do such a thing. I mean, Ryland didn't seem hungry or frightened, but then again, maybe his parents aren't as strict as Mother. Maybe they don't beat him if he gets out. His little voice is chattering loudly on the other side of the closed door. He's brash and sounds happy. Maybe he likes his closet? Maybe it's not as scary for him as I think it is? But a little boy doesn't deserve to be left in the dark. I could help him, bring him food, talk to Alyssa and let her know how petrifying it is inside. They can't be monsters. They can't be like Mother.

The chilled tile cuts through my worn cotton socks like I'm barefoot. His playful noises drag me across the bathroom, and I move like a puppet on strings.

Who do you think you are? You can't even help yourself. How can you save that child? Mother's voice mocks me in my mind.

I don't know! I shout mentally. The ringing in my ears is back, and my foot slips on the polished tile. I steady myself with the doorknob. There's a button lock on this side of the door, just like the one from last night, and as far as I can tell, it's unlocked. Shaking, I test the knob, and it turns.

Mother's phantom voice is right—I'm not equipped to help anyone. But I can't just leave him. I wish someone had opened my door a long time ago and let me out of the darkness.

I twist and yank, prepared to see a little person curled up on the cold floor, scared or lonely or resigned. But when the door swings wide, it's not a closet or a whimpering lump that meets me, but a vast room, twice the size of my own, painted a dark blue. Toys litter the floor, and a full-size bed with a twin-size bunk on top of it fills only one corner of the vaulted room. It's Ryland's bedroom. I've seen it before online, but usually it's clean and he's opening toys with his sister in one of their unboxing videos.

What was I thinking? I shake my head. Of course the Feelys wouldn't put their son in a closet, especially not Ryland. They love him. They're not Mother.

Ryland is halfway under his bed looking for something or hiding his marbles and hasn't even noticed my grand entrance. He doesn't need to know. I leave the way I came in, the anxiety of a new day starting to download into my body. I lock the door to Ryland's room and to the guest bedroom and flick on all the light switches, illuminating the bathroom in a flood of white and turning on a loud whooshing fan in the ceiling.

Secured between two locked doors, I find the small confines of the bathroom comforting in a way. The fan makes enough sound to muffle Ryland's playful shouts and the other, even more remote sounds of the house. As close to safe as I've felt since before I wrote the first rebellious email, I strip off my dress and drop it into a pile on the floor. The dirt is obvious now in contrast to the clean, bright tile.

I wrestle out of the prosthetic belly and lay it down with more care than the dress. It smells. Ugh. I gag as I turn it over and open the damp zipper on the side. I hope this isn't the stench I heard Alyssa and Stan joking about in the hall last night. It's downright repugnant. Out of the pouch, I recover my belongings, including a change of clothes and little

Angela, hair matted and body twisted from when I hastily shoved her inside before my escape.

"There you are," I whisper, and pull her into my arms. "I have so much to tell you about." I kiss her forehead and hold her tight. She smells like home: musty, like dust and a touch of Lysol from when Mother got into one of her cleaning rampages. I lean back against the cold tub, shivering in just my shorts and sweat-soaked tank top. I imagine what Angela would say to me if she really was my best friend or sister.

What the heck happened? I laugh at the imaginary exclamation.

"Yeah, I know. I went a little crazy, didn't I?" I say out loud, not just to the doll in my arms but to myself.

We got out? she would ask if she were real.

"Some of us did," I answer, ashamed that I could only save one of my companions.

Oh goes through my mind, and I'm sure she's as deeply ashamed of me as I am. And with that small, imaginary sound, something that's been keeping me going since the closet, since Mother's outburst and running away and the library and Henry, breaks inside of me, and a sound comes out of my mouth that's neither words nor a scream but something in between. It's not calm, like when I talk to Angela or Ryland. It's not fierce or shattered like when Mother hurts me. This is a wail of pain and a sigh of release happening at the same instant— acknowledging I am free but also unsure if I am okay with leaving so much behind. It's a soundless cry and a flood of tears for the Tara I was, and fear of the Angela I must become in order to survive.

CHAPTER 17

"I'm not doing another slime challenge. Those are getting so old." Voices spill out from the kitchen as I tiptoe down the stairs. My hair is still wet. The bath didn't make much of a difference, since my clothes and pregnancy suit still reek, but maybe they'll appreciate that I'm at least trying.

The door is right in front of me. This time, if I reach the bottom step, I can just keep walking and leave. They'd never know. I don't have any place to go and very little money, but I could be myself and get rid of this whole pregnancy lie.

But Angela is on the bed upstairs, and my bag with cash and clothes that Henry dropped outside my door last night is hanging up in the closet. And Ryland—his cheeks and dimples are just too adorable. He said I'm his friend. I think of the marble I tucked under Angela's satin ribbon and his crooked smirk when a little wiggly giggle echoes out of the kitchen.

"If I never touch slime again—"

"You have to do what you're assigned, Kels," Connor cuts her off, and he sounds annoyed. I guess I understand. I'd be annoyed too. Why is she complaining? I thought she liked slime. They call her the slime queen because she's the best mixer in the family. Her videos always get tons of views.

"I want to do a fashion show with all those clothes Crumpit sent me," she argues back.

"It would be good to give them some coverage. There were a lot of clothes in that box," Alyssa's voice adds.

"Fine, you can do a fashion show," Stan agrees, and I cringe. I always hate posts that seem like they've been sponsored.

"That should be on Kelsey's channel. That's not an AllTheFeels product." Henry is already here. I can't believe I can pick out his voice as easily as each member of the Feely family. And what's more surprising . . . I agree with him.

"Shut up, Henry," Kelsey snips. I can't tell if she's joking or actually mad.

But instead of walking into the kitchen and joining the discussion, I shift my weight backward, craving the bolted bathroom. What if they don't like my ideas? What if they find out I'm not even a high school graduate? What if just a few more minutes in conversation with me lets them see it all? I should wait in the guest bedroom until someone comes to get me. I don't want to walk into the middle of something that doesn't involve me. It's not my place.

"Hey you, girl," Ryland calls out, and I jump.

"Hey," I whisper and wave.

"What are you doing?" he asks in a crazy-loud voice for such a small person.

"I forgot something upstairs. I was just going to head up and—"

"Angela! You're awake," Alyssa says, coming up behind me.

"I was just getting tidied up. I'm sorry if I'm late."

"Oh, not late," she says. I like her smile. I hope that's what I look like when I smile. "We wanted to let you rest after your busy day yesterday. How are your hands and knees?"

"Fine." I hide the glaring red gashes on my hands against my thigh and in the folds of my skirt. They're not pretty, but I don't want to go through more of a fuss getting bandaged again. What really hurts is my head, and my vision is still slightly fuzzy, but they don't know about that injury, and I plan to keep it that way.

"Come on in the kitchen. We put some breakfast aside for you, and we're having our morning meeting right now. I'd love for you to meet the kids and give some of your thoughts. Henry will get you set up with a phone and computer and a list of your duties. Then we'll go from there."

There are two entrances into the kitchen, and Ryland runs around to the one that must meet up with the rear family room. Alyssa takes me a different way, through the living room and dining room, until we walk into a nest of activity.

The kitchen is exactly how I remember it. Brilliant white cabinets and sparkling countertops. Five stools lining one side of a giant kitchen island, a massive dark wooden table to the right with chairs around all sides except for the one that backs up to the large picture window. A bench there could fit another four people, especially if they're children. It's like they're prepared for an army to move in and ask for PB&Js for lunch. The brightness of the ceiling lights surprises me, and I flinch and instinctively cover my eyes.

"Sorry, the lights in here are a little over-the-top, I know. They're LED, for the videos. Now we just need one ring light, and . . ." She must notice the blank look on my face because she stops. "Lighting isn't really a day-one discussion, huh? How about you meet the crew instead?"

The people in the room come into focus, and every face is well-known to me, though they appear slightly different in person than they do through the heavily pixilated, ancient computer screen. Kelsey is as adorable as ever—actually, more adorable with her green eyes and jet-black, purple-streaked hair coming through in person in brilliant color. Even in her pajamas and with her hair in a fuzzy halo around her head, the ten-year-old is an older, female version of Ryland, and I want to pinch her dimpled cheeks like I used to do with my doll Sally. They have the same eyes.

Next to her is a different set of eyes that look up from a bowl of soggy cereal. These are dark and, according to an "Ask Me Anything" vlog, actually a deep shade of gray. But from here they look almost black. Connor. I've always been fascinated with the oldest Feely child. He's an excellent big brother and loving son, and he seems to be pretty smart. AllTheFeels videos with Connor are my favorite, even though he's several years younger than me. I think of all the Feely family members, Connor and I will be friends. I let myself give him a little smile, testing out the limits of my boldness. He makes the briefest amount of eye contact with me and then glances away. He must be shy.

Little Ryland bounces up and down, peeking over the corner of the granite countertop. Connor rubs the four-year-old's head. Stan, still in his tight shirt and baggy flannel pants from the night before, leans against the counter. His salt-and-pepper hair is disheveled and might be greasy, but I can't totally tell from this distance.

"Hey! Everyone!" Alyssa calls out to the collection of people in the kitchen, but no one reacts. "Hey! Guys!" she tries again, but it's almost like they don't want to hear her. Stan slaps the counter, making the ceramic bowl of serving spoons jangle and teeter.

"Shut it and listen to your mom," he roars, and Ryland's little head disappears. "Damn it. You guys never stop talking."

I'm not used to a loud male voice, and I understand Ryland's desire to hide. My hands clench at my sides, and the scratches sting, but I kind of like it. I have a carefully decorated, hidden place inside my mind where I go when Mother gets angry. My thoughts rush into that safe spot. The figurative door opens easily and slams behind me quickly. But then a voice from behind the kids yanks me back through to the real world.

"Pretty sure you pay the bills with all that talking," Henry snarks, coming out of a side room, which I'd guess is a bathroom, rubbing his damp hands together. "I know it pays mine. Come on, kids—talk more."

I'm sure that I'm the only one who can hear Alyssa chuckle. I'm slowly compiling a cheat sheet in my mind about each family member and, in Henry's case, employee. I find it interesting that Alyssa would laugh at Henry teasing her husband, and I find it even more interesting that she wants to keep it under wraps.

I don't look at Henry fully, but I can make out some of his features and movements. He's freshly showered, his dark hair curled up on the top of his head, a part down one side the only clue that he did anything to style it this morning. His glasses are a little different, a dark brown and light brown mottled together in round frames. He has on a plain green T-shirt under a dark zip-up hoodie, and a pair of worn-out jeans. It's the most casual I've seen him, and he looks closer to the first half of his twenties than the second. My stomach flips, and I put my hands in their anxiety spot on my belly.

"You're a smart-ass sometimes, you know that?" Stan says, teasing this time, but there's definitely a tension I can't explain just yet. I'll figure it out eventually, if I watch long enough. I might not be great at doing my hair or putting on makeup like Alyssa, or even picking out the most stylish outfits like Kelsey, but I *am* good at knowing when someone is angry. It's hard to focus with Stan's negative energy leaking out from his corner of the kitchen, but everyone else seems to be able to move on and let it go. Alyssa naturally takes the reins during the half-second break after Stan's last barb.

"Anyway! This is our new intern, Angela." All the kids seem to relax and turn their attention to Alyssa's soft, trilling voice. Ryland climbs up on Connor's lap and gives me a little wave, which I can't help but return. Henry doesn't glance at me and returns to a computer and pile of papers at the table where he must've been stationed before his break.

"Angela is my friend," Ryland says to his siblings. "I gave her a present."

I blush at the attention. Connor, who had a hard time looking at me before, says to Ryland, "Yeah, RyRy? That's so nice of you."

"She was on the floor sad, and I made her happy," he says, putting his tiny hands on each side of Connor's face like it's the only way to get the message through properly. Alyssa continues her introduction.

"Well, she'll be everyone's friend now," Alyssa continues. "Connor, Kelsey, you know your mini-channels? That was her idea. I think Angela will be a nice addition to our little team."

"Oh, that's awesome!" Kelsey smiles at me.

"Yeah, Kelsey loves her camera," Stan adds, back to the friendly dad persona that's always seemed to be his norm.

"Hey," Connor adds and nods a hello.

Heavens. Connor and Kelsey are talking to *me*. The heat in my face creeps down my neck and into my shoulders. I know I should say something, anything, but I can't. The awkward pause that follows is enough to make me want to hide, but Henry chimes in.

"I can get you set up with your tech over here," he says, and the rest of the family breaks into activity. Alyssa throws together a last-minute lunch for the kids, and papers fly in from all directions for parental signatures. It's all a lot more frenzied than it seems on the screen, but I watch even as I cross to Henry at the table.

It seems like a comfortable chaos, though, like everyone knows where they are in the middle of the madness, like they're all signed on fully for the ride. It's a bit like the birds I could see from my window. If I lay on the floor of my bedroom, I could see the sky, just a rectangle, but it was enough. I don't know how they did it, those little sparrows like Sampson, flitting through the air like they'd practiced the intricate dance that could easily have been put to a great symphony and made more sense than the silence of Mother's house.

Sampson. His broken body and the bloody fingerprints on the wall flash through my thoughts. A chill runs down my arms, and I shake off the memory. *Old life, that's my old life.*

I sit down at the table with my back to the activity, distracted by their beautiful ballet. Henry is staring at his computer screen, tapping at the keyboard like I don't exist. I sit with my hands in my lap patiently. The screen reflects in his glasses, and if I were braver, I could probably make out what he's looking at, but instead I stare ahead at the large picture windows that look out to the screened back porch and the large pool in the backyard. I haven't been this close to a pool since I was a little girl. The amount of water is overwhelming, and I try to remember what it's like to have water cover every part of my body.

"All right, I have it all set up. Here you go." Henry shoves the shiny laptop in my direction. I've never seen anything so ridiculously beautiful this close. It's a superfuturistic great-grandchild of Mother's computer. I have absolutely no idea what to do with it.

"You can set your password. It's a company computer, so I'll have remote admin privileges, but as long as you stay away from porn and don't download any pirated movies or something, I'll mind my own business." A blank line stares back at me, and the cursor blinks impatiently. "Seriously, you can put anything. I have like ten firewalls, so your account should be just fine."

My hands hover over the glowing keyboard, and I can only think of the password I used for my email back home. I type slowly, using one finger: *FeelyFan5*.

It comes out as stars across the screen and then asks me to write it again. I type it in even slower this time, just to be careful. When a green check mark glows next to the anonymous passwords, I place my hands back in my lap and look at Henry, breathing shallowly, hoping I did it right. He's watching me, his head cocked to one side.

"Huh. So, that's done. Do you . . . do you know how to work a laptop?" It feels like he wants to say, *Do you even know how to turn on a computer?* but must've known it would sound rude.

"Uh, I've never had one like this," I say. He leans in like he can't hear me. He smells good again, like he did in the car. I repeat myself, trying to talk louder, but it's so hard. "I . . . I had an old computer be . . . before."

"Huh, you're a strange creature," he says. He doesn't know what to think about me. I can read that in his voice even if I can't make myself look at him again until he finally leaves my personal space and slides a smaller black rectangle across the table. It stops when it hits my elbow.

"That's yours too," he says. It's a cell phone, a touch-screen one made of glass and metal. The only thing I know less about than computers is phones, but I pick it up anyway.

"Thanks."

"Do you know how to use that?"

"Of course," I say immediately, and put the device in my lap. A blank screen with no buttons confuses me, and I have no idea how to turn it on, but I'm not going to admit that.

Henry plops a pink Post-it down in front of me.

"This is your phone number and temporary passcode. You can change that when you have time. Once again, I have admin access, but I'm not too worried about you doing anything illegal. And your official Feely family email address is on there too."

Henry sounds bored or annoyed, maybe both. Then another long pause like maybe he's expecting me to say something.

He sighs and continues, "So, today why don't you just get a feel for the computer and the house? We'll be shooting a segment after the kids get home, but there's a planning meeting at noon, and then we'll need to go shopping for supplies. You have a driver's license, right?"

I shake my head. The list of things I'm not useful for is just getting longer.

"Shit, okay, I'll drive you today, but we'll have to figure out an Uber account or something." I have a vague idea of what Uber is from other videos but refuse to show my ignorance by asking outright. He takes out his phone and taps at it like he's checking items off a list. "Oh, while we're running errands I can also take you by the college. There are some rooms over there reserved for summer school students and interns. Or there might be some options through Airbnb."

Housing. I guess I already knew I couldn't stay here long-term even if they offered it—how long could I change and shower and sleep here before someone found out the truth about me and my "baby"?

I researched shelters briefly at the library, but most had waiting lists or applications, and a few needed a referral from social services. Social services—those were the people who placed me with Mother. She said they could come take me away again and put me in a house with other kids who might hurt me or foster parents who would make me beg to go back to her. I'm not a child anymore, and I'm hundreds of miles from home, but there's always the possibility she could know someone there. I'll find somewhere to stay, and I'll do it without Henry or any contact with social services.

"I don't need help," I say, my voice gravelly from being quiet for so long.

"You don't even know the area, how can you . . . ?"

"I have a cousin who lives close by," I lie, saying the first thing that comes into my head. I need to stop making up human beings. It's going to become increasingly hard to make them appear out of thin air.

"I thought you said you didn't know anyone," he says, like it's an accusation. I rush to explain.

"Well, we aren't that close, and she doesn't know I'm here. She travels a lot for work and . . . and if she called my mother . . ." When I say the name, Mother, that spot on the back of my head pulses, and I lose track of my thoughts. Mother. She knows I'm gone by now. She must be furious. She must be looking for me. Did I delete the history on the computer? Did I log out of my email? Will she look for me? Will someone at the library tell her they saw me? Will she call the police and tell them about my crimes?

"You're really scared, aren't you?" He's watching me again. I hate his eyes on me. It's a gross, crawling sensation, like when a fly lands briefly on my bare skin and then flits away, just barely registering but also putting every nerve on edge.

I'm so transparent. This man can see right through me. He probably knows I'm not pregnant too. That I'm a shoplifting fraud of a person. That I don't deserve to be here.

"No, no. I love my mom," I say, shaking now like I've caught a chill.

"You're scared of something, I know that much," he says, the creepy fly feeling compounding. I need to get away. I can't sit here and let him learn any more about me.

"I'll come down at noon." I stand up and collect the computer, Post-it, and phone in a pile that I clutch.

Henry watches me. He's always watching me.

The kitchen is now empty, backpacks, lunches, and the banter all gone off to other parts of Santa Barbara. No one is around to see my rushed, rude exit. I don't fit in here. I only remember tiny pieces of family life from before Mother, but it was nothing like the dynamic busyness of this place.

Henry calls to me as I charge up the stairs, but I don't stop. I need some time alone, locked in my room. This new world I'm in has so much beauty it almost hurts to look at it, and right now I miss my modest life of nothingness. I had the rules, my dolls, my room, my work, and Mother. As long as I did what she demanded of me, my life was so simple, so easy. I thought being free of Mother would feel like freedom, but I was wrong. It feels like falling and not knowing if anyone is going to catch me.

CHAPTER 18

Henry starts the SUV. It smells fresh and clean, and the blast of tepid air from the vents is just the right temperature on this mild spring afternoon. We're headed out to run errands together, but he was quieter than usual in the planning meeting, and I haven't figured out why yet. Usually in the car he's talking shop about cameras or lighting or props or even his thoughts on the channel. Sometimes he shoots off a personal question, but in general he has more opinions than he has use for. Something is on his mind today that has him so pensive, but I guess I shouldn't assume I have his temperament figured out already.

I've been with the Feelys for almost three days now, three mornings with Ryland chittering in my face as soon as I open my eyes, three days of breakfasts and noon meetings. Three days of Henry politely asking for the references Alyssa requested in her first emails and Stan asking if I needed help moving anywhere. Three days of lies about texting with my cousin, who supposedly is out of town and will be for a little bit longer, and panic because I have no clue where I'm going to live, since it turns out that the shelters that have open spots also require a background check, which I'm sure is the same reason Alyssa wants all those documents.

Thankfully, unlike the shelters I've contacted, Alyssa hasn't pushed the issue since hearing about my mostly fictional escape from my boyfriend and mother. But maybe that's not enough for Henry, and one of my notable incongruences is behind his silence.

"You don't like me very much, do you?" he asks, out of nowhere.

"What do you mean?" I ask, arranging my dress under the seat belt like I'm unfazed by his strange question. If anyone should be worried about being liked, it's me, not Henry.

"You talk to Alyssa and Stan just fine, but then get all quiet and weird around me." He's not wrong, and that's exactly why I hate being alone with Henry—when he gets tired of talking about the job, he skips the boring and half-hearted conversation that comes with small talk and goes straight into personal questions.

"I don't know you that well."

"But you feel like you know Alyssa and Stan?" It's a question and a statement.

"Well, kinda." I shrug, confused why snarky Henry cares.

Henry grumbles, annoyed, and pushes a button that puts the car in reverse. His hand goes to the back of my seat, like he wants to touch me. I jerk away. If he touches me, he might feel the straps for the body suit or the swollen places on the back of my head and neck that are still tender.

"That's just how I back out," he says, defensively. He shifts his hand lower on the back of my seat, and I stare forward at the garage door, so tired of having to hold it all together when he seems to see everything. It's utterly exhausting.

"You know they're just people, right?" he asks, and the car lurches backward into the street and then forward again, faster than he's supposed to. Mother never went too fast; she didn't like doing anything to attract attention.

"I know," I say, gripping the armrests. "But they feel like friends."

"Friends?" he says, clearly skeptical.

"Uh, um, like family, maybe." My mouth is as dry as it was the day I got out of the closet.

"Damn. I see why they like you so much. You think they're per-fect." He runs a yellow light at the exit of the subdivision and makes a sharp left turn onto the busy thoroughfare. I glance around for flashing police lights.

"Not perfect. No one is perfect," I correct, holding on tighter.

"Just don't get your hopes up, okay? Alyssa and Stan are not the Cleavers." He turns on his signal this time and takes a right into the Walgreens on the corner, finally slowing down.

"I don't know the Cleavers," I say, distracted by the red curly letters on the storefront. "Is that another YouTube family?"

He parks and looks at me like he can't tell if he should laugh or be serious.

"You know, *Leave It to Beaver*. That old show where the family is all perfect—Dad comes home from work at five, and Mom has a roast in the oven. Black and white. The family's name is the Cleavers. Sound familiar?" I don't answer, and he continues. "I guess I'm getting old. It's a saying that means people aren't always what they seem like on TV. You know what I mean? The Feelys look perfect online, but they're just people."

He is watching me again, but I'm still only halfway paying atten-tion. I don't want to go into this store. Mother loved doing jobs at Walgreens. She could get good money for over-the-counter cold medi-cines and the overpriced beauty products, and sometimes we got lucky and found an unlatched security lock and brought home some decent electronics. What if they have my picture somewhere, and it gets passed around electronically? What if I walk in the door and alarms go off?

"Huh," he says, as though he's responding to something I've said and not awkward silence. I think he's going to say something else, but he picks up his phone and starts typing instead. I don't know where to look. I'm not used to this phone thing where people go from talking to looking at a screen. If I'd ever done that to Mother, she would've smacked the phone out of my hand. She's not here, but my wrist stings anyway.

My phone dings and buzzes in my dress pocket. I jump and then pat around until I find it.

"I just sent you the shopping list for today and the notes from the planning meeting. We need to get back to the house by two o'clock so we can get packed up before the kids get home. It's very important when we go shopping for the show that we take a picture of every receipt and then put the paper copy in this folder." He walks through the steps of taking a picture and then points to an accordion folder on the armrest between us.

"Okay," I mumble. I kept track of records for Mother, accordion folder and all. Finally, something I know how to do.

"And," he continues, "we have to use the corporate credit card; you'll get one in a few days. We can get lunch on it and little things like that, but that's it. I don't think I need to worry about that with you." Henry chuckles like he made a really good joke and then starts collecting his belongings. The joke's on him. I'm exactly the kind of person he should be worried about, and he might find that out as soon as I walk in those sliding glass doors.

I have to go in. It's clearly part of my job. But if Mother gave the police my name, my picture, if she did all the things she always promised me she'd do if I got caught or left, I'll be put in jail. I'll lose my internship. She'll find me.

I take a deep breath and blow it out and then nearly gag. My breath is stale and gross and fills the close confines of the car. I blush, mortified. This morning, I ran a glob of toothpaste over my teeth using my finger and some paper towels, but it obviously wasn't effective. I pop the door open, and stumble out of the car.

"Damn it. Why won't you ever let me help you?" Henry grumbles as he rushes around the front of the car, trying to get to me before I fall down. This time I right myself and find my balance all on my own.

I have the door closed and my rumpled dress smoothed by the time Henry gets there, out of breath.

"I'm ready," I say, and I can't hold back a rebellious smile. He looks me over, one eyebrow raised. He turns his back on me and walks into the store.

"You coming?" he calls back, and it sounds like a challenge. I can't help but accept.

Inside the store, Henry grabs a basket, and I take a cart out of habit. A cart is good cover. He suggests I take the first half of the list, which includes simple items like note cards and markers, cleaning supplies and sponges. I'm not sure how all of this relates to the stupid fashion show we're supposed to be filming with Kelsey later today, but I just do as my list instructs.

It takes six or seven minutes to get all the items listed on my phone. I'm careful when I take it in and out of my pocket because very little holds the fabric pouch together other than a set of snaps that make the false belly accessible during shopping trips. Unlike my other maternity dress that we used at department stores, Mother altered this one specifically for smaller items. Both had their usefulness, but right now I'd give anything to not look like a huge tent of material.

As I wait for Henry, I stroll up and down the aisles with a cart full of items I'm actually going to buy. It might not be my money, but it's still liberating. I slow to a stop, the front wheel squealing against the waxed vinyl flooring.

I've ended up in the oral hygiene section, and columns of flavored toothpaste and multicolored toothbrushes call to me. Until recently I had no idea that my body odor might be different from any other human's. But then I met flowery Alyssa and musky Stan and bubble gum-y Kelsey and woodsy Connor. And their teeth are straight, white, brilliant. My fingertips tingle. If I had money with me, I'd buy so many good-smelling things. I could come back later and purchase all the items I need, but I don't want to ask someone to drive me back for deodorant. Then again, I could just take it . . . but no . . . I'm giving that up, right?

Mother's words come to mind. She'd give me this lecture at least once a year for the first four or five years after I was adopted. It took a while to learn how to mute that nagging voice of guilt that gnawed inside of me back then.

No one is there for us, Tara. We can't wait for handouts. Plus, these stores have insurance. They basically get paid twice as much for missing items. If they knew how hard our life was, they'd want us to do it.

Mother couldn't have been *all* wrong, could she? That part of me she trained from the time I was a small child to palm tubes of lipstick and hide bracelets up my sleeve is activated. I check for any onlookers without moving my head, like Mother taught me, and then I put several articles in my cart like I'm stocking up a supply closet. In the basket are things I need, like toothpaste and toothbrushes, deodorant, and shampoo, but also other bulkier items from the list on my phone, like toilet paper and a six-pack of soda. Thankfully I don't see Henry, but I have to work fast. As I push the cart, I fish out the few items I've targeted and slip them through the snaps in my pocket to the zipper opening of the belly pouch. Just as I get everything hidden away, Henry calls my name from another aisle.

"Angela?"

I take out all the unnecessary items from the cart and ditch them on a side shelf. With Mother, I'd abandon the cart and leave the store, but I have a different job to do today. As soon as I'm left with only essentials, I rush to the next aisle, that pesky wheel squeaking as I go.

"I'm here." I'm out of breath, and he's looking at me funny but doesn't say anything.

"Okay, is that everything?"

I gulp and nod, that odd, irritating feeling of guilt from my youth tugging at me from inside.

"I grabbed you a water." He passes me a cold plastic bottle and the car keys. "Why don't you head to the car and catch your breath; I'll pay." I'm about to say no and tell him I'm just fine the way I am, but the contraband inside of me is as significant as my fear of getting caught, and I crave the safety of the outside.

"Thanks," I say, and walk away from my cart with my eyes to the floor. Don't look directly at the cameras; that's another Mother rule, but I know where they are. When the doors swish behind me, I let out a heavy breath, slapping the sweating bottle against the palm of my other hand. I'm a thief. No one made me do it today.

It takes a few tries to figure out how the buttons on the keys relate to the locks on the car doors, but when they pop open, I hop inside quickly. The water-bottle cap opens with a crack, and the whole fifteen-minute shopping trip comes over me in great detail. Shame fills me like the cold water I'm drinking, and I wish I could take it all back.

"Stupid. Stupid. Stupid," I chant, eyes closed, rocking slightly in the front seat and hitting my head on the headrest behind me. It's padded but still sends enough pain through my damaged scalp to make it feel like a punishment. "Stupid. Stupid. Stupid."

The rear hatch opens with a gust from the back of the car. I have to look normal. The tinted windows hopefully kept him from seeing my crazy act in the front seat, but I can't be positive. Henry hops in the driver's seat, and we're on the road before he makes a sound.

"I paid for it," he says, keeping his eyes on the road.

"Okay?" I say, unsure what that comment means. I thought he was supposed to pay for the supplies because I don't have a credit card yet.

"The toothpaste, I paid for it." His features are calm and still.

He knows.

"I . . . I . . . don't know what you're talking about . . ."

"I saw you," he says firmly, his gaze on the road.

"Saw me do what?" I toss back. Mother taught me how to talk to a store clerk if questioned. Deny. Deny. Deny.

"I saw you put it in your pocket."

When we get to the red traffic light, my instincts tell me to open the door and run. The car is a moving prison, and Henry is my warden. But if I run, it's as good as a confession, and then . . . I have nowhere to go. I need this job, this family. I have to stick this out.

"No, I didn't," I say with a touch of outrage. Mother taught me to always tell the simplest lie possible—easier to remember than easier to believe. Wish I'd remembered that tip during my first interview.

"I saw you," he repeats, and I can tell he really did. I'm caught.

"I didn't take it," I say, digging in, refusing to submit to being called a liar even if I am one.

He shrugs. "Whatever. I don't care that much. It's just a tube of toothpaste."

"That I didn't take—see?" I wrest my phone out of my pocket and then turn both pockets inside out. I can't help it. I can't tell the truth. I can't let him see me.

He glances at my empty pockets and then back at the road, taciturn and sure.

"Okay, guess I was wrong," he says, unconvinced but surrendering the fight.

"Yeah, you were," I insist, maybe too forcefully. He's given up—I should too. I put my pockets back to normal and leave my fists inside so he can't see them shaking. We turn into another strip mall with random stores strung together like pearls on costume jewelry.

He parks a few rows back from a party store. A woman with a cluster of multicolored balloons rushes across the lot and disappears into her fancy black car, off to some celebration I'm passively envious of. There are so many normal things in this world that feel like mysterious wonders to me, and I both relish experiencing them and hate feeling so brand-new. When he speaks again, I'm prepared for more accusations, maybe a consequence. I don't think he'll hit me, but there could be yelling or perhaps tense silence. Both hurt the same. I brace myself by assuming the most submissive posture Mother taught me.

"You don't have any money, do you?"

His question takes me by surprise.

"I have enough," I whisper, shame blocking an honest answer.

"But not very much." He fills in the blanks of my response, sitting patiently for a moment before continuing his thought process. "If you can't move in with your cousin, there's no way you can afford a place around here. Maybe Stan and Alyssa could—"

"No." I cut him off but then rethink it. He's not yelling, and he isn't silent. In fact, he sounds like he might actually care for some reason. I try again. "I mean, thank you, but no. My cousin will be back soon."

"You really don't like letting people help you, do you?" He turns off the engine and checks his phone, the indifferent attitude back.

"I *can* take care of myself," I say, studying the side of his face. He pities me. I catch my reflection in the passenger's-side mirror. My hair, despite my efforts to wash it with the bar soap in the bathtub this morning, is straggly and still greasy at the roots. My eyes are wide and dark, like a wild animal caught in a floodlight. I look like a pale, skinny, frightened child. If I were Henry, I'd probably pity me too. And he's right. I can't shoplift an apartment, but I'm not going to let Henry or any member of the Feely family far enough into my world to help me.

"If you say so," he says, reinterested in his screen, which works in my favor. "We'd better get moving."

He starts typing, and I watch him. It's hard to predict what might happen from moment to moment with Henry. Mother was unpredictable in a predictable way. I knew she'd have extreme reactions sometimes, and I knew how to respond when she did. But I have no idea what Henry is thinking, and that's unsettling.

My phone dings and vibrates. He looks up from his device and seems to notice me watching him in the reflection of the windshield. Unlike in real life, in the reflection he seems genuine, maybe kind even.

But I guess that's what reflections do, reverse images, show the same picture but opposite in nearly every way. Tricky.

A roll of thunder in the distance draws my attention. I might get to feel rain again.

"You ready?" he asks, placing his phone in his pants pocket. I focus on the real Henry this time, instead of the reflection. He's the one who sees too much and is willing to ask me hard questions. I can't let myself forget his reality.

"I'm ready," I lie.

CHAPTER 19

"Just stand here and hit the button when I tell you to," Henry says. A compact camera is attached to the top of a fully expanded tripod that keeps sinking into the mud on the rain-soaked field. After we finished at the party store and drove home in the rain, there was little time to get the running order put together, supplies organized into bins, and intros filmed before Stan started pacing and complaining that we were going to "lose the light."

While we were shopping, Stan postponed Kelsey's fashion show for the third day in a row and instead went with one of my ideas: a family trip to the park. Alyssa and Kelsey were arguing that we should cancel because of the storm, but Stan insisted that the muddy conditions would make for some great dramatic moments.

When Stan wants to do something, it usually happens. Right now he likes my ideas, but who knows how long that might last. And really, the way this video is coming together isn't exactly what I'd had in mind, anyway.

The shoot starts out like I suggested, the kids playing on the slides and seeing who can swing the highest. Connor's magnetism turns on when the cameras focus on him. I love seeing the Connor I've known for years. But after fifteen minutes or so of organic play, Henry calls cut, and everyone freezes.

"Let's do it again!" he calls out. "Places!"

The family scatters, and with a few instructions from Alyssa and Stan, everyone ends up back in the approximate spots they'd started from before Henry called action the first time. Then they start again.

What's happening? I stay by my assigned button and camera but watch a strangely similar scene unravel the second time around. This run-through is crisp, and certain moments, like when Ryland was too scared of bees to cross the bridge, are eliminated entirely. Over the next hour, the family resets three more times, and I'm left watching it all, confused and frustrated. This isn't what I was talking about when I suggested playing. This is anything but play—this feels like work.

The sun is low in the sky when Henry calls cut for the fourth time and sends the family off to get changed for the second half of the shoot. I've helped with two very simple vlogs over the past few days, but the scale of this shoot is immense and has me a little lost.

By the time Henry fills me in on the details of our second shoot, a simple obstacle course with a series of "challenge stations" dotting the open field adjacent to the park, the family has changed clothes. They emerge from the small cement bathroom in the middle of the park, each family member tucking a mic pack into a back pocket or chest strap.

They have on red shirts and yellow shirts, splitting them into color-coded teams. Kelsey and Connor are looking at their phones at the starting line, but Ryland is jumping up and down, his four-year-old body barely containing his excitement. I don't know if this will end up being anything watchable with the low light, muddy grass, and mostly worn-out kids.

"They're already tired of this," I say, self-conscious that this was connected to my idea. Henry shuffles a little closer, his shoulder rubbing mine.

"They're fine. They get like this. Don't worry."

I don't want to worry, but my first shoot can't be a fail. What good will I be to the family then?

"We should've done fewer takes at the park. I just wanted them to play together as a family like they always do."

"Play?" Henry scoffs, adjusting the camera a few inches to the right. "They don't play, Angela. That's just acting."

"Acting?" No, this family loves each other. Henry is jaded, a skeptic. I don't have time to rebut when Henry yells out, "Places!"

Stan tosses his hands in Alyssa's direction like he's dumping a tray onto the ground and then stomps away to where the children are milling about. I've been so busy with my assignments and keeping tabs on the kids that I didn't notice their interaction just out of frame.

Alyssa follows him to the starting line with a partial smile on her face, and even I can tell she's faking it. What are they fighting about? My suggestions must be messing up their well-oiled balance. Earlier this week the other two shoots went off without a hitch—this is the first one mired in tension.

"Push the button when I say action, okay?" Henry shouts out as he runs across the field toward the family. He's training me on the stationary camera. It's stupidly easy to use, and I'm ready to make my shots more interesting. I haven't tried anything yet, but maybe I will—eventually.

"Okay, everyone! Phones away," Henry orders. He holds out a Ziploc bag, and the children and adults alike place their phones inside of it as part of their preshoot to-do list. Their lives go from dynamic chaos to routine and businesslike in these moments. I almost wish I could close my eyes so the magic doesn't wear off.

I'm too far away to hear what Henry is saying to Stan and Alyssa; I assume he's reviewing the opening. He has the only headphones that pick up the portable mics, so I have to use my imagination. As he turns to the kids and goes through each of the steps of the obstacle course, my feet slowly sink into the mud, and the hem of my dress soaks up some of the dark brown. The storm cleared out the park, and we're the only ones here.

"Hey, we're losing the light. Let's get this in one take, okay?" Henry announces, walking toward me with the communal Ziploc. I drop my phone in with the rest before he runs back to his camera. No one but Ryland seems to have the energy to answer. One take? This is going to be a disaster.

"Quiet on set," he calls, and the tone suddenly changes. There is a deepening intensity, a grave, anticipatory silence. He points to me to do my one camera-related job—press record.

"Action!" he shouts, holding a small camera up in front of Stan and Alyssa, and the world comes to life through the viewfinder of my device. Only the family is in frame, Henry expertly off-screen.

Stan goes through the intro. I can't hear all of it over here, but I have a copy of the script. Even without it, I've gotten used to watching my videos on low volume, so it's not overly difficult to make out the dialogue. Low volume or not, Stan is a natural, and if I didn't have a paper filled with the words he's mouthing, I'd think he was making them up as he went. Is that the acting Henry was talking about? I don't like that idea.

"Welcome to AllTheFeels. Today we decided to get out and get moving with some friendly competition."

"Yeah, 'friendly,'" Connor barbs using air quotes, and I squint at him through the tiny camera screen. It's the Connor I've wanted as my best friend, the one I related to, who gave me hope that all men were not the monsters Mother made them out to be. Where has he been hiding?

Alyssa takes over the intro.

"That's right! Today is parents versus kids. Whoever loses does all the dishes . . . for a week." She lowers her voice to add drama, and Kelsey squeals at the revelation. "So, tell us below, who do you think is going to win? Kelsey, Connor, and RyRy, or me and Stan the Feely man? And don't forget to like this video and subscribe to our channel and turn on those notifications, so you can see when we have a new video." She points to spots in the air where links will be put in postproduction.

"This isn't really fair," Stan adds, with a ruffle of Connor's hair.

"Yeah, I agree. We're gonna wipe the floor with you guys."

"Yeah!" Ryland shouts.

"Well, then, let's get started!" Alyssa smiles into the camera for an extended moment before Henry says cut and puts it down. Everyone lets out a sigh.

"Okay," Henry says, "good opening. I think we can just go with it since it's getting so late. I'm going to film the course really quickly, so watch me go through it so you know what it will be like for you. Also, Kelsey and Connor, don't forget to include Ryland. He might slow you down, but Alyssa and Stan will give you a little leeway on their turn, okay?" Henry puts on a different personality when he's in charge. Everyone listens to him without a second thought. I can't believe he's been behind the scenes all this time and I never knew.

Unenthused heads nod, and the focus turns to the obstacle course and keeping Ryland quiet during the shots, though they will likely be dubbed over with music so I'm not sure if the silence is because of the camera or because no one wants to interact. Why does Henry keep shooting when no one is having fun?

In another ten minutes, the kids are on the starting line, and Henry calls action. The kids rush through the course, popping shaving-cream-filled balloons that Henry had me prepare on the back patio while it was raining, and then chugging a can of soda each from the pack we picked up at Walgreens.

Connor carries Ryland on his back for most of the two minutes and twenty-two seconds except for when it's his turn to do the challenge activities. Through the viewfinder it looks like the most fun any family could ever have, but when I step away from the screen it's not the same. Not acting, like Henry claimed, but something else I can't seem to place. Like when they were on the playground and the fun wasn't sinking in for anyone but Ryland. I shift back to watching through the camera, and my itch to play along rushes back instantly.

When the kids finish their turn through the obstacles with high fives and shouts of victory, Henry and I reset the field. The kids fish their phones out of the plastic baggie when Henry isn't looking. I notice but don't say anything.

"We have to run this fast," he says, like I have any idea what this all truly entails. He's talking to me like a professional, so I go with it.

"The kids did a great job," I add as we work.

"Yeah, we'll have to go through the raw footage, but it'll splice together nicely for a solid segment. I wasn't worried about the kids. Alyssa and Stan are actually harder to direct."

Oh, Henry is the director, not some intern or assistant. They've never called him by a title, but it's so obvious. How'd it take me so long to figure it out? I guess I never thought AllTheFeels had a director besides Alyssa and Stan. I have a million questions that I'll probably never find the courage to ask.

"Okay, wish me luck." Henry claps, running with his camera in hand.

Connor is perched on a slide, arms wrapped around the metal handrails at the top. Kelsey is taking a video of herself on her phone, blabbering away in a bubbly voice like she's talking to her best friend. Ryland is swinging on his stomach like he's Superman, and Alyssa and Stan stand in a tense hush that either means they've resolved whatever they were discussing or they've come to a stalemate. I don't like seeing them so disconnected. It reminds me of what happened to my birth parents after the babies were born—always fighting. Never smiling at each other and eventually never smiling at me. Is this all happening because of me?

CHAPTER 20

Henry works his magic with Alyssa and Stan and then calls the family back to their places. When he shouts action this time, the kids heckle their parents, but Alyssa and Stan look like best friends and teammates. They give each other a good-luck kiss on camera, and Stan gives his wife's bum a little smack. She flirts back by slapping at his biceps and flipping her long, curled ponytail in his face. I don't know what Henry said to snap them out of their funk, but the lead in my belly starts to dissolve as they look like *my* Feely family again.

The challenge goes entirely as planned until they get to the kid-die pool filled with slime directly in front of me, which Henry and I prepped while the family was getting changed. They're supposed to search through the sluggish substance to find a silver dollar. With three sets of hands and no worries about getting dirty, the kids found it in fifteen seconds. But Alyssa doesn't want to have anything to do with the slime. She's playful about it, but she refuses to get her hands in the muck. I haven't been able to hear much of their conversations till now.

"Come on," Stan pleads, trying to keep a smile on his face.

"Oh no! It's gross!" she says, like she's joking but with a hidden growl of meaning underneath.

Stan sighs a real sigh and then corrects himself.

"I need your help," he calls with one of his biggest smiles on his face. I know he must be frustrated, but he's also good at not showing it. Alyssa answers through gritted teeth. I hope we can edit it out.

"I told you I don't want to do this part," she mutters to him low enough that I can hear it, but I'm not sure anyone else can. She gets on her knees slowly, cringing when the mud squishes under them, the energy sucked from the scene.

"Come on! We've got this," Stan calls out, still invested in the competition, and then says under his breath, "Just do it, damn it!"

Henry must be catching this through the mics.

Alyssa digs her hands into the mush and swirls them around lackadaisically. Stan is up to his elbows.

Do something, I urge mentally, but he keeps rolling.

No one else seems concerned. Kelsey and Connor are hopping up and down screaming friendly barbs at their parents. Ryland can't seem to stay still, and he runs parallel to the start/finish line. Instead of shouting challenges like his big brother and sister, he calls out cheers of support and love for his mom and dad.

I have an idea. I leave my station by the camera and run around the outside of what I think is the frame and call out.

"RyRy!" I shout low enough that I hope the cameras and sound equipment won't pick it up. Ryland's head snaps in my direction and he smiles. I wave him over, mouthing, "Come here! Come on!"

He bounces to me, and I squat down to his level. His arms immediately go around my neck, and I almost fall over.

"Hey, friend!" I whisper in his ear and squeeze him back a little. He's the only person I feel comfortable enough to let touch me. "Can you help me play a little trick on your mom and dad?"

"I like tricks," he says. I put a finger over my lips so he'll listen and hopefully save this shoot from the virtual garbage can—time and money wasted.

I lower my voice. "Okay, this is your chance. Go on over and jump on Daddy's back, okay? And try and make your mommy laugh."

"Really? But Henry said . . ."

Finger on my lips again to make sure he listens, I say, "Ry, it's okay! They'll love it. Go, go fast!"

"Okay!" His eyes go wide and he hugs my neck again. He starts to run off and then turns back for a second. "Bye!" And then he keeps running.

"Ryland! Stop!" Connor and Kelsey yell out from their spots when they see him sprinting, but thankfully he doesn't listen. I jog a little back to my camera and get there just in time for Ryland to tackle his dad so he falls face-first into the slime. Alyssa gasps and giggles, her green hands going to her face, getting slime all over it.

"Ryland!" she cries out in a genuine laugh.

"I'm helping," he adds, completely sincere.

"I'll show you helping," Stan says, pulling Ryland into the pool with him, both soaked through with the goopy liquid instantly.

"Oh my gosh." Alyssa laughs at the two wrestling. Stan stops flopping around and holds Ryland still for a second, both out of breath and dripping.

"Ry, let's get Mommy."

"No!" Alyssa holds her hands up in front of her.

"Yes," Stan says, and Ryland echoes him.

"Yes!"

"Don't you even dare." She starts to back away when Ryland jumps out of the pool and into her arms, leaving a little-boy-sized print across her chest. "Oh, you're in trouble now!"

Taking a handful of slime, she chucks it at Stan, but he ducks at the last minute, and it whizzes past his face and lands in the middle of my chest.

"Oof." The mush soaks into the top half of my dress, staining it green and dripping down the strip of buttons on my front, but I hardly notice—I'm transfixed by the scene.

This is the Feely family I know.

As a trio, they finish out the challenge, Alyssa and Stan tossing Ryland back and forth through the obstacles. As their parents charge down the field, Kelsey and Connor break across the nonexistent barrier and try to physically keep Stan and Alyssa from crossing the finish line. The group is a ball of arms and legs and laughter, till they all crash over the line, with Henry filming them close behind.

I find myself clapping as they lie in a puppy pile covered in mud and slime, and my face hurts from smiling. After recording a quick sign-off, Henry calls cut and gives a round of high fives. Alyssa slings a duffel bag over her shoulder, and the chattering family heads off to the park bathroom. Henry sprints across the heavily muddied field with portable mics collected in the crook of his arm, his other hand raised.

"That was so great!" Henry shouts.

I think he wants me to hit it, but I've never given a high five. So I just raise my arm and wait for him to complete the greeting. When his hand smacks mine, I blush, and my heart races like I was the one running around. He hits my palm just hard enough that it tingles in a surprisingly stimulating way. "You so made that happen."

I smile at Henry's hyper banter. His face is flushed, and his glasses are steamed up where his frames rest on his cheeks. I wave him away and turn from his approving look. To seem busy, I click the record button to off and power down the camera.

"They sure got you good, didn't they?" He points to the wet stain running down my chest. It isn't a little splotch; my dress is soaked down the front. I have to hold it away from my body, the thin fabric clinging to every curve and threatening to reveal the secrets underneath.

"I can help you," I shout as he starts packing up the equipment. If he thought I was just a regular girl and not a pregnant, frail one, I could help pack and carry instead of watching.

He shakes his head as he works. "I've got it," he says, passing me the camera to hold while he closes up the tripod and cleans off the ends with some wet wipes.

"I'm pretty strong," I insist.

He takes the camera out of my hands like I haven't said a word.

"I told you, I've got it," he repeats, placing the cleaned items in their hardcover case, his face red from bending down and packing equipment. He knows I'm weak, and not because he thinks I'm pregnant, but because he sees things I don't want him to.

I stomp away, my feet squishing loudly. With a bit of rebellion, I collect the plastic rings Ryland dropped during his time as "helper" and slip them on my arm, where they stack up in a rainbow cast. They cascade off my arm into the large bin by the finish line, leaving streaks of mud. I'm a total mess, but I don't care. I'm invigorated, inspired, on fire with usefulness.

The end of the finish-line rope sticks out of the ground. It's semi-submerged in the dirt, and I give it a yank. The cord barely budges. I try again, harder this time, taking satisfaction in the resistance.

Voices approach from behind. Henry is headed my way with Stan stern-faced by his side and Ryland tripping along behind them. I've missed something, some sort of disagreement or tension that I don't understand. Henry doesn't stop or even look at me; instead he goes directly toward the line of cars where the SUV is parked. Stan is right behind and doesn't appear much happier.

"He made you clean up? I'm so sorry." Stan rushes over, concerned and speaking loudly, as though he wants Henry to know that he sees his errors. "I need to apologize for Henry. He can be lazy sometimes."

"No, no, he told me not to . . ."

Stan doesn't listen. He puts his hands around mine on top of the rope. I slide out from under his light grip, the mud making our skin slip like silk against each other. This isn't like my high five with Henry. That was fun, and I'd do it again in a heartbeat. Having Stan's hands around mine feels different. It's icky, dirty, like the mud on my hands and arms and dress is now also inside of my body, coating every surface with muck. But what's even more confusing is—I don't know why.

CHAPTER 21

"You've had a hard life, haven't you, Angela?" Stan asks like he really cares.

"Not—not that hard." I stutter a bit. A cleaned-up Ryland makes his third attempt to help Stan's packing efforts.

"Ry, I got this," Stan repeats. The four-year-old isn't supposed to get muddy again, so I take his hand and guide him over to the bench on the edge of the park a few feet away. Stan keeps talking.

"I can tell. You have a sadness in your eyes, did you know that?" He continues to extract the rope and collect the other items from today's activities as he asks me questions like he's known me for years. If Henry makes me feel uncomfortably seen in his silence, Stan makes me feel completely invisible with his assumptions.

"I'm happy to be here," I say, wishing I didn't have to talk. I really like Stan Feely. He's such a good dad and husband, but sometimes I think he's trying to say words I know he's not thinking. It's hard to blame him for his awkwardness. I mean, he's probably trying to stop himself from gagging at my smell.

"Well, we're happy to have you. Aren't we, RyRy?"

"Yes!" Ryland bounces up and down on his toes. He really does like me. I've never questioned that since we made our friendship "official."

"You were a superstar today!" I offer him a high five like I've been doing it my whole life.

"I was?" he asks, no idea that he pumped energy and authenticity into that video.

"Yeah, you were fantastic. You know, I've always liked your vlogs the best. Don't tell." I put a shushing finger over my lips.

He giggles conspiratorially. "Even better than Connor and Kelsey?"

"Well . . . I don't want to hurt their feelings . . . but . . ."

"Hey, what about my feelings?" Stan chimes. He's standing so close that his arm hair grazes my skin when I stand up from my half squat by Ryland.

"I know, um . . ." I start explaining, but he keeps teasing me and Ryland, tossing the rope into the bin with a thunk.

"Well, I've got feelings too, you know." He's doing his dad-Stan thing that I've seen so many times before, rewording a sentence to make it sound like an insult pointed at him and then being fake upset about it. It's funny on screen, but when he does it to me, I start to sweat.

"Uh, I was kidding around with Ryland. I'm sorry. Your videos are good too." My reassurance could come off as slightly patronizing, but Stan doesn't call me on it.

"Well, they might be 'good' but not your 'favorite.' I get it. I get it."

Ryland hugs his father's legs and plays along with the game. "No, Daddy. We love your videos. You're so funny. Right, Angela?"

"Yeah, they're great. I . . . I'm sorry. I didn't mean to hurt your feelings," I say, trying to play along, but Alyssa interrupts out of nowhere.

"What feelings?" she asks, floating down the sidewalk that leads to the bathrooms where she'd been changing. She's wearing her designer shirt and long, sparkling rose-gold necklace again, but her jeans are the same. They're smudged with dirt and grass, but on her model-like body, stains look like a fashion accessory.

"I was saying that I'm a little sore from the obstacle course," Stan says.

It's only a little white lie, and even though I'm trying to stop being like Mother, I'm relieved Stan doesn't repeat what I said to Ryland about being my favorite.

"Well, that's 'cause you're an old man." Alyssa smacks Stan playfully. She has the duffel bag over one shoulder and a pile of clothes in her arms. "Let's get out of here—it's almost dark, and we don't have a permit."

"Ooooo, no permit." Stan fake-shivers like he's spooked and then laughs in my direction as though I'm his new buddy. This must be what it feels like to have a dad.

"Connor, go dump the slime pool, and, Kelsey, pick up at least some of those popped balloons. And, Stan"—she smiles at him like he's the one thing keeping her afloat and not like they'd had at least five simmering-in-the-background arguments during the shoot—"can you help me out, hon?" She holds out her overburdened arms.

"Sure thing, hot stuff." Stan collects the laundry and encourages Ryland to follow him to the car, away from the mud pit. For a guy claiming to be sore, Stan sure is spry. With inconsistencies like that, he'd get picked up by cameras in a second if he ever tried his hand at shoplifting. What a weird thing to think.

Alyssa sighs heavily once we're alone.

"Hey, sweetie, how are you doing? You didn't work too hard, did you?" She talks to me like I matter. There's something intoxicating in that.

"I want to do more," I admit, a bit shy but still basking in the postshoot buzz enough to speak up.

"Absolutely. You should do what you feel you can handle. I was still running three miles every day when I was pregnant with Ryland. I always say you gotta listen to your body, right?" She shifts a chunk of my hair back over my shoulder, and I don't recoil. "Fact is, you're good at this. Really good. You've got instincts that are impeccable. I bet you have a million things going on behind those eyes."

If she only knew how many. Shame nibbles at my gut, but I can't let it take me down now. Alyssa has a knowing pride in her eyes, like she's vindicated in her decision to choose me, and that feels like sunshine. She sees things in me that I've never even considered possible.

"I have some ideas," I say, embarrassed at all the positive attention but also ravenous for more, but Alyssa isn't listening anymore. She's focused on the splotched and streaked front of my dress.

"Oh my god, you poor thing. We ruined your pretty dress."

My taupe tent of a dress *is* a disaster area; I pat the stains like I'm washing them off with air. But even before the mud and slime, there's no way she thought my dress was beautiful. No one in their right mind thinks my dress is beautiful. If she lies about little things like my dress, she could be lying about anything, including her faith in my skills. The sunshine feeling is extinguished immediately, like the sun plunged into the ocean.

"It's okay." I wave her concerns off. The dress is almost dry, and the mud will come out easily with water. I might have a neon-green splotch on my top if I don't rinse it soon, but really, what's so shocking about that? I'm already a mess in so many other ways, and my dress will obviously continue to be an outside representation of that, a lot like that book I swiped from the rack at the library that held all the high school required-reading books—*Dorian Gray*. Maybe my dress shows the filth of my soul.

"I've been meaning to tell you—I've got some great maternity stuff at home that you might be interested in. We got a lot of complimentary items from sponsors when I was pregnant with Ryland, and I couldn't even use half of them. I kept them around, you know, just in case, but if you'd like, you can totally come take a look when we get home."

A new dress. I've secretly been wishing for a new dress. Every time Mother and I would go into a mall or department store, I'd scan the racks of lovely non-maternity clothes wistfully. I don't need to be special like Alyssa, curvy in the right places, with clear skin, white teeth, flowing hair, and a natural grace that can't be learned. But I long to look somewhat normal.

"I'd love that."

There's a neediness in my voice. Alyssa flips the duffel in front of her body, digging inside. She holds out an oversize red shirt from the challenge today.

"Here, I know it's not pretty, but at least you'll feel a little more . . . covered. Why don't you let us finish up here, and you take some me-time in the bathroom?" I glance down at my own clothing, and sure enough, my dress is stuck to my skin, as good as see-through. Thankfully the only thing showing right now is the outline of the top of the maternity suit, which just looks like a bra. I silently take the shirt.

"We can get you really set up when we get home, but take as much time as you need here; we're in no rush." Once again, I know she's being delicately deceitful. They *are* in a rush. Alyssa just said they were. Why does she keep saying things I know can't be true? I don't like it. Her polite dishonesty throws me off-balance. I want to trust Alyssa, to let her in, but I can't seem to do it when she's always lying to me.

The bathrooms in the park are different than I'd expected. There's a massive steel door with a dead bolt on it and then three bathroom stalls. The mirror above the sink isn't actually a mirror but a highly buffed piece of sheet metal that gives off a dull reflection. The light is one simple fluorescent chamber on the ceiling that flicks on with any movement and off if you stand still for longer than two minutes, but it's supplemented by the dim evening light sneaking in through the open skylights. The room is dank and stale, but it isn't worse than the closet after a few days inside or the way my burned hair stank up the house for weeks after my ninth birthday. Bad smells don't seem to bother me anymore. I get used to them quickly, but I guess I get used to a lot of things quickly.

The stain is too formidable to tackle in a bathroom with cement walls and stainless steel sinks. I put the folded shirt from Alyssa aside in a dry corner of the sink so I can slip it on last-minute when I'm ready to leave. First, I'll wash up. I hit the button on the top of the faucet and then scan the walls and counter for soap, but there's only an empty hand-sanitizer dispenser and a pinkish residue on the sink where a spout protrudes from the surface. When I pump it, nothing comes out but a few splashes of watery liquid soap. Clearly this bathroom doesn't get much upkeep, which isn't surprising, just inconvenient.

This is a growingly futile attempt at cleaning up. So I quickly rinse my arms with water, rubbing the bit of soap on my skin till it starts to bubble up ever so slightly. After a few more swipes, my arms are soon the only part of me that's clean. There aren't any paper towels, and the hand dryer revs up only to sputter out a moment later.

Usually, I'd live with damp skin, but the Feely family seems to think pregnant women are the most fragile creatures on the planet. There has to be toilet paper in the stalls. The first two have rolls that are nearly empty. I can't leave the next person to come in here with nothing. I head to the final stall, the one that's meant to be wheelchair accessible.

"There you are," I say to a stack of unopened rolls and then stop myself. Talking out loud to everything like it's human is a bad habit I have to change. I yank off a few pieces and rub at my damp arms, the thin paper rolling up against my wet skin, when the light vanishes.

"Oh," I gasp as my eyes adjust, my hands full of wet toilet paper. The sensors must've lost track of my movements back here. It's not pitch-black, but it *is* dark.

I'm not scared like I used to be when I was little. As I got older the dark meant Mother was close to going to bed, which meant that was the time in my day that I got to live my true life with my dolls and the Feelys and Sampson. Comfortable in the shadows, I'm reaching for more paper when there's a loud pounding on the bathroom door.

"Anybody in there?" a deep, husky voice I don't recognize calls out. I freeze. I honestly can't move. Not one inch. Another heavy-handed pound on the door. "Helllooooo?"

The jangle of keys and then the only too familiar swoosh of a closing lock echo through the cave-like bathroom, followed by an electronic sucking sound. The thunking footsteps echo farther and farther away until he's either stepped off into mud and grass or he's gone. I hold my breath, waiting for his weighty footfalls again. Nothing. I let out my breath and toss the toilet paper into the empty bowl and hurry out of the back stall. But nothing happens. No lights. I wave my arms around, and still nothing.

I don't care about getting clean anymore; I've gotta get out. Tripping over the skirt of my dress, I rush to the door and jerk on the handle, but it doesn't budge. I yank hard until it feels like my arms might rip out of their sockets. I knew it—it's locked. I shove the door and shuffle backward toward the rear stall. The darkness makes everything seem closer together, though I can make out most details without any additional light, but it's all bland and gray, lifeless, like a fuzzy memory or a faded black-and-white photograph.

My cell phone. Thank heavens for technology. I'll text Alyssa, and she can find the guy with the key, and . . . I pat my pocket. Empty. That's right—I stupidly put the phone in the Ziploc bag with everyone else's at the beginning of the shoot. Do they even know I'm gone? Are they looking for me? Angry? Why hasn't anyone come to the bathroom yet? That's where Alyssa told me to go. Maybe I'm forgettable, annoying, a pest. Maybe they're better off without me. These thoughts batter the inside of my head.

I slump against the cinder block wall, knees giving way, and I slide to the floor like my old plush doll, Suzie. The slightly damp tile is cold. Instinctively, I want to yank away from it, but I can't seem to move, even with ample motivation. The world becomes only half there, and I'm only half in it. I'm living in some alternate reality, some type of bubble outside of time and space where I don't exactly exist, but I haven't fully disappeared. It's strangely familiar, the numbness, the structure with no responsibility to make decisions because I don't have any to make. There's a simplicity here that I miss from my old life, a time when locked doors meant freedom and alone meant safe.

"Help," I chirp, but my voice sounds like the squeaking of a small animal. "Help," I squeeze out again, but if I can barely hear it, I'm sure no one else can. There's a ferocious rhythm in my chest, a relentless drummer with no melody. There's no sound other than its beat and my haggard breathing. I can't seem to stay here in the present. I find myself catapulted into another time, long ago. I don't want to go, but I can't stop . . .

CHAPTER 22

I'm awake. I don't know how; Mother gave me my sleepy medicine like she always does, but even with the yucky sweet taste finally going away, it isn't doing what it's supposed to. Usually I take my medicine, Mother turns off the lights, and then she goes to bed, and I fall into a deep, dreamless sleep, listening to her TV through the wall. But lately, it's stopped working right.

At least my hands don't ache anymore, and my hair is growing back. It's taking forever, though, and it's all funny looking, some parts short and some long. The smell is gone, that's good. Most of the time I forget how funny I look. I never noticed mirrors until I didn't have any around anymore.

I roll onto my side facing the door. She's snoring in the other room. The TV is turned off tonight; most nights she leaves it on, and I listen to the commercials and funny shows through the wall. At least some of it. The only other sound I can hear is the grumble of my stomach. Why am I always so hungry? Mother says I eat too much already, but it's never enough. I miss sleep. At least when I'm asleep, I forget the ache in my stomach.

I can't keep my mind off that pain. There are some pancakes in the fridge. A few bananas. I try to think of food that comes in multiples. If I snuck something from a group, then maybe Mother wouldn't pick up on what was missing. I curl up tighter, pressing a fist into my belly. The pressure relieves a tiny bit of the pain, but not much. Not enough.

A little voice starts in my mind. Sometimes this voice talks to me, tries to protect me. Usually the sleepy medicine makes that voice go to sleep when I do, but lately, it's getting louder.

Mother is asleep, the voice starts. *She'd never know,* it coaxes. *You can be quiet,* it whispers.

I roll up like one of those roly-poly bugs I learned about in Mrs. Moran's second-grade science lesson. But I don't have an exoskeleton to protect me. *You're just a little girl.*

That's it. I can't take it anymore. I shove the covers down and then kick them off the rest of the way. The bed squeaks very slightly, and I hesitate, but Mother's snores are so loud and comforting that I know I'm safe. *Don't wait. Do it now.*

One inch at a time, I make my way off the bed. My socked feet land silently. The more I move, the more my mouth waters in anticipation. I almost throw the door open but correct myself just in time, opening it just enough that I can squeeze out into the kitchen. I've never been out here at night. Ever. Between fear and the medicine Mother spoon-feeds me, until recently I've slept deeply nearly every night since I was brought home from the hospital that first day with Mother.

Mother might be a pack rat in some ways, but she keeps her kitchen spotless. It's one of the reasons I've learned to eat my pancakes plain—so much easier than fighting against gravity with every sticky drop. I'm learning how to clean the floor the way she likes it. If I can do it right, everything just right, maybe she will like me, or love me.

The door stays open when I venture out into the room. Even with nothing changed or missing, it's empty out here. It's Mother. Mother is missing. I'm never alone outside of my room. Ever. Mother is always with me. The refrigerator makes a soothing hum that calms, and a quiet dripping from the faucet sends shivers down my arms.

You're free. The voice answers my question. *You can do anything.*

Anything?

I forget about the refrigerator for a moment and get distracted by something far more enticing—the back door, rust red with carefully carved *x*'s inside raised panels of painted wood. Off-white lace curtains hang limply over a nine-square window.

You can leave, the little voice says. I glance back at Mother's room and then the refrigerator, and then back at that stupid door.

Where would I go? I'm in a flannel nightgown, and Mother keeps my shoes in her closet, so I can't get those. But even if I found them, who am I kidding? My birth parents signed away their parental rights. Mother adopted me. I have the certificate framed in my room.

Find them, that stupid rebellious voice says clearly. *They'll help you.*

What if I told them what life was like with Mother? They couldn't know. They couldn't want me to burn and starve and hide inside all day long. They loved me once, didn't they? I need to find them.

My hunger pangs are gone, and my fingers wiggle by my side. If I wait too long, I'll change my mind.

Go. Go. Go. Go, the voice chants like a cheering squad inside my head. I'm shaking now like I'm cold, but I'm not cold—I'm on fire with fear, and running from the flames.

I slam into the door, and I twist the handle hard—nothing happens. I turn it the other way and yank—nothing happens. There's a button on the knob and a dead bolt with a keyhole. It's locked. I should've known it would be locked.

Find the key. The tender newly grown skin on my palms stings, and I'm panting like when I used to run around the playground during recess.

I squeeze my eyes shut. Whenever we get home she locks that door, muttering about women living alone. The key is golden. The last time we came home, she had the keys in her hands and . . .

The cabinet. There's a row of keys hanging inside the upper cabinet to the right of the back door. I'm beyond stopping now. Cautiously, I curl my toes around the handles on the cabinet doors under the counter and then hoist myself up. My arms are weak and my skin is barely healed, but I keep going.

Not too long ago I was running around outside, playing on the playground, climbing to the top of my tree in the backyard. But I can barely shimmy my way halfway on the counter. Reaching as far as I can, I open the door with my fingertips, and it squeaks against the hinges. The key is there among a collection of several others hanging from a row of small hooks. Using my knee on the counter and pointing my toes to get a little more distance, I extend one more time, every joint stretching to its greatest length.

I touch the tip of the key; so stretched out like this it's almost hard to breathe, like my lungs are being crushed by my rib cage. *Almost,* the little voice says. *Almost.*

Then everything changes. A strong arm around my waist and a hard heave back forces any air left in my body out in a single poof.

"What do you think you're doing?" Mother demands. Her voice is deep, and there's a dark fury I can pick out immediately. I lunge for the key and the back door.

"I wanna go home!" Nothing good comes from screaming, but I can't stop; the little voice that's been urging me on is speaking through me now like it's a part of me I've been putting off for far too long.

"You *are* home, you ungrateful child. I thought you learned your lesson at your birthday party."

I wriggle and wrestle against her vise grip, and she puts her other arm around my waist to heft me in a half circle toward my bedroom.

"No! No!" I yell. "I won't go back in there. I won't!" Tears cover my face, and my throat hurts from the force of my protests. I grab the table leg and try to wrap my legs around it, but Mother just pulls the aluminum-and-plastic piece of furniture with us, and it screeches across the linoleum. She yanks me backward, raspy breath after raspy breath reminding me she has more to say but can't. But it will come, and I will regret this. I know I will. But maybe I'll regret not doing it too.

As we approach my bedroom door, I put my feet up on the doorframe and kick. "Let me go! Let me go!"

"Oh, that's it," she growls, and squeezes me so tight I have to pant in order to get any air into my lungs. It's getting hard to keep fighting; everything gets dim and dense. The little voice is gone. And so is my big one. When we get to the back closet, my feet are dragging, and I can't say much more than "No. Please, no . . ."

She lets go briefly, and I'm too fragile to even respond. With a quick shove she dumps me inside the tiny space, and I lie there, exhausted. She shakes her head at me like she's not even mad, but more like I'm a piece of garbage she's been saddled with. When the door closes and Mother's footsteps disappear, I take a few deep breaths and get up on my hands and knees and crawl to the door. Sore, tired, and defeated, I reach up to the doorknob and twist, but nothing happens. Locked.

I hang off the doorknob, my head against my arms, and in the silence that little voice fades off into the distance.

No way out. No way out. No . . . way . . . out . . .

◆ ◆ ◆

No way out. No way out. No way out.

After that middle-of-the-night escape attempt, Mother installed the dead bolt on my door. I don't know how much time has passed or how long I've heard the pounding, but it's dark and cold and the thumping I thought was my heart is coming from the metal door to the bathroom. I get up, my back and legs stiff from sitting on the ground and my dress damp, and stumble to the door.

"Angela! Are you in there? Are you okay?" Henry shouts through the wall.

"I'm here," I say back, hoping it's loud enough for him to hear.

"We've been looking for you. Stan is getting the key. Are you okay?"

"Yeah. I'm fine." I'm shivering both from the cold and from the memories that overtook me, and when I say that, when I lie about being all right, my eyes get damp and my throat tightens.

"I'm so sorry," he says, somehow knowing I'm telling a lie of convenience.

"It's okay" is all I can manage to say. The area under my eyes starts to tingle, and I know it's coming. I sniff and swallow repeatedly to make it stop.

"No," he says, low and sure. "It's not."

I can't talk anymore, or I'm going to cry. He doesn't try to make me. Instead, he turns on some kind of music that pours in from under the door. I don't know if it's for his entertainment or mine, but it's pretty and serene.

Honestly, Mother could've removed the locks a long time ago. I wasn't going to leave. In some ways dead bolts and rules and punishments are the only things I truly understand. The only reason I got out was because I had something else waiting for me, something better. But even this, the Feelys, this facade of my pregnancy and my attempts to prove I'm competent, are doors and locks of their own. I don't know how to let any of them in. I'm not sure I want to.

"You still with me in there?" Henry asks in the slight pause between songs. I think he's sitting down now, because the location of his voice has changed.

"I'm here," I say, calmer now.

"Good," he replies, the music starting up again.

I rest my head against the cool metal and close my eyes, submitting to the subtle bass buzzing against my back and the unfamiliar melody that accompanies it. Henry is somewhere on the other side, hearing the same thing. It's not as scary to like Henry when there's a steel door between us. I just don't know what happens when that door opens.

CHAPTER 23

"And then the park guy got all defensive and said that it wasn't his fault and that Angela should've said something, but I was like, nah, man. You should've done your job."

Stan has already retold the story five or six times since we finally got home late last night, and it gets grander with every telling. He's going through it again at our morning meeting. Another staff member is here, a twentysomething named Jen who does their graphic design and website, and sometimes helps with editing. Henry and Jen seem familiar with each other and have been whisper-chatting since she sat down next to him at the kitchen table. I'm at the head of the table, and Henry leans over close enough for me to hear his whisper.

"He's telling it again?" Henry asks, still smiling from his conversation with Jen. Jen has short, straight brown hair that curves into a bob just under her chin, and glasses that almost match Henry's. She looks so casual and normal.

"I . . . I think he's funny." I don't find anything he's saying humorous, but my first instinct is to defend the Feelys above all else.

"You're too nice," Henry says, and sits back when I drop his playful volley. Everyone lets Stan finish his tallish tale. And I'm not too nice—Henry's the one being too nice, such a sudden change that can only be explained by Jen's presence.

I don't exactly like Stan's story, and I can't stand that he's talking about such an embarrassing situation over and over again. I want him to stop, but I don't have the courage to say it. I wish I could think of something clever to say back, but Henry is already making Jen laugh so hard she has to cover her mouth to stay quiet.

I kinda slump back in my seat, annoyed at the pretty new girl and annoyed at myself for not being nearly as fascinating. If I could find the right words, I'd tell him that I don't have a say in a whole lot of things in this house right now, and Stan's storytelling is the least of it.

When the three of us got home last night, Alyssa was waiting with a box of new clothes, and she gave me a pair of oversize flannel pants and a warm sweatshirt, which helped stop the shivering that had set in. She washed my hair in the sink with warm water and gave me a facial, with my arms folded around my body the whole time. I don't think I would've allowed it if I'd been in my right mind, but I still felt fragile, fuzzy, and easily influenced. When she started talking about painting toenails, I had to finally speak up and ask to go to bed.

Going to bed also made my blood rush in a different way. The soft mattress and the delicate smell of flowers from the air freshener plugged in to the wall were suddenly unbearable. This isn't my home. It can't be. The Feelys have let me stay out of obligation and kindness, and that thought makes me cringe. I hate being a burden. I know how hard it was for Mother to have me as her responsibility. I don't want to be a weight to the Feelys.

And then there's Henry's accusation in the car, which seems like it happened weeks ago. He's watching my every move like I'm some monster in disguise. Now with Jen as a sharp contrast to my awkwardness, despite the small soft spot I have for Henry's kindness last night, he's becoming my greatest nemesis.

Stan finally finishes his story, and Henry chuckles at something Jen says, and a knot tightens in my stomach.

"Hey, Henry says you're the new intern." Jen taps my elbow, leaning across Henry to reach me. I wince away from her touch.

"She's a little shy," Henry answers for me, and guides Jen back a bit with a soft hand on her shoulder.

"I'm not shy," I blurt, wanting to prove him wrong.

"Oh, well, then it's nice to meet you. I'm Jen." She puts out her hand. Two pewter rings rub against each other on neighboring fingers, and her nails are a picked-away teal that makes her look like the coolest person I've ever been around.

"I'm Angela," I say, and shake her offering, but I'm still not used to these kinds of human niceties, and her grip crushes mine. I grimace internally but keep my face still, absolutely unwilling to balk in front of Henry, who's watching us with a smirk like he has a secret.

"Everybody! Everybody!" Ryland shouts across the room and hops up onto the stool he's been sitting on eating toaster waffles.

"Ugh, it's King Ryland again," Jen says and rolls her eyes. "They let that kid do whatever he wants." I want to say something about how he's a good kid and loves everyone and that it's mean to pick on a four-year-old, but Ryland's speech breaks through.

"I have a story too. It's about my new friend, Angela." He says my name with a *w* in the middle instead of an *l*, and it makes my insides warm and mushy.

"Go ahead and tell it, RyRy," Stan says and then winks at me knowingly.

"Yesterday, Mommy and Daddy were slow in our game, and, and, and Angela said, 'RyRy, you can help!' and I did. And I ran over and jumped on Daddy and Mommy, and we got all icky in the slime, and it was so funny." He laughs as he's talking, and I smile along with him. Is this what it would've been like if I'd been there to see the twins grow up? Ryland makes me feel like a hero every time he says my name or takes my hand.

"I have to agree with Ryland. You two saved the day." Alyssa puts out her arms, and Ryland jumps into them and hugs her face against his. I'm sure I'm blushing and end up looking at my hands. "Now, no more stories, because we have to get out the door, and you guys"—she points over to the three of us at the table—"have to get to work. I want to get a backlog of videos now that we have an extra pair of hands behind all this. I want to hit 2.5 million subscribers by the end of this month. Oh, and take a hard look at increasing our watch time and shares on social media."

She sounds almost boss-like in that moment. She's so changeable, like she's five or six different people inside the same body. I keep thinking I've found the real Alyssa, and then, bam, she changes.

Jen starts complaining under her breath again. "Maybe they should just have *another* baby to get more subscribers. Worked last time."

Henry snorts and then pats the table like he's telling her to be quiet.

"And, Angela, don't let all this overwhelm you. Henry will show you where we measure this stuff online, and maybe it'll spark some new thoughts for you." She puts Ryland on her hip, collects three sagging cloth lunch sacks full of food, palms a set of keys, and then calls out to the front room without stopping for a breath, "Kelsey, Connor! Time to go!"

Stan, coffee mug in hand, joins us at the table but remains standing.

"I'm going to head to the gym. You guys have this under control, right?" He pats Henry's shoulder hard enough that I can hear it. I don't know Henry that well, but when his jaw clenches and he starts cracking his knuckles one at a time, I'm positive he's forcing himself to stay quiet. "We're shooting right after school today, so no lollygagging. Don't want to be chasing the sunset again."

"Got this covered. Go do your squats and stuff," Jen snarks, biting the side of her lip like everything she says is funny.

Stan doesn't acknowledge her little remark. He gets deeply serious instead and raps a knuckle on the table like a judge's gavel. "Good, 'cause yesterday was nearly a disaster. If I hadn't slipped that park ranger some cash, we would've had a fine for shooting there without a permit. Do you know that was the first time he'd heard about someone getting stuck *inside* a bathroom? It was a stupid mistake. When we rush, we get sloppy. I expect more from you guys."

As I really focus on what he's saying, my ears ring. He's talking about me. I'm the stupid one. I'm the sloppy one. I'm the disaster. I bite my lip; the fall from success to failure is a steep one that knocks the breath out of me.

"Would you just leave already? We have actual work to do, and you're bothering us," Henry grumbles, shrugging Stan off.

"What? What did I say?" Stan throws up his hands, and I want it all to stop. "I'm just telling the truth. Alyssa was supposed to bring it up during our morning meeting and didn't, so I thought it needed to be said."

"Come on, this is ridiculous; last night was *not* Angela's fault." Henry's back is straight, like he might end up on his feet at any moment.

"I agree!" Stan says immediately, and puts that heavy hand of his on my shoulder this time, and I sink deeper into my seat. "Angela, I wasn't talking about you, sweetheart." He sounds like AllTheFeels Stan right now, my loving father figure. But then he continues, and his words have barbs. "I was talking about Henry."

Henry shifts in his seat and readjusts his computer like he's determined not to acknowledge Stan's existence. Jen is playing the same game.

"I'm just saying, if you'd kept on schedule yesterday, none of this would've happened." Stan lifts his immense grip. He picks up his coffee mug and takes a long swig.

"Oh my GOD!" Henry mutters fiercely, turning in his seat like he's going to stand up. "It rained, damn it. Are you going to blame that on me too?"

"No, but you've never really been strong under pressure, have you? I'm sure Sheila would have had some thoughts on that."

This new name and meaning hang in the air for a second. Jen, who I'm still not exactly a fan of, is now my new ally in this awkward moment. Her eyes widen and meet mine, like I should know what these new fighting words were supposed to invoke, but I don't. All I know is the effect they have on Henry.

"Don't you *ever* say her name."

"I try to avoid it whenever possible," Stan says with a casualness that doesn't match the tension in the air. "Hey, I'm not worried. Looks like Angela here knows how to step up. You could learn a thing or two from her."

Part of me loves that Stan Feely thinks I'm a good addition. And even after seeing the pain on Henry's face, for the briefest moment I feel a shocking conceit that Stan finds me more competent than Henry. But then I remember how Henry sat with me as I was locked inside the bathroom and how this argument started when he tried to stand up for me.

Henry's fists ball up at his sides; he looks angry enough to stand up and hit something or someone. Stan is unfazed.

"Hey, I'll see you all at noon." Stan lifts his mug toward Jen and me and walks out. Henry visibly relaxes, and I do too.

"Oh my god, they are so weird," Jen blurts out as soon as Stan is out of earshot. "You okay?" She caresses his arm and leaves it there.

"Same old, same old, right?" he says and shifts in his seat so her hand slips off his elbow.

"I know, but still. Maybe you should say something?"

"To who?" Henry asks, shaking his head in tiny little stutters and squinting at his computer screen like he wishes Jen would drop it.

"Yeah, good point." She clicks a few buttons on her keyboard, maybe taking the hint. "I mean, I don't know why you still work here. These people kinda suck." Jen's voice turns distracted. I'm getting used to the change that signals someone is only a little invested in the conversation while mostly focused on some version of technology.

"Watch out, Angela here is a true-blue fan," Henry says as he types something on his computer keyboard and uses the touch pad to navigate, clicking every few seconds almost like nothing dramatic has just happened. I know this method from my life with Mother: normalcy over discomfort.

"You are?" Jen asks, adding several *r*'s to the question. She stares at me across the table like I have seventeen heads. I stare back. Our momentary connection is gone.

"She thinks they're a nice 'family.'" Henry uses air quotes. There's a mocking tone to his comment that makes me feel like he's saying I'm an idiot. Stan called me stupid by accident, but Henry can make me feel it to my core in his own way.

"Well, what can I say, Hen, our movie magic must be working." Jen wiggles her fingers. "Poof!"

"Right?" Henry sounds bitter, and he's staring at his computer screen so intently it's like he can see right through it. Jen starts typing on her keyboard at a regular pace.

"Uh, what should I do now?" I ask after a few minutes of quietly watching them work, my hands in my lap.

"You know what, come on over here. I'll show you how to check the numbers on YouTube, and then we can start you in on our editing software." He moves his chair over with a scratch, and I drag mine beside his, but far enough away that we aren't close to touching. Having him too near brings back those warm feelings from last night. I wish I had that door back between us.

"Henry!" We all jump at Stan's call from the foyer, like kids caught trying to steal a piece of birthday cake a day early.

"Oh shit," Jen says under her breath.

Henry's energy is tense, and the veins in his neck stand out, throbbing. He bolts to his feet and sighs deeply. He's trembling.

"Good luck," Jen says to Henry and then adds in my direction, "he's gonna need it." I wish I had the ability to silence her with a switch, like on my phone.

He walks off, straightening his glasses and adjusting the hem of his shirt a few times. I want to listen to the conversation in the foyer, but Jen doesn't let me. She starts talking again, and I can't make out the rumbling male voices speaking back and forth on the other side of the wall.

"I honestly don't know why he's still here. He's a genius, and with his résumé and graduating from UCLA, he could do so much more than this. I keep telling him he should go to LA. Or at least think about being a consultant. He'd get paid way better than in this f-ing job."

Henry seems competent, creative even, but I guess I haven't been around long enough to pick up on all the rest of her declarations, if they're true. She does seem to have a crush on Henry. I guess they'd be good together—both innovative, artistic, attractive.

"I'm sure he's grateful for this opportunity," I say, and sit up in my chair. I have to pretend I'm busy, or she's going to keep talking.

"Ha, I know Stan thinks so, but the Feely name can only get you so far. They're just YouTubers. It's not like this is the Ron Howard family. A YouTube pedigree doesn't carry much weight."

The front door slams, and Jen looks at me, eyes wide with anticipation and almost excitement rather than concern. I focus on the hallway, waiting for Henry to emerge, anxious to read his body language, but he doesn't return to the kitchen immediately as I'd hoped. Jen is still talking. I don't think I can sit here with her all day. Henry's got to come back, or I'm going to need to feign some pregnant-lady ailment to get out of here.

"You know, when his dad offered him this job after he graduated, it was just supposed to be for the summer, kinda like you. But three years later and, boom, still here. I don't know, part of me thinks he'll never leave."

Never leave. That phrase, I've said it to myself or out loud to Angela many times before, basically anytime Mother walked away from me at a store or let me work on my own. It was my motto, my life, until it wasn't.

"Wait," I say, finding something off in Jen's sentence now that I slow down and think it all through. "His dad?"

Jen takes a swig from her aluminum water bottle, chokes, and wipes her mouth. "Yeah, his dad. You know"—she points at the front of the house—"Stan."

What? The question echoes inside of my head before I can find words.

"Stan?"

"Oh my god, you didn't know?" She screws the lid back on her water bottle and plops it in her canvas messenger bag, runs her nearly picked-off nails through her hair, and then talks to me in a whisper like we're best friends. "Henry is a Feely."

She starts in on some intense gossip about Alyssa and Stan having an affair while Stan was still married to Henry's mom, Sheila, and how the pregnancy with Connor was the reason they got divorced. I barely hear any of it, and she stops midsentence as soon as Henry reenters the room. He doesn't seem to notice the conspiratorial whispers.

"Well, that sucked," Henry says, red around his eyes like he's been crying. I stare at the M key on my keyboard, uncomfortable knowing so much about him that he didn't tell me.

"Not surprising, Stan is an ass," Jen says, like it's a fact she's reading out of a book. "Work heals all wounds, or makes you forget about them at least. Am I right?"

"I don't want to talk about it," Henry says, plopping into the seat next to me. He's different now, like some outer shell has fallen off, like the bugs that used to crawl in when I'd leave the window open a crack for Sampson.

I study him out of the corner of my eye, looking for hints of Stan. I see a few. His hair is the same, now that I'm really taking notice, and the few times I've seen his full smile, it's had an electric quality to it just like Stan's. But more than similarities, I notice differences. From the color of his eyes to the angle of his jaw to the way he looks at me most of the time with a boiling suspicion, when he had his own secret he was hiding.

"Are you sure you're okay?" I ask. He licks his lower lip thoughtfully, and I wonder if he can feel the stubble that lines his mouth.

"Yeah." He nods with a slow bob of his head. "We don't always get along. Clearly." He tries to laugh it off, but I can hear what he's really saying. I can put it into words I understand: he's hurt, and it isn't a new pain; it's an old one. It's a wound that never heals and keeps getting reopened every single day.

"Thank you," I say, not knowing how to pack all of my thoughts into words. If I were Jen or just about anyone else in this world, I'd reach out and touch his arm or shoulder or hand.

"God, for what? For getting into a stupid fight with the guy who signs our checks?" he asks, and I realize that I might not be supposed to know Stan is his father.

"No, thank you for saying it wasn't my fault. It was . . ." I hesitate. "It was nice."

He doesn't respond at first. He squints at his computer like he's doing math in his head. I can't imagine what he thinks of me. Since he caught me shoplifting, I know it can't be all good.

"Let me get you logged in to YouTube as an admin."

"Okay," I respond immediately, agreeing to the game of "pretend everything is okay" that he wants to play. He participated in that farce with me yesterday after our shopping trip, so I in turn try the "half-paying attention while looking at the computer" game he and Jen are so proficient at playing. So many games. So much to lose.

As the morning progresses, after my brief tutorial, very little is said out loud. Most of the time Jen and Henry communicate with a few verbal prompts, the rest coming through shared email messages and texts that go to the whole team, including Stan and Alyssa.

I like the pleasant blur of work and get lost in it easily. But then, when Jen is up refilling her water bottle and it's just me and Henry at the table, I get a single buzz. This one doesn't light up Jen's phone or ding on Henry's computer. This one is just for me. It's from Henry.

All it says is: **You're welcome.**

CHAPTER 24

"No, I'll be fine," I say, palm on my hand-me-down Kelsey backpack and a new duffel bag on my shoulder full of the clothes Alyssa gave me, plus containers of shampoo, conditioner, face wash, and other beauty products the Feely gals shared with me before I left. "Drop me here."

I point at the gate to a two-story apartment complex with outdoor stairs reaching up to the second level on both sides. Aspen Apartments. I can see why Henry is unsettled. I could've picked a nicer building, but if I did, I doubt he'd believe my cousin lived there. Plus, these apartments are only two blocks from the park, and an easy walk is really all I was looking for besides believability.

He looks at me and then back at the building. The sun has started its descent and will set in the next twenty minutes, so I need to make this quick.

"I can wait till your cousin gets down here. What was her name again? Jane?"

He thinks he can trick me into messing up, still acting like a detective nearly every time he's around me. I haven't made any big mistakes in the past two days, and I plan to keep it that way. And now that I'm ready to move out, it should be easier.

"Yup, Jane Evanston. Second cousin from my mother's side." I quote the backstory I've made for my fake cousin, matching the name to the one I looked up online. She's lived in this building for two years and is between twenty-five and thirty. A perfect match. "And she told me to come up when I got here. I'm fine."

I readjust the strap on my shoulder and then heft the backpack out of the car and onto the ground.

"Thanks so much," I say with too much excitement. I'm being strange, and Henry can sense it, but I hope he'll give up and go away since he has absolutely no reason to stick around. I get out of the car onto the curb, not allowing him the opportunity to help. I'm getting better at this, doing things on my own. There's a power in independence. Almost as much power as having secrets.

"Well, okay, if you're sure," he says, leaning over so he can see me better through the open door. He has plans for tonight, which works well for a quick escape. He and Jen have been talking about some open mic they're going to with friends. Henry invited me to come along, but I didn't want to extend my stay at the Feelys' any longer, and if I'm going to make my new place work, I have to get there before dark.

"I'm sure." I close the door and then squat to pick up the backpack from the ground. I've been paying more attention to how pregnant women move than when I first got here. I've learned a lot, watching YouTube in the guest bedroom with headphones on. I always wonder if Henry can see my viewing history, so I'm careful to only watch videos that could look like research.

Like, last night I was watching videos on this little girl in Nevada who disappeared last week, Tracey Monroe. Alyssa wants to do a stranger-danger video because the abduction story is all over the news. But in doing research on the efforts to find her, I've found lots of information about staying safe on my own and how to spot dangerous people. I think that's why I'm so prepared to move out today.

"Do you want me to pick you up on the way in tomorrow?" Henry asks, squinting at the lines of apartments behind me.

"Jane will take me." I say it with my hand on my belly, like Jane and I have had a fun ole conversation about the driving schedule. Today I'm wearing a baggy maroon shirt hanging over the softest pair of stretch pants I've ever experienced. It's strange to wear pants, but if the shirt is big enough, I'm not as self-conscious.

Everything handed down to me is slightly too big for my scrawny frame, but I'm enjoying the variety of wearing different outfits and nearly obsessed with keeping myself free from the smells that come out of the latex suit so easily. I still don't like mirrors or cameras, but it's not as stressful passing by one now. Alyssa says that next on her list of new things is makeup, but I'm not sure I'm ready for that.

"Text me if you need me, then."

"Will do. Have a good night." I complete the circle of niceties and walk toward the open front gate. Inside there's a cloudy pool with a strong chlorine smell and leaves spotting the bottom. Two little girls in brightly colored swimsuits play on the stairs to the shallow end, and a mom with oversize sunglasses watches, only kinda interested, from a reclining chair on the side of the water.

I'm glad she doesn't notice me, pretty sure I look like the creepy stranger someone would call the police on in one of the videos I was watching last night. When it seems like Henry is long gone, I step out from behind the palm-tree-like bushes. I've thought through this moment a thousand times, but there's no guarantee it'll work.

When I leave the gates I'm exposed, but with the sunset chasing me, I have little time to worry. Henry is gone. There aren't any police officers patrolling as I travel down the sidewalk toward the park. Thankfully, the playset is empty when I cross the street to the grassy area I haven't been to since I was locked inside the bathroom last week.

It's risky, but I guess it's a calculated risk that I'm willing to take. See, according to Ranger Bob, all he's required to do each evening is make a quick inspection, secure the cement structure for the night, and turn off the power to the building. So I'm thinking that if I can get in there before sunset and hide, then I may have just found the solution to my housing issue.

The ground is dry and firm, unlike when we shot our video. I made good time, and I still have several minutes to loop around the exterior of the park a few times, close enough to make a quick inspection of the bathroom from a distance.

On my first pass I can see that the motion-activated lights are off inside the women's bathroom. On my second pass I drop my duffel bag in a bush just outside the bathroom so I'll look less obvious pacing the park with luggage. And on my third pass, the sun now so low that the one woman sitting on a bench reading a book by the street has left for the night, I open the bathroom door, snag the hidden bag, and then duck inside. The door slams shut behind me with the full force of steel. The lights flick on, and I jump into a bathroom stall with my belongings, my erratic panting more of a potential giveaway than the glowing light bulbs.

I'm inside, but that doesn't mean I'm safe. The lights flick off as I stand in the stall, unsure of what to do next. In my mind, I scold myself for not hiding my belongings or getting into the handicapped stall or something less conspicuous than crouching in the first stall by the bathroom door.

Oh good. The sensors don't seem to pick up movement inside the stalls. I shove the duffel bag under the partition to my left and slide it slowly with my foot. Still dark. My breathing slows a notch. Okay, now I have a plan. I slip my backpack into the other stall and shift both bags back with my foot as far as they will go. With a touch of regret, I look down at my clean, nearly new outfit. I have to try. The ranger will be here soon.

Inch by inch I lower myself to the rough cement floor, the smell slightly dank and slightly sour. I hold my breath and flatten my body to the ground, the front of my shirt soaking up the unidentified dampness like a paper towel on a spilled surface, and I crawl like a snake under the partition. The lights stay off.

Footsteps. I swear there are masculine footsteps outside, getting louder with each second. I can't measure how far away they are because my pulse is so loud in my ears that it's sending my thoughts into a frenzy. I stay on the ground, ignoring the mold I'm sure is growing along the base of the toilet and the sting of ammonia, and crawl, pushing both myself and my belongings along the floor and into the back stall.

Breathing hard with both bags in my arms, I stumble my way up to standing on the black toilet seat, squatting low enough that my head shouldn't show if the ranger looks inside.

Thump. Thump. Thump.

There's a pounding on the door, just like last time, and an authoritative voice asks, "Anyone in there?"

I hold my breath. The door squeaks open what sounds like just inches. The light flicks on, and I squeeze my belongings to my chest, refusing to move in that moment. *Don't fall. Don't fall. Don't fall.*

Then the door closes. The bolt scrapes shut. The lights turn off. The building powers down. And . . . I'm alone.

I did it.

I let myself breathe again. It's the same rancid room, and I'm still standing on a public toilet, and I've just rubbed myself across a disease-ridden floor, but I'm on my own. For the first time in my entire life, I'm spending the night alone. It's not exactly freedom, since I'm locked inside, but there's something electric about this moment. No one can get in. No one is trying to hurt me, no one is watching my every move, judging me. I can just be me in here, Tara or Angela, it doesn't matter what name I go by. In here, I'm free.

CHAPTER 25

I'm a block from the Feelys' house and sweating through my pink maternity shirt and ankle-length skirt, late for the first time ever. I mean, all my other mornings started in the Feelys' upstairs guest bedroom, so not a fair comparison, but I'm still consumed by that terrible embarrassment I hate so much. Especially showing up looking like such a mess. Alyssa will be horrified. But it's not easy to stay clean in a public bathroom when you aren't supposed to be there. I'm scared to run the water, even at night, and I'm sleeping on the floor with just half an inch of yoga mat between me and cement.

In the light of the morning, my new home seemed less magnificent than it did last night in the darkness. Even with the folded yoga mat to sleep on and a fleece blanket with the name of an unfamiliar prescription drug on it, the night was uncomfortable and long. And I shivered through most of it, even with the glowing feeling of triumph to keep me warm.

Today I took both my bags, unsure whether they'd be safe in the bathroom. I stashed the duffel behind a cluster of bushes at the apartment complex where I'm supposedly staying and keep the backpack with me. I wished I could take a dip in the pool or find some nice person to let me in and use their shower, but it's only a passing fancy. If

I've learned anything from my new obsession with the Tracey Monroe abduction case, it's that there are creepy people everywhere.

But I do smell. Of all the things I'm most self-conscious of, it isn't my hair or my skin or even my oddly shaped belly. It's my smell. Even with brushed teeth and a healthy coating of deodorant, I reek.

Finally at the front door, I pause. I've never had to stop here before; I've always walked through without waiting for an invitation, like I belong inside. The doorknob isn't mine; I don't own a key to this door.

I ring the doorbell.

When the door opens, no one from the Feely family is on the other side—it's Jen.

"Hey, there you are. 'Bout time," she jabs. The air-conditioning chills my damp skin as it wafts out of the house. "Damn, you're a mess."

"My cousin went to work early, so I had to walk." I wipe my brow and step inside without an invitation. This isn't Jen's house any more than it's mine, but Jen stops me with a look.

"The morning meeting is over. You and I are heading to the library at Westmont to scout a shoot and get a permit. C'mon."

I stare longingly over her shoulder into the living room. I want back inside that world. Jen takes me by the elbow and points me toward her car.

"Where is everyone?" There's no sign of Henry's car or the family SUV in the driveway or street.

"Kids are at school. Alyssa's at the salon. Henry is out today, and Stan is inside"—she pauses—"sick or something."

"Do we have a meeting at noon or a shoot tonight?"

We stop by her car, and she seems annoyed at my questions, flipping her hair and tossing her messenger bag into the back seat.

"Nope. Gonna have a Saturday shoot at the beach. Didn't you get the texts?" She gets in the car, and I fish my phone out from the pocket on the side of my backpack. I swear I can tell just by touch that it's dead. A quick check of the screen confirms it.

"It's dead," I say, holding it up, walking around to the passenger side.

"Whatever, I've got a car charger." She exchanges her dark-rimmed glasses for oversize reflective sunglasses. "Let's get the hell outta here."

As we drive way faster than the speed limit allows, she keeps her windows rolled down, the radio blasting. The car is much older than the SUV that belongs to the Feely family and has a similar radio to Mother's van, though I never actually saw her use it.

I like the shifting speeds of the manual transmission, and the carefree attitude Jen lives by. The music is louder than the songs Henry played through the bathroom door, and the bass in the car is all-encompassing. I could use a little bit of Jen in my personality.

When the song on the radio ends, the newsy-sounding voice takes over, droning on about weather, stocks, and politics. Jen flicks it off during the only bit that even makes sense to me: ten-year-old Tracey Monroe.

"God, that missing-little-girl thing depresses me. I wish Alyssa would let it go. That video she wants to do is gonna be a bummer."

"I think it's a good idea." I actually give my opinion, which doesn't happen often.

"Until they find her. Then it's old news. Or if they don't find her, or what if she's dead?"

I shake my head, cringing. Does Jen think anything she doesn't say?

"Fine, I know no one wants to say it, but that girl is probably not coming home." She parks in an empty space in a large parking lot. "Why do we want to be in that business?"

"It's not about business. Alyssa wants to help people. Kids." I know what it's like being abandoned by your family as a little girl. I wasn't kidnapped, but the immense aloneness of losing all that's familiar has to be the same. She's isolated, hurting, scared—but unlike me, she has a family waiting for her. Which might make it worse for a ten-year-old wanting to get home.

Jen swaps out to her regular glasses again and combs her hair with her stubby nails and folds a stick of gum into her mouth. She gets serious.

"There's something you gotta get through your brain, Ang. These people, the Feely family or whatever, they don't care about you. Anyone. They just wanna pay their bills."

I shake my head and work to find the right words, but Jen isn't interested in hearing my rebuttal, or doesn't expect it maybe. She hops out of the car, squinting up at the sun. I'm supposed to follow her, but I unplug my phone, charged at 19 percent, and open to my texting app first. I don't normally send texts other than *okay* or *yes* or *no*. But right now I open a new chat window for Henry only.

Where are you? I type, and hit send before I can rethink it. I barely slept last night. I'm dirty and smelly and I now have to spend the day with Jen. How can I get out of this?

I put my phone in my pocket, the sound turned on so I can hear it ding when I get a text. Jen has a small handheld camera and films as we walk. She stops talking—thank goodness none of our awkward conversation can get recorded. I don't know what we're even thinking of filming here, which is what we *should've* talked about on the way over instead of kidnapped kids and Jen insulting the Feelys.

The building is huge, multistory, and far more impressive than Walnut Creek's public library. Inside, the shelves of endless books overwhelm me, stairs leading up and down on both sides. It's like a playground of words and stories, and I'm like a kid who wants to explore every ladder and slide.

"What are we filming here?" I ask in a reverent whisper.

She pauses the camera and whispers back, "Looking for a place to film that lock-in challenge against the Palmer family. They're getting locked in a mall overnight. Henry thought this place might be an option if we can get the bigwigs to give us a permit. Stan wants us to see if the size of this place translates on screen." She clicks the camera back on.

I go on tiptoes to ask in her ear, "What should I do?" She must smell me because she pulls back and rolls her eyes.

"I don't even care. You have a phone—go film something." She bats me away. I don't know why she brought me with her today. I shouldn't complain, but I don't want to spend any time with Jen. She's a know-it-all and so negative. I don't understand negative people, even with all the hard things in this world.

I slink away, a little rejected even though I'm not concerned with Jen's approval. I don't know where to go right now—so many books, so many quiet people reading and working. There's an intense learning vibe here, and it feels so right. I wander up the stairs and to a new level of activity: treadmill desks, computers in a cluster, a café where people eat and work. This place awakens something bubbly in my midsection. I click some pictures and then find a few angles of areas where I think the family could have filming opportunities.

There's one more set of stairs, and I follow them up again, hungry to know what could be next. Another floor of books and offices, light pouring in from walls of windows. I can't take enough pictures, my brain creating a story line for the lock-in. We can start on the bottom floor, Connor giving a boys-against-girls challenge for a race on the treadmill desks. Then maybe Kelsey will up the ante with a relay using the staircases. I shake my head. A story line? I'm doing it—just like Stan and Alyssa and Henry.

Why is it so hard to let that family exist and film their lives?

I put my phone down and drift to the window overlooking the college. Buildings dot the green landscape, empty sidewalks snake through the campus, cars intermittently meander around the circle drive that follows the perimeter of the school. A pair of students wearing backpacks head off together away from the library, and I watch them longingly. This could've been my life. I could be a naive twenty-year-old taking summer classes at a local college, spending my Friday morning studying and hanging out with friends, maybe even meeting a nice boy who'd find me interesting, funny, pretty.

I put my hand on the window, the transparent boundary keeping me from the future I should've had, want to have. But unlike the trails from one building to another that I can follow easily with my eyes, I don't see a direct path for me from the park bathroom and fake pregnancy to someone who actually belongs here. When I tire of watching the wandering students, I start counting the cars driving by, wondering where they're going, who might be inside, if they had a normal family growing up, if I'm a lost cause.

My eyes blur, staring for too long. I blink, clearing my vision and my head. I can't stand here forever; for the next few weeks at least, I have a job. I need to focus on that. I take one more longing glance over the campus, but as I'm about to turn away from my dreams, something catches my eye. On the road, one more vehicle meanders down the blacktop and makes me jump back from the window like it's charged with electricity.

A white van, exhaust billowing out behind as it coasts toward me. It's exactly like Mother's car, same make as far as I can see, same model. I step back again, clutching my phone in one hand, the other trembling like we are in an earthquake but I'm the only one involved. *Could it be? Did she find me? How?*

The van passes the turnoff to the library, impossibly far for me to see who the driver might be. I can't stay here. I have to hide. I don't know how she's here, but . . . could it be? Suddenly the room that used to be so enticing is too cramped with people, and the stacks of books feel like they're about to fall down on me. Someone taps me on my shoulder, and a scream stops in my throat.

"Excuse me." A college-aged girl stands in front of me. "Oh, I'm sorry! I didn't mean to scare you."

I gulp and try to focus on the person in front of me and not the floating feeling fear brings to my body. She's about my age, with blond hair and shorts that barely cover her more than a swimsuit bottom would.

"Yes?" I manage to say.

"God, I'm so sorry. I totally freaked you out!" She laughs, and looking at her I wonder if she's ever experienced a day of hunger or felt afraid for her life. "But I saw you taking pictures, and I was wondering if you're in Dr. Lopez's lit class? I wasn't gonna do that extra-credit scavenger hunt thing, but is it hard?"

"Uh, no," I say, wanting the conversation to end so I can find someplace to hide till I can think straight. I look past the girl, trying to pick out the cars on the road through the windows on the opposite side of the library, but it's all fuzzy from this distance.

"I have a C in that class, and my dad said that I have to get my grade up by fall or I'll have to take out loans." She rolls her eyes, and I nod like I know or care what she's talking about. "I haven't seen you around. Do you live on campus?"

I can tell she's just noticed I'm pregnant and that maybe I'm not as pretty and clean as she is. I can't talk anymore so I default to nodding.

"Oh, you must be in Page Hall," she says with a scrunch of her nose. I don't know what she's referring to, but apparently it's bad. "I'm in Van Kampen," she says, with a hint of pride, like I should pay homage to her. "Anyway, do you wanna work together? On the extra credit, I mean?"

My phone dings, loudly, and more than one head whips in my direction. I open my phone to look at the notification, relieved when Henry's name stares back up at me.

I'm here.

I don't know if he means the Feelys' house or the library, but I don't care—I have a way out.

"I'm sorry, I have to go," I say, holding up my phone as evidence, no longer afraid of being rude.

She takes my unlocked phone out of my hand, and I lurch forward, trying to stop her, but she's already busy typing a number in my contacts. She calls it, lets it ring twice and hangs up, then hands the phone back to me.

"That's my number. I'm Payton. Let me know if you wanna team up, k?"

I put my phone away fast in case she tries to grab it again, but she starts to walk off, lost in her own device. I take a quick glance out the window behind me—no van. I'm in a fishbowl; I can't be out in the open anymore. As I take my first step down the staircase, eager to find a better hiding place, or maybe the safety of Henry and Jen and work, Payton calls out.

"Wait, what's your name?" she whisper-shouts.

"Tara," I say back, already halfway down the first flight, and then cringe at my moment of distracted honesty. Shoot.

It's okay. She doesn't know me as Angela. I'll never see her again. She doesn't need to know my name. Instead of attempting any kind of correction, I turn to run down the stairs and away from Payton. But I'm also running away from the image of a white van hurtling toward me when I slam right into Henry.

The items in my pregnancy suit dig into my abdomen, and I clutch there instinctively. He looks almost as stunned, holding a spot by his ribs. He doesn't recognize me for a moment.

"Angela! Oh my god—are you okay?" He comes at me with both hands open. The wind's been knocked out of me a bit, and there's a sore spot where something jabbed me from inside the suit, but the thing that has me petrified is not physical. Henry must've felt my stomach when we crashed.

"Yeah," I say, cradling my stomach, mostly to keep him from getting too close to it again.

"Oh my goodness! What happened?" Payton thumps up behind me and meets us on the landing of the staircase. "Watch where you're going next time, asshole. She's pregnant." She glares at Henry like he's a murderer and then puts her arm around me like I'm her sister.

"It was an accident. I'm fine." I'm calm and straightforward, putting space between us.

"Are you sure? 'Cause I can take you to the Health office."

"No, no . . ." I wave her off. Henry stands there, hands in his pockets and forehead scrunched. Payton's face is so close to mine I can smell the fruity scent of her gum.

"Maybe you should go," Henry adds, garnering a dirty look from Payton.

"We've got this, buddy." Her eyes go wide at me. She thinks she's doing me a favor, woman to woman. It's so oddly kind and strangely fierce.

"Actually, Payton, Henry and I work together," I say.

Henry gives one of his rare, sparkling Stan smiles, and Payton lets out a little "Oh." The defensive buzz that's surrounded her like an electric fence powers down. She looks at Henry with clear eyes for the first time and laughs.

"Oh my heavens. I'm so sorry. I'm the *worst* today." She takes a step back. "I just thought . . . well, she's pregnant, and so . . ."

"Girl code. I get it," Henry says, invoking some secret joke I'm not privy to. Payton laughs again and crosses her arms and then uncrosses them.

"You know, we girls gotta stick together," she banters back, and their easy repartee makes me stare at the metal railing, holding my midsection tighter.

"No, you're right. It's a crazy world out there." Henry keeps his charm turned on, and it's totally working.

"Yeah," Payton says, getting shy now, and then addresses me. "Well, if you're not hurt, then I'll let you go. But you've got my number. Call me whenever."

I sense that message isn't meant for me.

"Thanks" is the only contribution to the conversation I can manage.

"Nice to meet you, Henry." She smiles directly at him. "And I'll talk to you soon, Tara."

I wince and brace myself for Henry to correct her, but he doesn't. He stands still, with his hands in his pockets, smiling idiotically as Payton bounces back up the stairs. Once she's out of sight, he steps toward me.

"Seriously, now, are you okay?" He checks me over visually, and I wonder if he's trying to figure out what exactly he felt when we slammed into each other. I don't answer; instead I keep walking down the stairs, showing him I'm fine instead of telling him again.

"Jen is downstairs somewhere." I steer the conversation away from the interaction on the stairs, wanting to get away from Payton, who knows my real name, and the probably paranoid idea of Mother's van roaming the streets of Santa Barbara. He rushes to keep up.

"I know. I saw her on my way in. She's going to the administrative building to apply for a permit, and I'm taking you home."

"Home?" There are so many places that word applies to right now, and no place at all.

"Sorry, I'm taking you to Alyssa. She has a proposal for you." The words sound positive, but his tone is stormy, like he's been sent on an errand he isn't the least bit interested in. Why would Alyssa send Henry all the way over here to get me? Why not talk to me at the afternoon meeting or tomorrow morning? Unless . . . she knows.

"What does that mean?" I ask, hoping to finagle a bit of information out of him. But he doesn't know much more than I do.

"Who knows. More clothes?" he jokes, holding the door to the library open so I can exit first.

"Mysterious." I try to keep the joking going like when he was kidding around with Payton, but I'm too distracted to be truly clever. When we get outside, the sun has warmed the air, and sweat builds up under my suit instantly. Once my eyes have adjusted, I search the parking lot for the van row by row and remove one worry from my list. It's not here.

"Not as mysterious as you are."

"What does that mean?" I toss back at him, defensive, scared.

"You know what I mean," he says in that way that makes a chill go up my spine.

"No, I don't." Why do my conversations with him always end up this way—me hiding, him seeing things too clearly?

"How did she know you? She has your phone number?" We get to the Feelys' SUV and stop short, the heat reflected up from the blacktop making my skin tingle.

"We just met." I squint, telling as much of the truth as possible. "She saw me taking pictures and wanted them for some school project."

Lately I've started to talk too much when I'm covering something up, far more than any other time I'm talking to Henry. It should be a dead giveaway. Maybe it is. He's taking in my explanation and weighing it inside that impenetrable mind of his. The car doors unlock.

"Okay, I get that," he says, getting in the car. He's accepted my story, for now at least.

Thank heavens. With Alyssa waiting at home with some unknown purpose, and dealing with Jen and the van and Payton . . . I don't know how much more I can take of this constant fear. Are there people who live without this racing heart and looping mind? I've existed in a state of nonstop anxiety for so long that I don't have any idea what my life would be like without it.

Henry stops halfway in, halfway out of the SUV, his dark hair blowing slightly in the breeze.

"I just have one question, though," he says as an engine revs in the background. I know that sound.

Panic crushes my shoulders, and the sun sends flares of light across my field of vision as I whip my head around, searching for a glimpse of rusted white. Nothing on the road. Nothing behind me. I turn away from Henry, pretending to look at the library but searching the circle drive in front of it. Also empty.

"Angela," he calls behind me, but I can barely make it out. "Angela, what's wrong?"

I tune him out and listen again for that sound: the roar of old gears grinding, the whine of a belt that always needed replacing.

"Tara," someone shouts, and I spin around nearly 360, expecting to see Mother. But it's not her. It's Henry.

CHAPTER 26

The ride back to the house is uncomfortable and silent. Neither of us acknowledges the fact that I responded to the wrong name, the same name a girl was calling me inside the library a few minutes earlier. I was sure he'd press me for answers like he did when he saw me stealing the toothpaste, but this time he stares at the road and puts the radio on at full volume—wordless, pounding melodies. I wish I could read Henry's mind as easily as it seems he can read mine, but I have no idea what he's thinking about behind those dark-rimmed glasses and bottomless blue eyes that match the deepest part of the ocean.

Alyssa is waiting at the kitchen counter when we get back home, papers spread out in front of her and an iPad propped up, attached to a keyboard. Her hair is pulled back into a high ponytail like it is only on non-filming days, nails long, perfect, and pink. Each family member gets one non-filming day a week, and recently Alyssa's been taking two. I don't blame her—the schedule is intense, and she has to take care of a family and have a major hand in the business side of the channel on top of her time on camera in AllTheFeels.

She doesn't look upset, but it's not until she lifts her head and smiles that I know she's not about to kick me out of her house.

"Hey, you two!" She waves Henry and me into the kitchen and points to a stool next to her. When I sit, Henry goes to leave, but Alyssa stops him. "I want to talk to you too. This involves both of you."

Both of us? Henry, still silent, joins me on the stools lining the marble top of the giant kitchen island.

"First of all, how you feeling today, sweetie? You look kinda . . . rough." Alyssa has stopped mincing words when it comes to my appearance. I wonder if this is what normal girls feel like when their mothers get critical. I try not to let her assessments hurt me. I'm not sure why Alyssa is so concerned about my appearance. She never seemed worried about it before I started using some of her old maternity clothes, but now I feel like a project. I shouldn't complain. She's given me clothes, skincare products, shampoo, and conditioner, and even tried to sneak a tinted lip balm into my bag. I should be grateful. I *am* grateful, I guess.

"Jane's shower is broken." I make up a lie on the fly. Risky but also an important skill.

"You can always use the one here," she says, providing a temporary solution to my smell problem.

"Thanks. It should be fixed soon." This excuse will work for a few days, but I'll need to find a long-term shower solution. I refuse to go back to the way I looked and smelled before.

"Well, before you go do that, I want to talk to you about something that I think would be beneficial to everyone involved."

This is business Alyssa talking now. She turns the iPad around and touches the screen. A full-screen picture of me with Ryland on my lap during a shoot last week pops up. Neither of us were looking at the camera. I had no idea anyone had taken a picture of me . . . ever. A thrill of betrayal goes through me. They'd promised to keep me off camera. Business Alyssa keeps talking.

"Angela, we have so enjoyed having you join our family. You have fit right in and put in more than your share of work, brainpower, and heart."

I don't like how impersonal she's acting, especially with that picture glaring up at me. My arms cross defensively.

"Not only have you been a joy professionally, but we've all enjoyed being a part of your changing life and transformation."

She touches the screen again, and another picture flicks up. It takes a second to realize the smiling pregnant girl with flowing blond hair and a bright smile is me. In this one I'm wearing one of the billowing maternity dresses Alyssa gave me and looking away from the camera. My belly fills out the front of the floral dress. I look pregnant, for-real pregnant.

"I don't like my picture taken," I say, wobbly on the stool like I'm losing control. Pictures can be shared and spread all over the internet with a few simple clicks. I can't tear up a JPEG—if it's out there—and I can't do anything about it. Mother must be looking for me. All it would take is one misstep, and she could find me again. What would I do then?

"You are *beautiful*," Alyssa says passionately, flipping to another photo of me in the same dress, laughing, holding my belly. Beautiful? The girl in the photo looks happy and comfortable. She looks safe and clean. Beautiful, though? I shake my head.

"Can you delete those?" I need to make sure she hasn't put them somewhere online already. If I forgot to delete one cookie, one search, one link, that van I keep imagining will become a reality. I know it will.

Alyssa cocks her head, confused.

"Delete them? I thought you'd like them. I thought . . ."

"I don't like my picture taken," I say firmly this time, my neck and hairline sweating, red-hot from anger and anxiety. I always took off the keystroke recorder, right? Every time? Could Mother know about my love for the Feelys? Is she watching?

"Angela, hey. Hey. Okay. Okay. I'll delete them." She pats my hand across the counter and turns off the screen. It doesn't matter that it's off, though. It's still there, wound up in my mind like a venomous snake waiting for the right moment to attack.

"Why am I here?" Henry interjects, casually leaning back in his stool, watching our interaction, detached, almost like he's in cameraman mode.

Alyssa sighs and straightens her oversize mauve shirt, unbuttoned low enough that the very top of her bra is showing. She seems to have some kind of repressed emotion hidden under her smooth skin and layer of expensive foundation.

"I wanted to pitch a new segment. Stan and I have been brainstorming, and I think it would be big for our channel." She looks directly at me this time and says, with more emphasis, "Huge even."

Why is she telling me? I blink and then turn to Henry, hoping maybe he's done a better job putting the pieces together. His features are fixed, hard. He knows something I don't.

"Show us the rest of the presentation," he says—no, he orders, and clasps his hands behind his head. He leans back in his seat again.

"Presentation?" I ask, slower to understand whatever Henry has divined.

"Okay," Alyssa agrees. She resets her smile and centers herself on the stool. She quickly flicks past the picture I rejected and then makes solid eye contact—with me. Only me.

"Angela. We care about you and your future, and because of that, we care about your baby too. I know this internship was proposed for a ten-week duration, but Stan and I have been thinking about it a lot. We'd love to help you out in a more long-term arrangement."

She pauses here, and I can tell she wants me to acknowledge her offer. But I'm confused.

"Long-term?" I repeat her phrase out loud. What does that even mean? Henry is watching me.

"Yes, long-term." She flips to the next slide. There, Alyssa is holding a baby wrapped in a white blanket with blue-and-pink stripes. She's staring into the sleeping infant's face like she's discovered gold.

"Stan and I have always wanted to have another baby." Alyssa's bottom lip trembles for a second, breaking through her businesswoman mask. Her voice cracks as she talks through the emotion. "I had two miscarriages before Ryland and three after. We haven't shared this with our subscribers because"—she swallows like she's trying not to cry— "it's too hard."

I want to say I'm sorry or offer some words of comfort, but something else is coming. I don't think I'm going to like it. Alyssa powers forward.

"It's like you were sent to us by fate," she says like she believes it. "We want to take care of you, Angela. We'll give you a place to stay, we'll pay for your health care, your education, and keep you on here under full salary."

Take care of me? A wall of water pours across my vision, and I blink hard to hide my tears. No one has ever wanted to take care of me, no one. Not my parents. Not Mother. Gosh, not even myself most of the time. A little whimper catches in my throat. Safety, security, family. No more fear. No more shame. I could be like one of those girls on campus today. I'd have a future.

Henry interrupts my grand fantasy with a thought that freezes my dreams in place.

"In exchange for . . . ?" He lets the question trail out like the smoke jets would leave across the little blue rectangle of sky I could see from my room at Mother's house.

Exchange? What does that mean? Alyssa stares at Henry for a long moment, her smile faltering for only a second. She flips to the next slide, and like she's hitting a reset button, boss Alyssa is back.

This slide is a beautiful picture of the Feely family on the beach, and above them, written in bubble font, a title—**ALLTHEFEELS: BABY ON BOARD**.

"We'd be honored if you'd allow us to follow your story for AllTheFeels. Things like doctors' visits, ultrasounds, and maybe even a segment on the birth. All in good taste, of course. And then after the baby is born, we'd like to invite him or her to join our family for activities and special moments. Your baby would kind of be an honorary Feely."

The room spins, and my throat gets tight. *The baby. She wants to use my fake baby.* She taps to another slide, and pictures pop onto the screen one at a time of brand names and logos I don't recognize.

"As you've seen, when I was pregnant with Ryland, we received sponsorships from several baby brands. Back then, we were a relatively small channel, but now . . . a baby would provide us with countless options for episodes, sponsors, product placement. What do you think? Great idea, right?"

She's watching me eagerly. I have nothing to say. Absolutely nothing. I'd only imagined my new life for a few moments, but the idea of losing it now feels like someone has died. She doesn't love me or care about me. She wants to use me, and not because I'm smart or clever, but because I have a baby that doesn't exist.

When I don't respond, she rubs her lips together, dulling the glossy shimmer.

"I mean, I know you *said* that you didn't want to be on camera, but you've gone through such a transformation. And you're so relatable. It wouldn't take much. We already made that episode about finding you as our intern. The Feelers would be ecstatic to meet you on camera."

Feelers—that's what they call us—the superfans. And she's right. They'd love this. Is that why she hired me? Is that why she's put so much effort into helping me? To make money?

Her manicured nails clack on the counter, and I blink endlessly. Blink. Blink. Blink. No words make sense to me right now.

"Thoughts?" she adds, including Henry in her question this time, giving up on me.

"I think that's a no from Angela," Henry says, after holding for my reply for several endless moments. He's talking for me, and I hate it, but he's right, and I'm glad I don't have to say it.

"Henry!" Alyssa snips, and there's a message of disloyalty conveyed in her glare. I don't like the change in her demeanor or the way it affects her stepson.

He clams up and presses his lips together.

Alyssa leans toward me. "Angela. Listen. I want what's best for you. This way we can help you and the baby. And I *know* you'd love helping us just as much."

Henry's and Alyssa's eyes push at me, for different reasons. I know she's right; a baby would help the channel and the brand—but I'm not pregnant. And even if I *were* pregnant, I can't be on camera. Mother. I can already feel her looking for me. Even if that van wasn't hers, it reminds me that I'm not safe. Mother could find me. It probably wouldn't be that difficult. It only takes one mistake. One. Or maybe I've already made one, and she's on her way to pick me up right now . . .

"I can't," I mumble, shaking my head. Alyssa reaches out across the counter but doesn't make contact.

"If you're worried about being on camera, don't be. Your skin is clearing up nicely, and you look so cute in your new clothes. We can go to the salon and get your hair and nails done and—"

"No thank you," I say, kind but firmer this time. She thinks this is all about my looks, that she can fix my damage with a few drops of foundation or repair my brokenness with a bottle of hair spray, but all I really need to keep covered up is my true identity.

Alyssa tsks, drops her shoulders, and flattens the iPad onto the counter. Even though she's expressionless, the vein on the side of her neck is pounding, giving away the emotions that must be trapped inside. I must look so vain and self-centered in her eyes.

"I think you're making a mistake," she says, packing up the electronic devices and putting them into a black bag. "I mean, Angela, how long has it been since you've seen a doctor? Have you even had an ultrasound or blood work done? Do you know what it takes to care for a baby? Can't you see that I just want to help you?"

Each question slaps at my conscience, her disappointment painful to watch. I want to make her feel better. I *need* to make her feel better. It's an old, familiar desire from when I was a little girl with my birth mom, and then even more intensely with Mother. Consumed with the desire to please someone else, I start to lose my grip on my outrage and the betrayal of her offer.

"She said no, Alyssa," Henry says, shoving away from the island and gesturing to me. "Come on, we've got some errands to do."

I look at Henry and then back at Alyssa, conflicted. He wants me to walk away without making this better, while she's still mad. If I leave now, she may never talk to me again, or even worse, she might hate me forever.

But, then again, I can't make this better. I don't have anything she wants—no baby, no pregnancy, no boyfriend sob story. I thought she wanted me because of my skill and passion—what if she only wanted me for my marketability?

I stand up next to my stool, just like Henry did.

"I'm really sorry." I stare at my feet, both hoping I won't break down into tears and also wondering why my eyes are now dry. I wish I could explain myself. One day, maybe, but not today.

She doesn't say anything back, but I can make out a rustle of fabric and a shuffle of soft shoes on tile. Then a slender arm wraps around my shoulder, and Alyssa's motherly voice croons in my ear. "No, no. Please don't be sorry."

I keep myself together, every muscle and joint fused in place. Her touch is frightening in its potential to discover my secrets, and I don't know how to trust it. But it's also tender and welcoming, and reminds me of my old comforter from home that I'd bury my face into after taking the sleepy juice when I was very little. I haven't been hugged in a long time. My body longs to lean in, but no. I stiffen, hold my midsection with a protective grasp, and make my spine as straight as a rod. I can't trust Alyssa.

Henry tugs at my elbow.

"We should go."

"Yeah," I say, stepping away from Alyssa's touch and falling into Henry's gravitational pull, sensing a path to escape.

As I turn into the hallway, Alyssa rushes up behind us from the kitchen.

"Hey, hey, Angela. Wait up!" she calls, trying to catch up. I lengthen my stride to keep out of hugging range. She talks rapidly like she's desperate. "Sweetie, I didn't mean to upset you."

"It's okay," I say, slowing to a cautious stop by the front door.

But it's not okay. None of this is okay. She made me think she cared about me as a person, and I believed it, I really did. How am I so incredibly stupid? I must be as unlovable as Mother always said, because if I were good, someone as smart and beautiful as Alyssa Feely would've seen it by now. We stop by the front stairs, where Henry snatches his canvas shoulder bag.

"Oh good. I'm glad you aren't upset with me. It was just an idea Stan and I were tossing around. You know how that goes, brainstorming and all." She rushes to explain, and I let her, dizzy like when I'd first stand up after several days in the closet. So it was Stan's idea too . . . Stan and Alyssa—the third time in my life I'm not good enough for the people I love.

"No, I understand." I continue to lie and try to smile. Henry is waiting with his hand on the doorknob.

"No hard feelings?" she asks, flipping a chunk of hair off my shoulder and smiling her motherly smile that first made me love her. So, this is where my lies have gotten me, just outside the gates of heaven.

I shake my head. "No hard feelings."

"Good!" She pats her hands together in a muffled clap. "I really do want the best for you, Ang. When you get back, let's look into finding you a doctor. We gotta keep you healthy, on camera or not, right?"

I step toward Henry. He reads my intentions and opens the front door. The hot air floods in like we're walking into an oven. I don't want Alyssa or a doctor anywhere near me.

"I have a doctor." I offer the first excuse that comes to mind.

"Oh yeah? Good for you." She seems surprised and a little disappointed but also like she knows she shouldn't be. "Well, you can tell me all about it when you get back."

"Sure," I say, finally stepping over the threshold, preferring the oven air to the unexpected pressure cooker I'd been stewing in.

"Angela!" she calls out when I'm halfway down the front path.

"What does she want now?" Henry mutters. I shrug and turn to face Alyssa, still eager to please in the midst of my bewilderment.

"Let me know if you change your mind!" she calls across the front lawn. Henry tugs at my elbow, and I back away from Alyssa. She stands there, framed in the doorway, watching us leave like I've always imagined mothers do when they send their children off to school in the morning.

She's beautiful in her flowing shirt, smooth hair even on her day off, and relatably barefoot with painted toes. This is the woman I came to love through my computer screen. I used to hope she'd love me back.

When Henry drops me off at my "apartment" that night, he walks me to the gate like he did the night before. After a full day of work-related errands and no mention of the slipup at the library or Alyssa's proposal, Henry slows and clears his throat.

"Don't do it," he says.

"What?" I ask, distracted. The sun is starting to set, and I can't cut my timing too close or I could get locked out for the night.

"Don't sell out to the Feelys. That's all I'm saying." He's nervous, hands in his pockets and shuffling back and forth.

"You mean the baby-on-board thing?" I ask.

"Yeah, I mean, easy for me to say, right? You're the one with the baby." He readjusts his glasses and taps his foot. He still thinks I'm pregnant, so that's something. I rub my belly to reinforce his belief.

Henry seems sincere, but then again, even if he's a spy for Alyssa, it won't change anything. I know what my answer has to be.

"No way," I say, with finality. He kinda smiles a bit.

"Good," he says, visually checking the wraparound two-story porch of the complex like he's trying to figure out which unit is mine. "Her offer was creepy as shit, but—you can do better than this."

Better than this? My eyes narrow, and I flinch like Henry hit me. I wish he'd stop complaining about his cushy life. Even living where I do and wearing what I wear and smelling like I smell, and even with the Feelys' growing list of quirks, his family is better than mine has ever been.

"Maybe I can," I say, anger bubbling in my stomach in a way I'm not used to. He shrugs, like he's done the best he can or something, and turns to walk away, stopping when I blurt out, "But so can you."

"What did you say?" he demands, spinning around on one foot, his defenses stacking up like bricks. Yeah, right now he definitely looks like Stan's son.

"I don't know." I hedge momentarily. Why am I antagonizing this man?

"No, you know what you said," he pushes, with a giant step in my direction.

My mouth goes dry, and I can't swallow. I should let him go. I should avoid him. I should be silent and fade into the background. But I can't.

Fine. If he wants to know what I think, I'll tell him.

"I said—you can do better too. I mean, if you hate it here so much, why don't you just leave?" I hurl the question at him like a javelin. He flinches when it hits.

"It's complicated," he says, his brow furrowed tightly like his problems are so insurmountable. What arrogance.

"You mean about Stan?" I don't know where that question comes from. I guess I'm tired of Henry acting so superior, how he's always trying to figure out my secrets when he's keeping plenty of his own.

He opens his mouth and closes it.

"So, you know," he says finally, with a heavy resignation.

I nod.

"Jen?"

"Yeah."

"Of course," he says, swearing under his breath, looking past me down the street and then seeming like he's going to say something, but he shakes his head and takes a step back. "You know what, Angela, you wouldn't understand."

I wouldn't understand? Like he would understand my life if he knew it?

"Whatever you say." I reach for the gate, and he doesn't wait for me to get inside this time like he did last night. It's a relief to know I've pushed him away but also unsettling.

I need him far away from me. The rest of the Feely family seems oblivious to the inconsistencies and oddities of the stranger they've brought into their lives. But not Henry. It's terrifying to be seen under all my disguises, terrifying and a tiny bit thrilling.

I swear he revs his engine a little louder than usual as he drives away without a goodbye. As I stand here alone, just about all my worldly possessions gathered at my feet and on my body, the loneliness is heavier than the baggage I carry.

No one is looking out for me. My birth parents failed me. The system put me with Mother. Mother used me, hurt me, controlled me. And now the Feelys . . . I thought they'd be different, but . . .

A couple comes through the gate, and it nearly hits me. They don't notice. I hold back tears and gather my belongings from behind the bushes, holding more than my arms are strong enough to carry. Once I find my footing, I step out from my hiding place and wiggle my way through the partially opened gate. The sunset's pinks, purples, and oranges have started to invade the sky and give me a renewed strength. I used to only see the sky through a tiny, slanted window. Now, I walk underneath it freely.

I've survived on my own this long. If no one wants to take care of me—I guess I'll have to take care of myself.

CHAPTER 27

Three weeks later

I pull down my tank top over my stretch pants and squeeze some extra water out of my hair. Another girl is in the shower stall next to me, and I want to get out of the bathroom before I have to talk to her. I haven't had many issues in these dorm showers; I get here early enough that most of the girls are blurry eyed, or I shower on the weekends, when they're still asleep from partying the night before.

All I have to do is keep my phone in my hand and my head down like I'm texting, and then link up with any group of girls returning from breakfast or an early workout. Or what did Jen call it when she came in wearing the same thing two days in a row? A walk of shame. As embarrassing as the concept is for me, they're the easiest targets because they want to avoid eye contact and get back to their own rooms as quickly as possible.

I can't come every day, but I've worked out a schedule that seems to be effective enough at keeping me tidy even after sleeping on the floor of the park bathroom stall. Plus, I like having a somewhat unpredictable schedule.

I know I'm probably crazy, seeing things—well, hearing things too—but I can't get rid of the feeling that Mother is watching me. The blur of white out of the corner of my eye, the engine sputtering up behind me; it's always there just out of reach of confirmation.

Bent in half, I tie my shoelaces and arrange the contents of my backpack, keeping my phone in my hands. I stand up and toss the straps over my shoulders, and all the blood rushes from my head. Queasy, I lean against the sink. I've been fighting off this crawl of nausea since last night. I couldn't choke down more than a few nibbles of dinner, and I'm sure my empty stomach isn't helping. There will be food at the shoot today—that's gotta help.

I rub my flat abdomen as it clenches. With a deep breath in and slow breath out, I get control over my body.

You've got this. I take one more look over my reflection in the mirror. I'm like any other girl here, maybe a little skinnier than most, but with my skin nearly clear and the pregnancy suit hidden out in the woods behind the dorm, I look my age. I look like I belong.

Appearances can be deceiving, I guess. I might seem like one of these girls, but it's all an act. When I first met the Feelys, I thought I was different because of what I looked like, but now I'm not so sure. Once I don't have to pretend to be pregnant anymore, I'll still be scared little Tara inside normal-looking Angela. Then again, imagining this alternate version of my life in these early morning moments leaves me longing to change for real, if that's even possible.

The water shuts off in the back stall. I toss my toothpaste and brush into my bag and slip out the door as I hear the whoosh of the shower curtain opening.

It's a Saturday morning, and the dorm hall is dead. I always pick a new floor when I shower so no one recognizes me coming too often, and I stay as far away as possible from Payton's hall on the other side of campus. She knows me as a pregnant girl named Tara, and I could never explain my flat abdomen if I ever ran into her here.

I feel so free without that contraption, though. I nearly fly down the stairs, the muscles in my legs stronger than I knew they could be. It feels good to work them hard, and to own the vigor inside of my own skin instead of acting tired and weighed down like a woman entering her third trimester would normally be.

I'm still careful about where the cameras in the dorm are located, but right now I'm freer than I've ever been. Okay, 90 percent of my life is a lie, but they're all perfectly balanced on three cornerstones. Number one: never let anyone get too close; number two: keep it simple; and number three: tell the truth as often as possible. I'm less stringent in following them now, but they're still incredibly effective.

The only person I still worry around is Henry. After that moment of understanding in the library parking lot three weeks ago, when I responded as Tara instead of Angela, I knew I'd made some kind of terrible mistake. If it had been anyone other than Henry, I would've found some simple explanation, or told a joke about pregnancy brain, but not with that man. Henry knows my secret. Okay, he doesn't know what my real secret is, but he knows I have one. And I can tell he knows it's big.

But I've also found out something fascinating—Henry is just as scared of me as I am of him. Ever since I challenged him outside of my apartment building, he's looked at me differently. More like he wonders what I'm thinking and less like he wonders what I'm trying to steal. This unspoken understanding between us, my secret versus his, has created some sort of relational counterbalance that makes me feel safe from his suspicious eyes, at least temporarily.

I duck into the small wooded area that borders the northern edge of Westmont's campus and find my stashed bag. It takes very little time to get my uniform on. That's how I think of it now, my uniform, something I wear that helps me do my job. My hair is drying rapidly in the summer air, and I know Alyssa will make a comment about how I should really use a straightener. She gave me one last week, but I pawned it. I don't need a hair straightener, but I do need enough money to get some non-maternity clothes.

Without a pregnancy to film or baby to share with the Feely family, my time with them is limited. At some point I need to figure out what's next. But whenever I think about leaving, an elephant-like pressure crushes me, and so far I've only been able to come to one conclusion—I won't ever put on this fake belly again.

Today, I've dressed as lightly as I dare. We have a shoot at the beach, a follow-up to the viral stranger-danger video we did two weeks ago, and though I can't wear a swimsuit or even a tank top, I button up a loose-fitting cotton blouse and let it drop over the thin khakis I've just started to wear instead of skirts or stretch pants.

Everyone else is excited for a beach day. I'm excited for a whole different reason. Today, I'm bringing along my new ultrasound picture. In the shade of the trees, I check the image of my supposed baby one more time and double-check all the details.

My name: Angela Sampson. My birthday: the same as on the fake transcripts I printed out at the college library and handed to Alyssa two weeks ago. My due date: six weeks after the official last day of my internship, giving me plenty of cushion for disappearing before the supposed birth.

The paper doesn't match the kind used for ultrasound machines, but I've come up with an explanation for that too—the doctor made a copy at the clinic and kept the original for my file. I'm getting almost too good at lying.

I wad up the second maternity dress I brought from Mother's into the side zipper and mush the sides of the prosthesis with both hands. I'm technically a week into my third trimester as of today. The extra fabric makes the belly lumpy, but the weightiness of it is off. I keep thinking someone will notice, but so far my rules have kept everyone far enough away that I'm safe. *Safe.* What a strange and ever-changing concept. I'm starting to wonder if I'll ever feel safe.

I jiggle my whole body like I'm trying to shake off the questions that always follow. Nope, can't think about big concepts today.

My phone buzzes in my hand. My alarm. If I leave now, I should get to the Feelys' in time for the morning meeting. I don't know how I used to live without a phone. It's become such an important part of my daily life and routine that it's hard to imagine a time when it wasn't what kept me in touch with the world and on time, and what now feeds me information like I'm a ravenous creature that's been kept in a cage for weeks without food.

If I'm going to hear my alarm in the morning, I've learned I need to leave myself a good 20 percent of battery power. I also need to be ready for the scrape of Ranger Bob's key. He's yet to come in, only occasionally peeking through a crack in the door, but I always climb on top of the handicapped toilet just in case. I've only been locked out once because of shooting deadlines. That first night I spent at the college library till it closed and then walked around Walmart until I could tell the checkout ladies were wondering if I was going to buy something.

The main road that leads to the Feelys' home isn't far from Westmont, and I'm running ahead of schedule when I hit Claremont Road. This is my least favorite part of my day. On the sidewalk of the busy thoroughfare, I get plenty of looks, and I've been offered a ride by well-meaning locals more often than I like to think about. But it's not the attention that's most difficult for me; it's the van. I never really get a good look, ever, but every few days it's there, driving down the opposite side of the road with thick clouds of exhaust puffing out the tailpipe.

I stare far up Claremont, and then back down the opposite direction. A shiny black BMW, a nearly silent Tesla, an older silver minivan, and a few random vehicles disappear into the distance. The air is clear, and I can smell a bit of the salty breeze blowing in off the ocean. No exhaust. No oil. No white van. I step out cautiously.

Mother isn't here. I say the same things every day, trying to convince myself. *She doesn't know where I am. She hates leaving home. She hates worldly places like Santa Barbara.*

As I cross the street, an engine rumbles in the distance. I spin around. At the bottom of the hill, a small white dot lumbers toward me. There's a row of bushes to my right, and a street that leads to a dead end is a few feet in front of me. I step back. I can't run to the Feelys. I won't make it.

A car horn blares next to me.

"Ahhhh!" I scream. I trip over my own feet, not knowing which way to run.

"Oh my god, Angela, it's just us. Get in the car." Stan Feely is hanging out the driver's-side window of one of the Feelys' SUVs. He's wearing a light-blue tank top showing his tan shoulders. I clutch my chest; it's tight like I've been running.

"You scared her to death!" Alyssa scolds in the front seat as Connor helps me load my bag into the car. He hefts me in with one yank. As I settle into the seat Connor just vacated, a large white vehicle zooms past in the opposite direction. I can't see the driver, and the back windows are tinted, but I sink deeper into the leather upholstery anyway.

"Dang, you're like a feather. Do you even eat?" Connor says, calling out one of the many inconsistencies in my fake pregnancy. I drop another inch. Alyssa speaks before I can put together a response.

"Connor, that's rude. All women's bodies are different. You should apologize," she says in her mom Alyssa voice. I still haven't figured out which personality is the real Alyssa. I'm starting to think that even she doesn't know.

"Sorry," he says, blushing while fumbling with his seat belt.

"Thank you, Connor," she answers for me, again. "Now, Angela, Henry is at the house waiting for you. I'll text him." She starts typing on her phone. "You should really let him pick you up more often. This is a long walk for you."

"Leave her alone, she likes it," Stan says like he knows my thoughts too. And so I sit back and let Stan and Alyssa have the conversation for me. Between the two of them, they make me sound quite interesting, and the more they talk, the less I have to lie. They chat until they come to a question neither one has an answer for.

"Oh, honey, how did your appointment go? That was yesterday, right?" In general, she's stopped asking about the baby proposal but hints at it often enough to keep me diligent in my pregnancy care and baby prep. The more independent I seem, the better. I hand over the ultrasound. My stomach couldn't be more unsettled if I were actually pregnant.

"Oh my god! Is that the baby?" She takes the copy paper. I hope my research was right and that my editorial eye caught any issues.

"Yeah, I had them make a copy for you guys," I say hesitantly. I hate the way I lie, all nervous and stuttery. My stories are strong, and they think I'm shy, so that covers most of my uncertainty, but I'm getting comfortable with the family, and soon enough they'll notice a difference between my lies and my genuine interactions.

"Look at that little one," Alyssa gasps, holding the page like it contains the secrets of the universe. I can't stand to watch the love in her eyes for a baby that's likely some random four-year-old kid now. "Look, Stan." Alyssa displays the ultrasound, and Stan gives it a cursory glance.

"Nice" is his only response. I can't tell if he's holding back because it brings up feelings from their previous losses or if he really doesn't care.

"Can I see?" Ryland asks from the back seat. Strapped in, he can only lean forward an inch or so, but his fingers wiggle with desire.

"Sure, bud." Alyssa passes the picture back, and Kelsey takes a quick look before holding it up to Ryland.

"Careful, Ry. It's very important," Kelsey says, with more patience than her normal interactions with Ryland. She watches me with the curiosity of a little girl who's starting to understand that her body might create and carry humans one day. "Is it a boy or a girl?"

"I don't know." *Keep it simple.* Another rule.

"You're not going to find out?" Alyssa asks from the front seat.

"No, they don't do that kind of ultrasound there." I've done my research. I don't want to let a tiny detail throw everything else off. *Tell the truth as much as possible.*

"Huh," she says, like she has something on her mind. The kids pass the ultrasound around, and Connor hands it to me after a longer look than I'd expected.

"You can keep it," I say, holding it out to Alyssa again. She takes it but doesn't look at the image again. Nervously flicking the corner of the page with her nail, she asks me the question that I'm sure she's been wanting to ask.

"Did you know that there are some specialty places that will do a 3-D ultrasound and get a real picture of the baby's face? You know, you can even find out the gender there. We could go together sometime . . ." She doesn't say what I know is the rest of that sentence. She doesn't say "if you let us film you," but the connotation is there.

"Oh, maybe," I say, noncommittally, pretending I don't understand the unspoken caveat.

"Just think about it," she adds, with a flip of her wrist. That's what she always says when it comes to the baby stuff—"just think about it." I keep waiting for her to check back in on all that thinking, but thankfully she hasn't gotten to that next step in her new and slightly more covert plan.

The beach is just ahead. The glistening blue of the ocean rushes toward us as we approach. I don't like lying. Every night I pray for forgiveness like Mother taught me. I don't know if it does anything, the praying, or if God is even listening, but I hope He is. Because I can't stop, not yet. Even if I have to break some of the rules for now, at least today I can step out of the car and put my feet in the sand. I can ignore the Feely family's bickering and imperfections, and instead take in the salty air, enjoying its feel in my lungs.

Even as Stan and Alyssa fight over where to set up and the kids zombie out on their devices, I get to watch the waves and listen to Ryland laugh. It's not perfect. It's not what I thought it would be. But right now, in this moment, I get to be free. Yeah, it might not last, but then again—just like summer or a sunset or ice cream or innocence—nothing lasts forever, does it?

CHAPTER 28

"Hey!" Henry catches up to us at the beach. Running toward the cluster of blankets, he sends sprays of sand up with each step. Stan finally won the argument on where to set up a little oasis of blankets and umbrellas a few yards from the waves. Henry is wearing colorful swim trunks and a light T-shirt. Stan is already shirtless, and Alyssa is draped in a transparent wrap that barely covers up her bikini. The kids seem just as comfortable in their swimwear, but I'm having a hard time relaxing into the moment.

I'm massively overdressed next to all the scantily clad beachgoers, but that's not where my main anxiety is coming from. Once I got past the excitement of being at the ocean with the Feely family, the reality of our day settled in. The kids think we're taking a day off for some family time at the beach. But Stan has other plans—a new abduction awareness video.

This one is a follow-up to the first Tracey Monroe video we posted soon after her disappearance. Every news outlet has been obsessed with the missing ten-year-old girl from Sparks, Nevada. #KeepTheSparkAlive is still a trending hashtag on social media.

In the first video, the Feely family went through all the basics of stranger safety, breaking down tips for both children and their parents. Then Alyssa boldly posted it with the #KeepTheSparkAlive tag. Jen said it was opportunistic and so did a few online trolls, but overall it was well received and was spread widely around Facebook by concerned parents who wanted to educate their children, as though child abduction were contagious. Other vloggers followed with their own videos, but when it came down to it, AllTheFeels was the first.

Now Stan wants to do a follow-up where an actual stranger approaches the kids, and we film their reactions after the stranger-danger training. He thinks it'll hit an all-time high for the channel in views. I'm sure he's right, but I also don't think it's nice to scare children. Especially his own children. But I don't know how to share these thoughts with Stan so instead I've silently gone along with the planning. Part of me wonders if my conflicted conscience is the reason I've lost my appetite.

After saying his hellos and giving Ryland a quick ride on his shoulders into the water, Henry drops him off with Alyssa for lunch and then gestures for me to join him walking in the waves. I go down to the edge of the beach, where the sand meets the ocean.

"Come on, walk with me. The kids can't hear us out here."

I roll my eyes a little, pointing at my long pant legs.

"Pull them up or something. It's just water," he says, like he finds my hesitation funny.

"Fine." I clumsily roll the khakis up to my knees. It's strange to have my legs—any part of them—exposed. Fine white hairs coat my calves, and I hope that he doesn't look closely enough to see them. Alyssa tried to convince me to shave my legs when she first started her makeover attempts, but I've never liked the idea—until now.

It's a good reason to get into the water faster than I'd planned. The waves come to greet me before I get all the way in. They tickle my toes, pulling sand out from underneath my feet with each lap. The water is cool but not cold, and even that slight chill goes away within a few minutes after my lower legs are submerged. I can smell the salt in the mist and taste it when I open my mouth.

"They're gonna be out here in a few minutes," I warn once I reach Henry. The water almost hits the fabric gathered at my knees and lands a little lower on Henry's elongated legs.

"Eh, Alyssa is supposed to feed them lunch to give us time to get set up. We're good for a while still. You've never been in the ocean, have you?" he asks, watching me shuffle through the water next to him, afraid I'll fall down if I move too fast.

"No," I answer. "Is it that obvious?"

"Uh, kinda." He's being nice. It's not my favorite thing. I think I trust him more when he's short with me. "How have you lived in California your whole life and never been to the ocean?"

It sounds like a sincere question, though with Henry I can never be sure. But, well-meaning or not, the mention of my life before brings back some hazy memories of my birth family, good ones, the ones I usually try to ignore, though more and more often they're finding their way back in.

As a child, I think I did go to the beach. Built a sandcastle. Maybe ate sandwiches with little grains of sand in them that crunched with every bite. But I'm not sure, and if I say yes, he could ask for my story, and I don't have one I can share with him.

"Mother didn't like the sun. She said it was dangerous." *Tell the truth as often as possible.*

"Well, it's not that hard to put on sunscreen or wear a hat," he says, his shoulders scrunching up and down under his oversize, faded T-shirt. He's wearing a baseball hat that smooshes his hair down till a few little strands curl up around the edge of the brim.

"True." It's easier to talk about work. This is too personal. *Never let anyone get too close.*

"What about swimming?" He continues with the personal questions before I find a way to transition the conversation into something more comfortable. "Have you ever been swimming?"

I blush, feeling even warmer in my layers.

"I don't know how to swim. My mother didn't agree with . . . you know." I gesture to the barely dressed women on the beach. I have a hard time looking at them in what looks like underwear and seeing them as innocently sunbathing like everyone else. To me, after how I've been raised, they look naked.

"Bathing suits?" He chuckles, glancing at the women and then back at me like he was looking at a sign I pointed to. "God, growing up most people my age live in a bathing suit in the summer. How did you even meet your boyfriend with so many rules?"

My smile falls away. I don't want to talk about this anymore.

"It's a long story." I squint up at the beach. "You know, maybe we should go over the plans for the shoot before Stan gets grouchy." The family is still clustered under their umbrellas, and Stan is playing with his phone.

"That guy makes me so mad," Henry says, peering down at the water sloshing around our ankles.

"Stan?"

"Oh no, I was still on the other subject, but never mind." He clams up, and I stop walking, frozen. Is he talking about my fake boyfriend? Oh gosh, what was his name? Searching my memory for that seemingly ancient detail, I watch my feet start to slowly sink into the silky sand underneath.

"Stan hired some guy from the theater department at Westmont to be the 'stranger.'" He drops the personal questions. I look up, and the guarded, withdrawn Henry is back. Thank heavens.

"The guy from the headshot you sent last night?'" I ask, far more comfortable with this kind of professional conversation.

"Yeah. Damn, this video is gonna be creepy, right?" Henry asks, and I can't help but laugh.

"Oh my gosh, I'm so glad you think so too," I say, a little too easily. "I tried to talk Alyssa out of it, but you know how she is."

"I know. It's like watching a car crash, and Alyssa is clapping in the passenger seat," Henry says in a low, sarcastic tone.

I let out a loud "Ha!" and cover my mouth when people on the beach flip their heads my way. It's strange to laugh at Stan and Alyssa like this. It's like they're different people than the ones I love on my screen. Or at least that's how I make it okay that more and more often I find myself in this confusing place of recognizing flaws in their off-camera personalities.

I think Henry likes that he made me laugh. His mouth goes up for a moment, and then he starts talking logistics again.

"I was thinking we should do this with Connor first by the changing rooms—he'll be easy to keep quiet—then Ryland on the beach while Alyssa keeps Kelsey distracted." He lays out the camera positioning and the few scripted lines we've given the "stranger" for the first two beach-centric locations.

"And then Kelsey?" I ask, a sick weight in my stomach as the details become more and more real.

"Her shoot will be up in the parking lot. Stan rented the exact vehicle that the girl was abducted in and other creepy shit," he says. "The actor is wearing a body cam; I put it on him when I got here. When Jen gets here with the van from the rental place, I'll put one in there too."

"So he's going to grab her in the parking lot?" Of all the scenarios, this one is the most uncomfortable for me. On the beach Ryland can call for help and Connor can run away, but a car can be a prison on wheels in a matter of seconds. Or at least that's how I see it. Strong hands, a quick shove, doors that won't open no matter how hard she tries. I want to warn Kelsey. I can't imagine how scared she's going to be.

"He's supposed to try," Henry says, lifting his feet one at a time to free them from the sand.

Stan's deep voice calls to us from the beach. The muscles on Henry's forearms tense up, and I feel the same tension inside of my own body. Listening to Stan's cry means it's time to film the video. My stomach rolls, and acid burns at the back of my throat. I'm not sure if it's anxious anticipation or hunger, but I have to swallow hard to make the gross feeling go away.

"We should probably head back," I say, even though I don't want to. The Feely family is collected together, Ryland shoving baby carrots in his mouth, Kelsey talking Alyssa's ear off, gesturing wildly, and Connor reclining in a folding beach chair watching something on his phone. This is what we should be filming—the Feely family doing normal things together.

"Can we make this good?" Henry asks as we emerge from the ocean in near unison.

"Well, we can try," I say with a shrug.

"So, that's a no, then," Henry says under his breath, raising one eyebrow as Stan rushes toward us.

"Hey! You two." His shoulders are browned from plenty of days at the beach. He's been at the gym more often lately after some comments on a pool video made fun of his "dad bod." Now that our views are on a steady climb, he seems hyperfocused on his appearance, and it shows. His muscles have more definition, and some of the girth at his middle has evaporated.

"We already went over the camera placement," Henry says before Stan asks any questions.

"Shh," Stan replies, patting down the air in front of him. "Change in plans. We're gonna do Kelsey first. Jen and the actor guy are set up in the parking lot. The rental car place let us rent by the hour, so we gotta get that in ASAP. How soon can you be ready?"

Henry looks at me like he's checking in with me as he responds, "With three of us working? How about fifteen minutes?"

I nod in agreement. If I can't stop Stan's plan, the least I can do is make it beneficial to the Feely brand, which seems more likely knowing that Henry and I are on the same page.

Stan glances at his phone to check the time. "I'll send Kelsey up to the car to get something and then . . . well . . . you know."

Yeah. We both know.

"Good luck!" he says, walking backward while giving us a subtle double thumbs-up. Henry waits until Stan pivots on the sand and runs back to the family gathering before talking again.

"Well, I guess it's showtime," he says, squinting up at the nearly full parking lot.

"Yeah," I echo. "Showtime."

"I've been waiting here forever, you assholes!" Jen shouts at us when we get to the top of the stairs. I can never tell when she's mad or just giving us a hard time.

"Sorry! Stan just sent us up right now." Henry is huffing a little from the rushed walk. I should pretend to be winded too, even if I'm not. I might vomit, but other than that the walk was easy compared to my trek every morning. I drop back and alter my breathing.

"It's fine. I fixed the hidden-camera work you did on the guy, Justin, or whatever his name is, and in the car. You two can set up the other cameras there and there." She points to the Feelys' SUV and then to the beginning of the long wooden dock that juts out into the ocean.

"I'll take the SUV so you don't have to climb over seats," Henry says, and Jen hands him a camera from her bag, attached to a stabilizing device with three bendable legs and then offers me the other one, listing off instructions.

"As of right now, there's a clean shot from that first pillar. Hardest part will be keeping Kelsey from seeing you. You'll figure it out." She checks the smartwatch on her wrist. "You've got five minutes. I'll text you when it's time. Justin will park behind the SUV. Just keep your camera focused there."

"Got it," Henry says, and I stay quiet, my default whenever Jen seems annoyed.

We spread out in three separate directions, and I get my camera clipped into place immediately. Taking in the shot through my display, I frame up the back of the SUV, trying to picture the various scenarios that could play out.

Out of nowhere, the scent of burning oil and gas hits me. I gag. I know that smell. Mother.

I look back over my shoulder. I search the rear of the parking lot, scan the rows of cars, take in all the vehicles big and small. No van. But that doesn't calm my sour stomach or quench the scorching in my throat.

The rumble of a large engine comes from—where? In front of me? I turn in a frantic circle until I see it.

It's there. The van. *Her* van idling in the beach parking lot by the entrance. I step back and cover my face, like that will do something to protect me. I should run. I should find someplace to hide. I should jump off the dock or do just about anything to get away. But I don't. I can't move, and I'm shaking, hard.

My phone buzzes. The text notification flashes across the screen, and another one quickly follows. I glance down as though whoever is reaching out knows about Mother.

Jen: Action, assholes. She's headed your way.

Henry: I see her. Angela, you see K?

Kelsey is at the top of the stairs, heading toward the SUV. Out of the corner of my eye, there's a flash of white. The van rolls forward, almost in perfect synchronicity with Kelsey's bouncy, distracted steps. She's typing something into her phone, and pauses for a moment on the sidewalk in front of the Feelys' SUV. My phone buzzes. I can't look away.

Mother's van lines up with Kelsey and stops. She doesn't even seem to notice. If Mother's found me, she knows about the Feelys. If she knows about the Feelys, she must recognize Kelsey. If she knows I care about Kelsey, then—just like my dolls, just like Sampson—Kelsey's not safe.

Kelsey! I scream her name in my head, the red of Sampson's blood on my fingers pounding through my mind in Technicolor. She doesn't look up. She doesn't stop. She's totally lost in her own world and can't even see the danger looming in her near future.

The sickening whoosh and thump of the side door sliding open reaches me up by the dock, and a black hole opens on the side of the van. I can't see inside, but I know she's there. Kelsey isn't prepared for this kind of stranger danger. Mother can look normal, maternal. She's a chameleon, adept at getting what she wants when she wants it. And I can only guess that if she's come all this way, what she wants is me.

But Kelsey isn't a worn-out doll or an insignificant bird—she's a sheltered, naive little girl. I can't let this happen. Immediately, I can move again.

"Kelsey, no!" I scream out loud this time. I don't understand this feeling rising inside me, consuming me and my fears like the forest fire scorching through dried-out brush in the hills by my house when I was a little girl, but I am driven by it. The sand makes the cement slippery, but I'm wild, frenzied, and keeping myself safe, keeping my secret safe, means nothing. My feet are still bare after walking in the ocean, but I'm not running away—I'm running toward the vehicle. I'm running toward Mother. But she's too far away, and I'm too late—right in front of my eyes Kelsey is swallowed up by the mouth of the van.

CHAPTER 29

"Angela!" Henry shouts into my face, hands on my shoulders, holding me back with all his strength. I don't let him stop me. I have to get down there, save Kelsey. My toes rub raw against the cement as I run against his straight arms. He continues to try to convince me. "Stop! You've gotta stop!"

"But Kelsey . . ." I can't complete my warning. How do I explain? Instead, I point, my finger shaking like an old woman's. Henry follows the direction I'm pointing and then looks back at me.

"Are you okay?" He furrows his eyebrows and tips his head to one side like he's concerned about me. But Kelsey is the one who needs help. Why can't he see that? I can't get away unless he lets me. I have to tell him. I stop fighting and look him right in the eyes.

"Henry, listen to me. There's a bad woman in that van. She can't be trusted. Look, she's taking Kelsey! We have to stop her." I'm out of breath and vibrating with fear. I point at the van that just gulped down Kelsey like she's a tasty snack. The doors are still open, but I don't see anyone inside or out.

"Angela," he says, hands tightening on my shoulders. "That's the actor. It's pretend. Alyssa's about to jump in and tell her it's fake. Remember?"

"No, no, you're wrong. It's her. It's Mother," I repeat, frantically working to see past him and get a glimpse of her silvery-white hair, proof that I'm telling the truth.

"Angela! Stop. It's a man," he says, still trying to keep his voice down but with a vocal shove that gets my attention. He steps aside so I can have a clearer view. The van is still there, and the door slams closed with a thump I can pick up all the way over here. Then a man walks around the front of the vehicle and climbs into the driver's seat. "Not your mother. It's a prank. Remember?"

A prank? A man? The van rolls past us in what feels like slow motion. The man behind the wheel latches eyes with me. It's the same face from the emailed headshot. Reality rushes in—the van is a newer model than Mother's, no rust or dents in the sliding door, no crack along the bottom of the windshield. It's not her. My knees buckle, and I think I'm going to throw up.

"Whoa." Henry grabs me under my arms before I collapse. "You're overheated. Sit. Sit down," he orders, and I listen, lowering myself to the sandy curb with his guidance.

"I'm fine," I say, leaning forward, head in my hands, hoping it will stop the world from spinning, but even with my eyes closed, I feel like I'm on a swing that I've twisted up on its chains and that's now spiraling in the opposite direction.

"What the *hell* was that?"

I can't open my eyes or I might lose the very loose grip I have on my bodily functions, but I know the voice. Jen is furious. I don't have an explanation, and I hope Henry will cover for me, though I'm not sure I can count on him.

"She's not feeling well—sunstroke, I think," he says, and I can feel that his body is between Jen's negative energy and me.

"Her shots have to be ruined. I mean, Stan is gonna f-ing kill us."

Henry's calm voice takes over, and I like the way he sounds. I almost believe him when he talks like this.

"We have plenty of other footage. It's fine."

"Hey, what's going on? Is she okay?" It's Alyssa. I hold my head even tighter as her voice gets closer, conversation about me taking place just a few feet away.

"I'm fine," I mumble, trying to get them to stop. I'm not sure if they hear me. I'm not sure of very much. The van wasn't Mother. None of the vans were Mother? Am I losing my mind?

"She needs to cool off and eat something," Alyssa says, with a calm, sure diagnosis. My stomach lurches again. There are too many feelings in my body right now: alarm, terror, some relief, and on top of it all is this undeniable nausea.

"I'm fine," I start to say again, but I can't finish before I lean to one side and finally lose control all over the curb. Even after my stomach empties, I continue to heave painfully. In the middle of it all, someone is rubbing my shoulders and holding my hair back.

"Oh, honey," Alyssa croons, and I like it, the pain in my midsection and the sting of bile in my throat making me immune to any suspicions of her kindness. When I finish, I sit stooped over, mouth wet, huffing.

"Here." It's Henry's voice. A paper napkin is pressed into my trembling hand. I wipe at my mouth with my eyes still closed.

"Jen, pass me your water bottle," Alyssa calls over my head.

"Uh, no way. She's probably contagious. She was already touching my camera."

"Are you serious right now?" Henry asks, and there's a jingling and a slosh of water behind me. "I'll wash it. Here."

"Thanks," Alyssa says. Some water splashes onto my elbow and then she pats me again, holding the bottle in front of my face. "Here, hon, take a sip."

I take the aluminum bottle and bring it to my lips, but even the taste of the slightly metallic water makes that sick feeling come back. Alyssa places a damp napkin on the back of my neck and then addresses Henry and Jen.

"Someone needs to take her home."

"We only have Justin till two, and half of Kelsey's shoot is total shit thanks to . . ." Jen has the presence of mind not to say my name, but we all know who she's talking about.

"Justin can wait. Honestly, the shoot can wait," Henry responds with a finality that reminds me of Stan. Alyssa stiffens beside me.

"No, no, we can't cancel the shoot. And we need you and Jen if Angela is sick. And this is Stan's project. And I need to keep Ryland out of the way . . ."

"I'm feeling better," I say, finally able to open my eyes. The evidence of my sickness is inches from my bare foot, and I slide away from its slow crawl in my direction. All this attention is painful. I can't think. I need space to think. "I can call my cousin to come and get me. I'll wait in the car."

I go to stand up but wobble on the way, and Alyssa guides me back to the curb. Henry's voice is closer now.

"It'll take me fifteen minutes round trip," Henry says. I wish they'd ask me what I want, but the nausea is back, and the few sips of water are building in my throat. If I talk, I'll throw up again.

There's a tense moment of silence that Jen breaks.

"Okay, okay, listen, we have to get the van back to the rental place. If you can take Angela to wherever, return the van, and then get the car back here in the next twenty minutes, we should be able to stay on schedule," she huffs. "Does that work for everyone?"

It's not really a question, more of a sarcastic demand.

"Sound good to you, honey?" Alyssa asks me as though I have a say.

"Yeah." I don't really care how I get out of here anymore. I just need to go.

"You have twenty minutes. Justin is waiting for me in the van down there." Jen pauses, probably pointing. "Send him over, and then you can go. But drop her off first, k? I don't want her in my car," Jen says, and there's a clink of keys. "And clean my damn water bottle."

"Jeez, Jen. You're a gem," Henry snipes. He's annoyed. Angry. I worry that part of the reason he's mad is because of my hysterics, and he's taking it out on Jen. Alyssa walks away and starts a hushed conversation with Jen about the rest of the shoot.

I can finally keep my eyes open, but staring off into the distance is the only thing that keeps me from getting sick again. Right now, I'm watching the stoplight out on the main road cycle from green to yellow to red and back again. The cars obey as if the lights control their engines, and I almost forget there are people inside of those machines making the ultimate decision to follow the color-coded messages or break the rules.

Waiting for Henry to get back with the van, I have a gallon-sized Ziploc from Alyssa in case I get sick again. She handed me another bag filled with snacks and juice boxes that I wanted to turn away at first, but she slipped it into my backpack when she brought it up from the beach and then left again to take Kelsey, who didn't seem that fazed by the prank, back down to play in the water.

But now Alyssa is back and Stan is with her this time, shirt on, shoes on, and keys in hand.

"Hey, Lyssa said you're under the weather," he says in that way I find comforting but that makes me feel like a child.

"Yeah," I say quietly, the words catching in my sore throat.

"We forgot the sand toys for Ryland so I'm running to the store to grab some. I can give you a ride." He hitches his thumb in the direction of the SUV.

"Henry said he'd take me," I say, not sure who I'd rather be alone with, Henry with his countless questions or Stan with his sometimes overwhelming personality. Alyssa steps in, sunglasses resting on the top of her head like a hair accessory. I hope I didn't get her sick—she's already so skinny.

"Don't worry about him, hon. Stan already called him." I have questions but not enough energy or interest to ask them. Instead, I let Alyssa help me get into the SUV and focus all my attention on not vomiting in front of my bosses. I tell him my fake address, and once it's typed into the car's built-in GPS, we pull away.

I clutch the clear baggie closer to my chin. I should've made some excuse earlier and then waited until they went down to the beach. Then I could've walked back to the park on my own. Anything would be better than sitting in this car feeling so weak and broken. I wish I could disappear, or maybe start over. Yes. I wish I had a time machine to take me back to . . . when? My first night here? When I ran away from Mother? The interview? When I was a little girl and my birth mother yelled at me and I ran away and—

Stan interrupts my thoughts, trying to make small talk.

"Is your cousin home?" he asks, hitting the gas like he's in a hurry.

"No, but I have a key." It's hard to think up new lies when I'm so sick and especially when I have so many other details to figure out that have nothing to do with lying to Stan. I'll have to find someplace to spend the rest of the day. A bench at the park? One of the quiet tables at the library? In the shade of the woods behind the dorms? I shift in my seat, the springs creaking like they used to in Mother's van.

"I heard Justin rocked the creepy stranger thing," Stan says. I don't remember anything about the actor or his role, but Stan doesn't need to know that.

"Kelsey was scared," I say, leaning my head against the window, the chilled glass helping me focus on something other than feeling ill.

"Awesome," he says, like it's a positive. "That van was, like, *the* perfect touch."

"The van?" Even in a filler conversation with Stan, I can't escape that thing. He takes a wide right turn that makes me hold the bag up closer to my mouth. I watch the greens and tans of passing trees and houses blur together. Maybe I'll just lie by the pool at the apartments for a few minutes. Just until I feel strong enough to walk.

"Yeah, you know, 'cause they had that press conference, like, this morning, and I called the car place right away," he says, like he's solved world hunger. Man, it's like Jen is in my head. I close my eyes for a second and then open them again.

Yes. I barely noticed it, that comment Henry made earlier today, smashed in the middle of all the other disturbing details of the faked kidnappings we were being paid to produce. It didn't mean anything to me then. And I was too hysterical and sick after seeing Kelsey disappear to put it all together, but yes, I'm starting to remember.

"That van was the one in the news?" I ask, sitting up, forgetting for a moment how puny and empty my body is after throwing up.

"Wait, you did see the press conference?" Stan asks, like I've missed some grand cosmic secret. It must be obvious I'm clueless. "I can't believe you haven't heard this yet," he says, making a U-turn in the middle of the road and then lining up next to the curb in front of the Aspen apartment complex. Stan dramatically wrestles the gearshift into park and turns to face me. He's such a large man, he fills all the space between the steering wheel and the headrest. He starts talking rapidly.

"So, you know how Tracey Monroe's little sister saw the whole thing? Apparently she kept waking up with bad dreams, telling her mom that a witch took her sister. They thought it was nothing, but after they subpoenaed the CCTV images from the surrounding businesses following the abduction, a street cam picked up an image showing a white van with an old lady behind the wheel who looked like . . ."

He pauses like he expects me to finish the sentence, but the only word that's screaming through my mind is *Mother*. I cover my mouth, and he fills in the rest of the sentence himself.

"A witch—she looked like a witch. And when they looked closer, it looked like Tracey's backpack was in the front seat. See why we have to get that video done today?"

No. I don't see why. I don't care why either. I have to get out of this car, away from Stan, who is far too excited about a missing girl.

Like a zombie, I unbuckle my seat belt and toss it over my shoulder, flinging the door open, lost in my racing thoughts. The van. The witch. A little girl.

My breathing accelerates, and I can't seem to take in enough oxygen. My head spins, and I know I'm about to vomit again. I turn so my feet dangle out of the vehicle. Stan is now in front of me like he teleported there. He's tall enough that even though I'm still seated in the van, his hands reach my shoulders and then slide down to my arms, but I don't let him help me out of the car just yet.

"Wait," I manage to say, gripping Stan's elbow now. "Are they sure? About the van?"

Stan shrugs and seems happy to stand there for as long as I need. He takes a step closer; his voice is less frantic than when he was in the car—low, calm.

"As sure as they can be, I guess." He shrugs again, and takes another mini-step in my direction, his hands again on my upper arms like he's urging me out. He must be in a rush, but it's hard to think about Stan right now. I have too many questions still.

"It was a woman?" I choke on the words, watching his eyes so I can read if he's telling me the truth or if he's joking around like he's known to do. But I don't doubt him; I wish I did, but I don't. I can see it clearly. The van, the silver hair in greasy curls, the yellowed dentures, a smile, friendly at first glance and terrifying as it gets closer.

He squeezes my shoulders rhythmically. He's too close, but my proximity alarms aren't working because my Mother alarms are drowning them out. He has a soft smile on his face, a subtle dimple forming in his cheek.

"The police think it's a disguise or an accomplice." He chuckles. "Or maybe they've got it all wrong, and they've got an APB out for somebody's grandma."

"Oh." I sigh, closing my eyes and leaning out of the car a little farther, sick for more than one reason. They do have it wrong. It's not a man. It's not a grandma. It's not a pedophile or a serial killer. It's Mother. And she's replaced me.

I have to tell someone. Stan will know what to do. Alyssa for sure. They can call the police, and they can get the girl and take her back home to her family and . . . my short-lived heroic fantasy ends there. If I tell them *everything*—it's over. This, all of this, is over. Who can I trust?

"Did I scare you?" Stan asks, closing any space between us. His body heat reaches out and touches my skin, and his breath dampens my cheek at a weird angle.

"I need your help," I say, wiggling my way out of the van with Stan's help. Names flash through my mind, a short list of people who might actually believe me. Stan is as good an option as any, better maybe because of his comprehensive understanding of the Tracey Monroe case.

I rest my palm on his chest and tap to get past him, but he doesn't step aside. Instead, he wraps his arms around me. It takes a second, but as soon as his heavy forearms tighten and his chest meets my face, his body wedges between my knees.

"I'm here for you," he says, his hands running up my back and into my hair. I'm yanked out of my looping mind, arms shooting up as a flimsy boundary between my body and Stan. Hands fisted, I push back against his chest, shaking my head, but I'm fighting against a brick wall. He kisses my hairline and then my cheek.

"Stop," I say, my voice muffled against his shirt. Why won't he listen? I'm still bolted against his chest as Stan flips back my hair and kisses down my neck. His mouth is hot, and he leaves a moist trail on my skin. I shove at him again.

"Please stop." I try asking this time. "I *need* you to help me." But it's like I'm not speaking, or like he's lost the ability to hear me. He drags me closer till there's no space between our bodies, suffocating me with his shirt against my mouth.

"I've got you, baby," he says, panting in my ear. I lean away, and his hands travel down my waist and around my hips and up my shirt. I wrestle against his touch, leaning back, shoving hard. He doesn't stop.

"Let me go," I shout, when his hand makes it up the front of my shirt. I wriggle hard against his grasp, and he steps back so suddenly I nearly fall.

"What the hell?" He's staring at me, not at my hot face covered in tears, but at my belly. I follow his gaze. My shirt is pushed up to my armpits, fake pregnancy suit entirely exposed. I yank down my shirt and hold it there, shaking. A slow, knowing smile grows on his face, and he nods like he's just gotten the punch line to a joke that went over his head.

"You're a little liar, aren't you?"

I cover my body and wriggle under his arm. It's over, this life with the Feelys, this effort at escaping Mother—it's over.

"It's not like that," I say, frightened of too many things to keep track. With my back to the fiery-hot black metal door, I slide around the exterior of the car until I'm out of Stan's reach. It's difficult to flip that switch from trust to distrust when it comes to the one man I've let myself feel at ease with.

"It sure is," he says, hands deep in his pockets, his shoulder muscles bulging up under his tank top. He's smiling like he's amused, and I don't know what he finds funny. He should be disgusted. Horrified. Angry. But all he can seem to do is smirk. "You've been playing a game here, haven't you?"

"No," I say, reflexively. Stan's kisses are drying on my neck at the same rate the image of Tracey Monroe riding in the back of Mother's van is developing in my mind. I can't go back to the Feelys. Stan knows my lie—soon they all will. I have nothing left to lose. "I need to tell you something. There's this woman, she's my mother, she . . . she . . ."

He shakes his head at me like I've seen him do on camera hundreds of times with his kids. I shrink myself down, crunching into myself as he slinks toward me again. He's still not listening, like this is some kind of twisted game.

"You did all this just to spend time with 'the Feely family'?" he asks, using air quotes.

I press myself farther and farther into the flaming-hot side panel until I can't make myself any smaller.

"Damn. I'm flattered."

"No, it's not like that. My mother, she . . ."

"Nah, I'm pretty sure it is like that. Don't worry," he says, reaching out for me again, dusting my hair off my shoulder, his thumb lingering on my collarbone. "I'm good at secrets. I can keep yours."

He's right up against me, touching me again, and I can't seem to do anything other than not watch. Not even fully present, I stand rigid, frozen, imprisoned by my own inaction.

He says he'll keep my secret, but I know it's for a price. Mother used to warn me about it all the time; she said it's all men really want. She said giving it away makes you a whore. But—if I let him take it, I don't have to leave. I can tell him about Tracey Monroe, and he can protect me from Mother. If I let him have me, I'll be safe.

My stomach lurches. I grab my midsection, but Stan's body is there, and I gag.

No. No. No. I lied and stole for Mother. I stayed all those years while she was hurting me. I gave and gave and gave because I believed her when she said she was keeping me safe. But I was never safe with her, and I'd never be safe with Stan. I'm not a currency used to buy safety. I'm a person.

My phone buzzes in my pocket. I shove Stan back with two hands and grab for my device.

"Ow!" he shouts, like I've hurt him, but I don't stop. I duck away and blindly answer the call on the third ring, rushing toward the front gate of the apartment complex.

"Hey, so, Alyssa said Stan was dropping you at home, but you left your bag at the beach. I'm taking the van back to the rental place, and, I don't know, I guess I wanted to make sure you're okay."

It's Henry. I'm almost at the twisting metal partition. Just hearing his voice makes me feel stronger. I gag back the bile in my throat and project myself through the entry into the pool area.

"Angela?" Henry asks, his anxiety pouring out of the speaker on the phone, but I can't answer. There's a slamming of car doors in the distance and the squeal of tires. I don't look.

I drop to my knees, phone clasped in my hand, the cement cutting at my skin through my pant legs. On all fours, it's like someone pushed an evacuation button on my insides. With so little in my stomach, the retching turns to dry heaving almost immediately, which hurts like my belly is collapsing on itself.

"Angela? Angela?" Henry's voice is far away and tiny. Even if I could talk, I don't know what I'd say, but I don't hang up. Just like when I was alone, locked in the park bathroom, and he stayed with me until Ranger Bob came to open the door, I like having him here—but also not here.

"Excuse me! What are you doing? Children play here." A middle-aged woman in a bikini that barely covers her parts is standing over me, sunglasses low on the bridge of her deeply tanned nose. She doesn't want to get too close, I can tell, and that's good. I don't want anyone close. I can still feel Stan's breath on my neck and the light trail of his fingertips on my bare skin.

"I'm sorry," I say, wiping my mouth with the back of my hand.

"You should be sorry. I'm not cleaning this up," she says, glaring at me like I'm single-handedly poisoning her children's drinking water. I haven't asked anyone to clean up after me.

"I'll clean it," I say, wiping away the watery residue in my eyes from the force of my dry heaves. I rock back and rest on my heels. The woman gasps, covering her mouth with long fuchsia nails.

"Oh my god, I'm so sorry. I thought you were a drunk," she says, with a nervous giggle tinged with embarrassment. That's right. I place my empty hand on my belly, remembering the power of this disguise.

"Can't seem to get rid of this morning sickness," I say with a weak smile. I wobble when I try to stand. The stranger reaches out for me, and I recoil, steadying myself against the stucco wall that surrounds the property.

"Hey, stop. You should sit down. Hold on," the bikini lady says, worry wrinkling her face more than the sun has over the years. She shuffles away, calling for someone named Carol, but I don't stop. She doesn't really want to help. I'm so tired of seeing that worried look everywhere I go.

The poor pregnant girl, what will happen to her and her baby? They're all so very worried, but no one wants to actually *help* me. It seems like no one has ever tried to help me in my life, not really. They do just enough to keep their guilt at bay, or to give themselves an ego boost, or worse yet—because they want something from me.

From this angle I have a clear view of the street—Stan's car is gone. I sag into the ragged plaster barrier, grateful he can't touch me again but wildly frantic that he knows my darkest secret. He might be on the phone with Alyssa right now telling her how crazy I am, convincing her to call the police on *me* instead of Mother. If only he had listened. If only I'd told him on my own before . . . but no one will believe me now. Alyssa will be disgusted, and Henry will finally have proof that he was right to distrust me.

Henry. I glance at my phone. I'd almost forgotten I was holding it. His name is lit up in white letters at the top of the screen. All I have to do is put it up to my ear and, boom, connection. What if Stan's already called him?

No. I tap the red decline button. My life with the Feely family is over, and that includes Henry.

I make it through the gate without using the bars to keep steady. The woman from the pool is calling after me now, but I'm regaining my strength and moving faster than I usually allow myself when I'm wearing the pregnancy suit. My phone buzzes again. This time a text pops up.

Henry: Worried. Stay put. Coming to get you.

I can't bear to see his name anymore. Clearly he doesn't know the truth. When he does, it will all change.

I drop the phone in my pocket, stumbling enough that I have to catch myself on the cement sidewalk. I don't stop. It's an advantage that I've just finished throwing up because the nausea is gone for a few minutes, and I can move swiftly and feel like I'm flying as gravity lends me a helping hand down the hill from the Aspen Apartments.

When I hit the stop sign where I need to turn, I wrap my arms around the thin metal pole, feeble from sickness and probably dehydration. I rest my burning face against the cool steel. The world is wobbly, and I don't know how I'll make it even a few more steps, much less all the way to the park. I slide down the post and crumple to the sidewalk. Allowing my body even that ounce of relaxation has a dangerous effect on me. I've felt it before, when I hit my head with Mother and when she left me in the closet for too long.

Maybe this is why I'm scared of water, because when the darkness drags me down it reminds me of something from before Mother and my head injury. It was Franny Dimil's eighth birthday party. I'm there again in my one-piece princess bathing suit from the summer before, a size too small and faded from chlorine and the sun.

My dad was inside grabbing beers with Franny's dad, and I bragged to Franny and Shannon, the most popular girls in our group, that I could swim across the pool all by myself. They cheered me on.

I jumped in without even a second thought, sure I could make it after a whole summer of swim lessons. I laughed and maybe called the other girls playful names like "scaredy-cat" and "wuss." Underwater, I shoved off the wall and swam easily for the first few strokes, but as I got a little past halfway to the other side, just far enough that I couldn't go back, I made a mistake. Breathing in at the wrong moment, I choked, and my mouth flooded with chlorinated water.

Gagging and sputtering, I chased another breath while trying to keep myself afloat. But I couldn't get air into my lungs. I flailed in the water, fighting like crazy to keep my head above the surface, but the more I kicked and squirmed, the more I craved oxygen that didn't come.

I wanted someone to just freaking help me, but no one did, and I didn't have the breath or the energy to scream. Submerging over and over again, longer each time, I felt my lungs fill more and more, like water balloons, and coughing did nothing to empty them.

I'm drowning, I thought, a little casually. The realization was clear to me, even as a small child. In circles of gray and black, the world went dark around me. I gave up and let the water and darkness take me, an unusual, warm, comforting peace replacing the panic until my dad jumped in the pool after hearing my friends scream once they realized I was in trouble. Even in the dark, faraway place, I felt it all. His arms were exactly what I'd been hoping for—strong, knowing, kind. I knew I was safe even before I took a breath and opened my eyes.

A shadow covers my body, yanking me out of my memory. My skin gathers into goose bumps, and I shiver at the sudden temperature change. How long have I been sitting like this? It takes a moment to recover from my daydream/memory, but when I finally open my eyes and they fully adjust, I find a wall of white blocks my view of the crosswalk. Tangy, dirty exhaust touches my dry tongue when I breathe. A white van idles in front of me.

Instead of the usual terror a white utility vehicle sends racing through my nervous system, an unexpected rush of calm sweeps through me, like when my dad carried me out of the water and filled my lungs with air.

I was wrong. Mother was wrong. Someone did come for me.

Henry.

There's still fear there—hesitation. Either he knows about my secret, or he doesn't and I'll have to tell him. But I can't run away anymore; I'm collapsing in on myself, and a broken me does nothing to help Tracey Monroe. The idea is still completely psychotic, that Mother kidnapped a child to replace me. But Mother steals; it's a well-documented fact. And Mother will replace anything that no longer serves her will, like how she took me as her foster child to replace her own daughter.

Walking my hands up the metal pole of the stop sign, I bring myself to standing and lunge for the door handle. A blast of embarrassment burns the top of my ears, and I know I won't be able to look him in the eyes, so I keep my head down as I use the running board to heft myself into the front seat. The action is uncomfortably familiar, especially wearing the latex belly.

I center myself in the bucket seat. The van is creepily realistic. The seat upholstery is worn, slightly tacky to the touch. When I shift my weight to grab the seat belt, the springs squeak, and the smell . . . the smell . . .

The automatic locks click on, and I whip my head around, no longer shy—but terrified.

"What a pretty little mess you've gotten yourself into this time, haven't you—Tara?"

Mother.

CHAPTER 30

I yank at the door handle, but it's useless. Pounding on the glass, I push the automatic button for the windows, but nothing happens.

"Let me out!" I shake the door with all my strength. She says nothing, silent, levelheaded, unfazed. Her confidence makes me wild to be free. Her tentacles of mental control are already working their way across the front seat, invisible but deadly and stronger than any real lock or restraint.

I have to get out before she gets them into me again.

I slam the window with both hands; she hits the brakes and I fly forward, smacking the side of my head on the dashboard and crumpling onto the floor. She continues to stare out the front windshield as I squint away bright flashes of light that blur my vision. We start moving again.

"I'm *not* going with you," I say, curling into myself, trying not to notice the stab of the random items inside the suit. I stay on the grit-covered carpet but turn my back to rest against the door slowly, ready for any attack she might have in store.

Nothing has changed in here—the broken radio, the grimy steering wheel, Mother's yellowed dentures and greasy white curls—it's all the same. I'm sick again and my head hurts. My head always hurts when Mother is around. Sometimes when I was in the bathroom stall unable to sleep, or when I was safe inside the Feelys' living room, I would try to convince myself that I remembered Mother worse than she actually was. But no, my memory was more forgiving than critical. Mother, the horror of my nightmares, was real—IS real.

She keeps driving, shaking her head slowly.

"Well, we sure are throwing a little fit, aren't we?"

I swear she chuckles, a little like I used to see Alyssa giggle at Ryland's outlandish demands. When she laughs at my courage like that, my power starts to drain out of me like a plug has been pulled.

"No," I say again, crossing my arms so she can see how serious I am, but this time I sound like a pouty little girl. "You can't keep me." I adjust my position so my palms are flat on the floorboard to give me leverage. I might be faint from throwing up and dehydration, but I'm not giving in. "It's different this time. I'm not a foster child anymore. You can't make me stay."

She tsks and turns on her blinker, trying to appear casual, but I can tell every muscle in her body is tight, like thick ropes wound taut.

"I see you've developed a nasty attitude around all these worldly people." She clenches those loose dentures, and I start to notice the little alarm bells that used to signal Mother's anger. Even through one of her baggy dresses, I can see her left knee bouncing in a furious rhythm, and she won't look at me.

"Get your know-it-all little ass off of that dirty floor, and sit on the seat like the grown-up you claim to be."

"No," I say again. She can't toss me around with the car's momentum if I'm already on the ground. She doesn't hit the brakes this time; instead, she revs the gas, and I have to readjust to keep from falling over.

"I don't know why I ever wanted such a selfish child, anyway," she says, voice dripping with disgust. "Look at what a fool you've made of yourself. You're lucky I'd even take you back. I mean, those people don't know the real you, Tara. They don't know that you lie and steal and you're ungrateful and selfish."

"They love me," I say, knowing it's not true, knowing that Stan is likely telling them about my lies. Maybe Henry will tell them about the time he thought I was shoplifting, and the girl who called me Tara at the library, and . . . they'll find out I don't live at the Aspen Apartments and that I don't have a cousin and that the Angela they thought they knew was just a carefully crafted mirage. My throat swells and tears burn at my eyes. She's right. They don't know me at all.

Mother makes a sharp turn that jostles me side to side and makes items in the back of the car slide around, and then she accelerates even further, the van engine rumbling in protest. We're on the highway. She's taking me home.

"You opened your legs for them, didn't you? I thought things would be different with you, Tara, but no. You're a little whore." She spits the accusations at me.

"No," I growl and clench my knees together, but I can't stop myself from remembering Stan's thick body pressing into me, his heat covering me, suffocating me. And that one single moment I considered letting him have me. I lean my head against the door to the glove box, the nausea filling me again.

"I'm saving *you*, you ungrateful child," she says, and for a fraction of a second I can see her logic, like catching a radio signal from some far-off station while flipping through the dial. I try to stay focused through the discomfort and the speed and the pain in my stomach.

My phone buzzes in my pants, and Mother's stone face cracks. I wrestle it out of the deep fabric pockets. I can call the police. I can tell them about Mother. I can . . .

"You wouldn't dare," she screeches, tugging the wheel hard to one side, reaching for the device. The tires squeal and I'm tossed backward. The phone flies from my grip and thuds onto the floor between Mother and me.

She's still driving at full speed, the van weaving as she works to get the phone with her fingertips. It takes me a moment to get my thoughts back together, panting to keep from losing myself to the gagging feeling in the back of my throat, but not sitting still. I toss my whole body forward, reaching for the one item that could possibly save me and Tracey Monroe at the same time. But I'm too late. Mother has it now.

"What has gotten into you?" she says, her smoker's lungs taking in air in short, raspy bursts. I'm also gasping like a fish on the deck at Fisherman's Wharf, drowning on dry land.

"You took that girl," I say, a little unsure but working to fight against the dragging, clinging suction of her control. As soon as Mother finds meaning in my words, I know I'm right.

"Is that what this is about?" Mother asks, leaning forward, the springs screeching against her increasing discomfort. "I saved that little girl."

"You *took* her," I correct Mother. "She's not like me. She has a family."

"She was playing in the street. What kind of parents let their little girl play outside all alone? She's not old enough. She could get hurt." She says it like she's already told herself these excuses a thousand times, chanted them to herself over and over again.

"She has parents," I say, getting up on my knees, stunned. "I've seen them on the news. They love her. She's not one of your foster kids."

She ignores me, turning to stone and unrolling her window a few inches. I slowly lean across the gap between the two seats like a pregnant cat that's about to pounce, eyes on the phone.

"Have you forgotten what I told you about prison? I'm not going back there."

What? Mother talked about the horrors of prison before but never let on that she'd been in one herself. How did they allow her to be around children? Why did they let her be my foster parent?

Unceremoniously Mother tosses the phone out the window.

"No!" I lunge forward, trying to stop her, but it's too late. She slaps my face, hard, like she used to do when she was angry. It hurts more now than before, or maybe I'm not used to it anymore. I cower like I'm a ten-year-old child.

"You'd best sit down and remember your place, or you'll be responsible for what happens to that little girl."

"Where is she?"

"Safe. She has a lot to learn, but she's a good girl. I want to bring her home with us, but if you keep playing these games, Tara . . . I don't know what's going to happen."

"You wouldn't hurt her," I say, hoping I'm right, but the residual sting of her hand on my cheek is proving me wrong. She sighs and rolls her eyes, and I feel like an idiot, though I don't know what I've said that's so stupid.

"I'm not hurting her, Tara. You are."

I recoil like I've been hit again. She's not wrong. None of this would've happened if I hadn't run away. She'll do whatever it takes to make me submit, even if it means hurting a child. How can I fight that?

Locked inside, no phone, going a million miles an hour down the highway, I have few options. I could drive us off the road or slam the van into one of those giant pillars under the overpass, but . . . then Tracey would never be found.

My will to fight leaves me like gas escaping from a balloon. It's not just about me anymore. Every decision I make now is linked with Tracey's life. If I die, she dies. If I run, she's trapped.

If I pretend to submit . . . I may be able to save us both.

"Fine," I mumble, stumbling backward into my seat in an act of compliance that makes me wish I could die the instant my body hits the threadbare fabric. The click of my seat belt sounds like the clank of a prison door slamming shut.

Mother continues to pretend I'm not there, like she always does when she's deciding how to punish me. I'm sure this will be the most extravagant consequence yet, but I won't let it happen. Not this time.

CHAPTER 31

"We should dump that disgusting thing you're wearing and anything else that would link us back to this place," Mother says, once I'm fully buckled in place.

She's clearly desperate to get rid of this chapter in our lives. I, on the other hand, want to cling to it fiercely. I stare out the window at the ocean as we speed past and remember how the wind felt against my skin just a few hours ago and the way the salt clung to my ankles when they dried.

I might never swim in the ocean, I tell myself. But maybe Tracey will.

"Tara, stop daydreaming and get rid of that getup—I mean it." She has on her wraparound sunglasses, and her hair is frizzing up in the dry air. I see why Tracey's sister thought she looked like a witch. I shift my weight in the fabric seat, and that one spring scratches at my leg.

It's not difficult to remove the maternity wear and the prosthetic belly. When I open the side zipper, very little of substance remains inside. I yank out the dress I'd been using as padding, and Angela's matted brown hair peeks out from the bundle.

"Hey there," I say. Mother sighs. She hates it when I talk to my dolls.

I stare into Angela's smooth white face and painted-on smile. I wriggle my finger up under her collar, and without revealing the bracelet inside, I check to make sure it's still there. The metal is slightly warm when I graze it, and right beside the crumpled chain is the marble from Ryland. I swallow. Ryland will miss me.

"Mother?" It's the first time I've called her that since I climbed in the van. The word burns my tongue, but if she's going to believe my submission, I have to play the part fully.

"Yes, child." She looks proud of herself that I'm already returning to my old ways so quickly. I hate giving her the satisfaction, but I know she won't answer me if she's angry.

"Why did you name me Tara?" I run my fingers over the italic letters, the bracelet still in hiding. I can read them without looking. A-N-G-E-L-A.

"I already told you that," she says, staring at the road. I remember when Angela was my name. I remember when she took away that name. But I don't remember very much in between. Why don't I remember?

"What did I forget?" I'm asking myself as much as I'm asking her. I wiggle the bracelet out from inside doll Angela's neck and hold it up in front of me. I haven't worn it in twelve years.

"Where did you get that?" she asks and grabs for the piece of jewelry. The van swerves and almost hits the yellow sports car next to us. The driver flips Mother off and speeds away, but I keep the bracelet far from her grasp.

"My dad gave me this bracelet," I say, starting to remember more about my birth father after that memory from the pool. It's like something has been rattled loose inside of me that's been hidden away for a long time.

"You should throw that thing out too. If you want to live like an adult and be treated like an adult, you can't have those creepy dolls anymore. Give it to me." She takes Angela by the hair and tosses her out the window just like she disposed of the phone.

I should scream. It should hurt, but something is coming, something that's been hiding for a very long time, and I can't stop it. I stare at that flat sliver of metal in my palm and read the name over and over again. It reminds me of something.

Tracey's dad gave her a necklace. They showed pictures on the news. My life and Tracey's life start to blur together, lining up, the gaps that my dodgy memory couldn't seem to hold suddenly filled with the details I know from hers. Tracey. Angela. Tracey. Angela . . . Tracey . . . Angela. Angela. Angela. Angela.

◆ ◆ ◆

"Stupid babies," I grumbled as I sped down Churchill Boulevard, the bell on my ten-speed jangling over each crack in the sidewalk. If Mom and Dad didn't want me there anymore, I was going to find someone who did.

No one asked me if I wanted any babies, but they came anyway, and I was just supposed to be okay with it? They'd told me like it was nothing, that after seven years of being alone my whole world was going to change forever. Then they wanted me to be happy about it.

I stood up and pedaled faster to get up the hill, my legs burning as I reached the highest part of the ride. It was getting a little chilly this close to winter, and the wind whipped against my jacket. I kept one hand on the handlebars and pulled the hood tight around my face. Mama said it got better, that they'd be fun and say my name and want to be my best friends one day, but that was before she yelled at me and hurt me. I didn't want to live with her anymore.

I didn't look both ways. I remember that now. My hood covered the left half of my face, and I thought it was too early in the morning to be worried about cars, and the openness of the early morning sidewalk felt like an invitation to zoom through the neighborhood, falling leaves swirling around my legs and frantically spinning feet.

I didn't see it coming. My wheels flew out from under me, and the ground came rushing toward me in slow motion. All the sound was sucked out of the world until I hit the asphalt with a thud and a sickening scraping as I skittered across the rough black pavement.

My temple cracked the ground again, and the blow vibrated through my skull like it was happening over and over again. At first it was all shock, falling, and confusion, but then the pain hit. The sting of my skinned arms, raw and bleeding, ringing in my head that hurt like I was the dangling part of a giant bell. And breathing, breathing was hard. I could barely get my lungs to take in any oxygen. The more I tried, the tighter they became, sealed off like when my goldfish jumped out of its bowl and onto my Hello Kitty area rug.

Then a tall figure stood over me. I didn't know what the person was saying. I stopped trying to understand and curled up into a ball, sure I was going to throw up, but I didn't want to ruin the new white-and-black kitten shirt my mom had just brought home from JCPenney's.

"Oh, sweetie, I didn't see you. Why were you going so fast?" The voice finally broke through the ringing. It was soft and feminine with a slight Southern twang. She sounded so kind.

"Mommy," I gasped. "Please . . . my mommy . . ." The salt from my tears stung as they fell into the wounds on my arms. All I could think about was my mom, her face when it was kind, her soft arms, her gentle whisper telling me it was all going to be okay. This nice woman would find my mommy.

"Oh, you're bleeding." The woman pushed hair off my forehead, and her face came into focus. She was older than my mom. She had deep lines around her eyes and mouth, like she'd spent a lot of time laughing or maybe frowning. Her skin was still a rich tan from the summer months, and the smell of stale cigarette smoke on the woman's breath made my tummy turn.

"Please . . . call my mom," I begged, my mind slowly putting together the numbers to my mother's cell phone. "Four one five . . . ," I forced out, trying not to sob, every slight movement sending shocks of pain through my nerve endings.

"Shh. Oh, of course, darling. Please don't worry." The woman patted the top of my head gently, then stood up and walked away. The nice woman would help. She'd get help.

I listened for a phone call to my mother or 911, or a siren or a concerned bystander, but all I could make out was the swoosh of a van door and the clank of broken metal. My bike. It must be torn to bits. Mommy would be mad. She'd say I was careless. She'd say I should know better . . .

I flopped onto my back and tried to sit up, determined to make this all okay, but my head pounded, and I fell backward onto the ground, panting for breath. Then the woman was back by my side.

"My name is Angela Stoneking. Angela Kay Stoneking. I wanna go home," I whined, the shock starting to wear off and the brokenness of my body hitting with full force. Something was wrong with my leg—it wouldn't move. And my head . . . It felt like it was four times bigger than it should be, heavier too.

"You're safe now, sweetie," the nice woman crooned. She bent over, her stringy, faded blond hair covering me like a curtain. The nearly white hair was stained red as the frayed endings rubbed against the wounds on my face. I closed my eyes so I didn't have to see the woman's bloody hair as she slid her arms under my back and side.

"I want my mom," I choked out, and vomit dribbled out the sides of my mouth. Too tired to wipe the bitter fluid away, I let it flow down my cheek and neck, my eyes staring unfocused at the sidewalk I'd raced up so carelessly just a few minutes earlier. I imagined my mother running toward me, robe flapping out behind her like a superhero's cape. Yeah, she'd be mad about the bike, about the blood on my new shirt, and probably about the money for the doctor's visit, but one thing my mom was also very good at was making everything okay.

"Mommy," I whispered, wishing the dissolving vision of my superhero mommy could take a message home and slip it into my real mother's ear. A splitting pain went through my skull, vomit rising in my throat and flooding my mouth again. My head lolled back and forth, and the agony was too overwhelming. Blackness nibbled at the edges of my vision.

The woman laid my broken body in the back of a large white utility van, the kind the construction workers drove when our basement flooded in the spring. The partition between the front seats and the rear of the van was painted black, no light coming in from any part of the van, dark, empty. There were no seats in the back, and the floor was covered in a rough, tightly woven carpet that scraped at the raw wounds on my forearms and shoulder when the woman laid me down. I didn't want to be inside the van, but I also didn't know how to stop it from happening. My limbs were limp, and I was barely able to stay awake.

I whimpered again, holding on to the light for just a moment longer as the woman stepped back and went to close the van's sliding door.

"Is my mommy coming?" I asked, my head buried in my hair and the curve of my arms. The woman froze with her hand on the door handle.

She must be kind, I thought, a great hope ballooning inside me. *She must be.*

"Oh, sweet darling, don't you fret. Mother is here." A slow, almost loving smile filled the woman's face. "I will take care of you now."

She yanked at the door and jerked it closed with a clank of finality.

The wail of sirens and a sharp lane change to the right brings me back to reality.

"Keep your mouth shut, or else," Mother orders as she organizes her papers and driver's license and tosses the pregnancy suit and dress into the back of the van, and the meaning of my memory settles in. Mother took me just like she took Tracey. I had a home. I had a family. She's not my mother. She's my abductor.

When an officer wearing mirrored glasses taps at the window, Mother rolls it down politely.

"Hello, officer, nice to see you." She bats her eyes at him like she's trying to flirt and then passes her papers seamlessly, like she couldn't even care that we've been pulled over. He can't know what she is; I've lived with her for twelve years, and I didn't know, not really.

"Yes, uh, we had several reports of an altercation and erratic driving involving this vehicle. Is everything okay in here?"

No, it's not, I think, wishing he could read my mind. I've been taught to fear police officers, but today I look at him closely and try to think of a way to tell him I need help.

"We are just fine. There was a bee. My daughter is allergic. I'm so sorry, officer. It was an honest mistake." He glances over at me as if to check Mother's story. I sit frozen, trying to send him a silent SOS.

Save me. Please, save me.

He returns his attention to Mother and takes a closer look at her driver's license and insurance and then taps it on the doorframe.

"Well, everything here seems in order and, uh, no one was stung? Everyone is okay?"

I am not okay, I think. *Help me.*

"Yes, we are both just fine. Thank you, officer." She is short but polite. How can he not notice this is the white van covered on the news? But I guess there are probably thousands of white vans in the area.

"Okay, well, let me go run this, just so I have a record of our conversation in response to that call, and then you can be on your way. Sit tight." He knocks on the side of the van as he walks away, and it makes a hollow echoing sound, just like I feel inside. What has my family thought for all these years? Do they think I'm dead? Do they even miss me? Will they be angry that I didn't remember, that I believed Mother, that I didn't try to escape?

"I know you're planning something, so you'd better keep your mouth shut, or you know exactly what I'm going to do."

"What, hit another little girl with your van and then keep her prisoner in your house? Just like you did with me and Tracey? Is that what you're going to do?"

I finally speak the truth. It may only be to Mother, but there is power in saying it out loud. It's the greatest moment of rage and respite of my entire life. This woman is a thief—she is an expert at stealing things, but she's also an expert at stealing lives, and I want mine back. I'm not expendable. Neither is Tracey. What makes Lila Saunders so important that she thinks she can own us?

"You don't know what you're talking about," she huffs, like I'm a fool.

But she knows. She knows that I've finally remembered. No wonder she's kept me under lock and key all these years. I'm a weapon, a dangerous weapon who, in the wrong hands, could lead to her destruction.

"You kidnapped Tracey Monroe just like you stole Angela Stoneking, didn't you? Angela Kay Stoneking. That's my name. I remember. That's my name."

My eyes fill with tears, and I'm smiling through the realization. I can remember now.

My mom, she would sing to me at night and kiss my head, and my daddy would call me "Angela bo-bangela" when he left for work in the morning. They loved me. And my room had little twinkling lights around my bed and smelled like blueberries, and at school I was smart and had friends and loved recess and math. I was happy.

"Would you shut up?" Mother says, eyes wide and spittle gathering at the corners of her mouth. Her pupils are tiny, the size of pinholes. "If you say *anything*, that little girl will die."

The officer returns with Mother's license, registration, and insurance card and then takes one more long look at each of us. Mother, then me, Mother again, and then back at me. I want to speak, but it's impossibly hard with Mother right beside me.

Then the officer lifts his sunglasses and looks me directly in the eyes. When I meet his gaze, I don't see a hard or murderous soul. He looks concerned, deeply concerned, like he cares.

"Miss, are you sure you're okay?"

Mother starts to talk for me, and he hushes her with a swipe of his hand.

"I want to hear what this young lady has to say."

I stare at him. Mother sits between us, her jaw clenching and unclenching. She's consumed by her absolute fury, and I can see it pouring out of her into a river I'm petrified to wade through.

She will die, and it will be my fault loops through my mind like a video on repeat. Mother's threat is real to me, and as desperately as I want to scream out for help, I don't know how to save Angela and Tracey at the same time. I could easily tell him what I've been trained to say my whole life: "I'm okay" or "I'm happy" or "I don't need help."

But then again, if I don't speak up, I'm still killing Tracey Monroe. Mother killed Angela Kay Stoneking the day she hit me with her car and took what wasn't hers. I became scared, submissive, broken Tara. I can't let that happen again. I know who I am now. And damn it—I need help.

"My name is Angela Kay Stoneking," I say frantically, like he should know me personally or something. As soon as I start to speak, Mother talks over me, leaning forward so he can't see my face, holding me back with nails in my forearm.

"She's mentally ill, officer. She's been pretending she's a pregnant woman and hassling people. She doesn't know what she's saying. I'm her mother . . ."

I rip my arm away and sit forward, not using my silent wishes anymore but using my voice.

"My name is Angela Stoneking. I was taken when I was a little girl. She is *not* my mother. She took Tracey Monroe—"

Mother clamps her hand over my mouth.

The officer orders Mother to let me speak, to take her hands off me, but she doesn't listen. I tear her hand away and I scream.

I won't let her silence me ever again.

CHAPTER 32

Six weeks later

There's a real film crew at the Feelys' house today. They belong to *Fireline*, a news program that's chronicling my story and transition into the real world. Yesterday was spent in interviews and filming segments around town. Next week they'll head up to Mother's house and film there without me. Today we film my family reunion.

Henry rubs my shoulders, and I can't stop smiling.

"Do I look okay?" I ask him for the fiftieth time today, and for the fiftieth time he kisses my forehead.

"You look beautiful. You can keep asking me 'cause I will keep telling you the same thing."

"Well, at least you're consistent," I joke, and poke his rib cage playfully, nuzzling into his side, wondering if he could sit by me through the whole interview. For the past six weeks, Henry has been there for me, always. I didn't even have to ask. He's just—there. I wrap my arms around his midsection and give him an aggressive hug.

"Whoa, you've got some muscles there," he jokes, and I laugh. He doesn't know I'm saying thank you.

Henry was the first person to show up at the police station.

They wouldn't let him in until they confirmed that my fingerprints matched the tiny ones the police pulled from my bedroom twelve years ago when I went missing. Then he waited while I was interviewed and debriefed, had medical attention, and finally got the news that Tracey Monroe had been found safe, locked in a motel bathroom.

He waited through it all. For ten hours that man sat in the waiting room just so he could be the first one to see me. But he wasn't the first—first I met my parents.

It was surreal, like I was standing outside of my body watching a scene from a television show, a blur of faces, tears, and questions I didn't have answers for. They were strangers to me, hazy memories that I still had trouble focusing on after the traumatic brain injury of that first night with Mother.

Claire Stoneking was a tired, older version of the mom from my memories. That day her eyes were red rimmed, and her cheeks were stained with watered-down trails of mascara. My dad, Scott Stoneking, was thin and frail looking, with wire-rimmed glasses and stooped shoulders like he'd been carrying around an invisible burden for too long.

He tried to hold my mom up when her knees gave out as they walked in the room, but I don't think he's strong enough to hold anyone anymore. I'm sure they wanted me to be their eight-year-old Angela, not the twenty-year-old woman wrapped in an emergency blanket, sipping on Gatorade and holding a trash can, still sick with a stomach flu.

My mom knelt at my feet and reached up to pet my hair and apologized for our fight from twelve years ago. She begged for my forgiveness, and I think she wanted me to comfort her, but I couldn't. I kept my arms around the blue plastic bin, overwhelmed by it all. Maybe seeing the lost, faraway look in my eye, my dad rushed in to help.

"Welcome home, Angela bo-bangela" was all he said as he took my mom by the elbow and escorted her out of the room, and I could breathe again. I didn't want to see them—my parents. I wasn't ready yet.

But I did want to see Henry.

He was almost shy as he walked into the conference room where I was being held, but as soon as I smiled, he rushed over, stopping short of hugging me. I understand why he didn't touch me—I'd kept everyone so far away for so long—but without a secret, I was starting to long for connection.

"Oh my gosh, you're tiny," he said. We still laugh that this was his first thought after knowing me as a massively pregnant woman for two months. He wasn't judgmental or angry, he was proud of me. Mother used to look proud of me when I submitted, when I was a good little girl, and I remember how proud Alyssa seemed that I'd left my "boyfriend" when I first moved in with the Feely family, but this was the first time someone looked proud of me because of who I really am. I liked it. A lot.

The whole Feely family came a few hours later, including Stan. He barely made eye contact, and I could tell from his posture alone that he hadn't told anyone about our altercation. I hadn't either. My parents offered to take me home with them and see how the twins had grown, but I still wasn't ready. And Alyssa wanted me to go home with her and Stan, but I couldn't go back there, keep pretending that nothing had happened, and live in fear that Stan might try again.

So I went home with Henry temporarily. He slept on the couch, and I hid in his bedroom, avoiding the TV and computer for days. Jen would come over, and they'd order takeout and offer it to me through the closed door. I knew that if I talked to Henry and the Feelys, I'd have to tell someone about Stan. I was done with secrets, and yet here I was hanging on to an incredibly important one. So I hid.

Until one night, about a week after Mother's arrest, just after Jen had left for the evening and the TV droned in the background, I snuck out of my room. Henry was already settled in on the couch and looked half-asleep, but when he saw me standing by the edge of the coffee table, he sat up with a start.

"Hey! I was wondering if we'd have to send in a rescue team or something," he said, sliding on a pair of glasses and sitting up to make space on the couch. "Wanna talk?"

I nodded. I was finally ready, and once I started telling him my story, the fuzzy bits becoming clearer every day, I didn't want to stop. We sat and talked for hours about my life with Mother, we reviewed all of my lies since meeting him, and I told him where I'd been living. He didn't interrupt or give advice. He just listened and sometimes cringed, and once or twice he looked like he was going to cry, but he never did. Eventually, at about two a.m., I felt ready, and I hesitantly told him about Stan.

"Are you shitting me?" Henry blurted out when all the details came together, hands becoming fists.

I shook my head. It was one thing for him to hear about what happened to me long ago or at the hands of a stranger, but with Stan . . . this was Henry's real life. I hoped I'd made the right decision telling him.

His face went red, fist slamming the armrest. "Oh my god, that asshole. No wonder you didn't want to stay at their house. Are you okay?"

"I'm fine," I said, a bit unprepared for his aggressive reaction. Too many other things had happened since Stan's unwanted advances. I was numb in so many ways I didn't know what I was feeling.

"It's not fine," he said, his face white, fury draining the color away. "Was this the first time?"

What a strange question. The first time? I wasn't sure what he meant, shutting down a little in response to his unexpected anger. I didn't expect the murderous look in his eye or the unmistakable rapid pounding of blood at his jugular.

"Yeah. The only time."

He nodded like he was calculating a math problem mentally, faking a cool disposition.

"Thank god," he huffed, rocking on his seat cushion. "When Alyssa hears about this, she's gonna lose it. You're gonna tell her, right?"

"I want to. I've wanted to since . . . you know . . . but . . ."

"You've got to," he said, reaching for his phone, like he wanted to do it right then and there.

"Wait, not yet. I'm not ready." I knew it was the right thing to do, but I also hated the heavy, slimy rock of shame that burrowed deeper into my stomach. Because I cared so much about my Feely "father," I think I'd let myself be blinded by my fantasies about what a father would be like in my life.

Henry was struggling too; he couldn't settle down, shifting and muttering.

"But he's not going to stop if you don't. This isn't the first time for him. He can't keep doing this to us."

There it was again.

"What do you mean, 'not the first time'?" I asked, nothing to lose anymore. Fists up to his temples, he took a deep breath through his nose and then out again, his eyes pinched shut.

"Stan, he keeps doing this shit. Like, he hit on Jen when she first started, but you know Jen, she's fierce. She told Alyssa, but Alyssa didn't want to hear it, not really. Claiming budget cuts, she downgraded Jen's position and started looking for an intern. At first I assumed that's why she picked you, 'cause you were . . . or looked . . . pregnant."

I folded my hands against my flat abdomen, surprised at how painful it was to think of Alyssa choosing me because I was the most undesirable. But I also know what it feels like to be Alyssa, a little at least. She wants to please Stan like I used to want to please Mother.

"If I tell her, will she leave him?" I asked, trying to reason through what he was saying. He opened his eyes, covered his mouth, lowered his hands, and made eye contact with me.

"Who knows? Maybe?" He shifted to face me. "You know what I can't stop thinking about lately? When you told me that I shouldn't be working there anymore. I kept asking myself why, why did I stay? You know what I realized? It's 'cause of my dad. I hate that man, but I still do all the shit he wants me to do. And we're all doing it, we're all letting that asshole run our lives. He hurts us. He hurt you. He hurt my mom, and she drank herself to death. Why do we stay with this man?"

Henry was bordering on frantic, and I knew exactly the futility he was experiencing. The stuck feeling that builds invisible barriers in your life, turning your world into a prison that seems impossible to escape. But I also knew something else—I knew it was possible to get out.

"Henry, stop," I said firmly, probably harsher than I'd ever spoken to him. I looked deep into his pleading eyes. There I found shame and regret; it was the same burden I saw in my parents' eyes and in my own. "It's not your fault. You know, I waited a long time for someone stronger than me to whisk me away to safety. No one ever came, but I still got out." A little unexpected sob caught in my throat. I coughed it away.

"I'm such a selfish asshole. I just made everything about me. I'm so sorry—your stuff is so much harder," he said.

"No," I said. I tried to reword my explanation, understanding something I'd been running from since I broke out of Mother's kitchen door. "It's not about the locks, Henry, or heroes. It's about feeling worthy enough to have something better."

"What if Alyssa doesn't listen? What if she won't leave?" he asked, still kind of missing my point. I turned and matched his posture, leaning forward, our knees close to touching.

"Then *you* leave and show her it's possible," I said, sure of one thing in my life: I would never sit by and let someone I cared about be hurt and controlled again. That meant Alyssa and her kids, and I was starting to find that meant Henry too. I'd thought I loved Stan Feely, but he wasn't the man he appeared to be through the computer screen. If I'd been watching closer in real life, I'd have recognized myself in Henry, a child, continually falling through the trapdoor of wanting to please his parent.

"Damn, you're so strong," he finally said, his eyes never breaking from mine as he slowly began to understand what I was saying.

Strong. I don't know why, but the word offended me. I was never some hulking giant with bulging muscles that pounded my way out of a bad situation. I was a frail, broken child who survived long enough to escape.

"I'm definitely not strong," I chuckled, lifting my bony arms as evidence. He laughed back, and it felt good to have a break from the enormity of the situation. "But you don't have to be strong. You have to be . . . I don't know . . . ready, I guess."

"I'm beyond ready," he said, leaning forward, his fingers twitching like he wanted to take my hand but knew better.

"Good." I put my hand on his. It was warm and slightly rough, but in a way that made me want to hold on tighter. I didn't let go, and he didn't try to make me.

It took a little while to settle into my new life, but once Tracey's discovery hit the news and my updated story of survival followed quickly behind, our world exploded. Subscribers barely noticed Stan's absence on AllTheFeels, and our numbers went through the roof as soon as the backstory of Angela Stoneking was linked to the family vlog.

Apparently, I was a pretty famous missing little girl. I'd disappeared early one morning in a "nice" middle-class neighborhood. There had been searches and pledge drives and candlelight vigils, and eventually memorial services. Everyone thought I was dead.

"They just pulled up," Connor announces, watching out the front window, and I get that old urge to hide. It's so hard to let myself be seen. By far the scariest thing I've ever done.

Ryland has decided to document the event with his handwritten "notes" of colorful scribbles that he keeps dropping all over the house. Alyssa snags a few to keep but recycles the rest when he's not looking, shooing me toward the front door and production team. I like this version of Alyssa. She's not nervous or sad all the time. I don't think she's reached happy yet, but ever since Stan moved out, she seems to be at peace more often than not.

Henry flips me around and puts his hands on my hips. I love his hands on me now. They're strong but gentle, and the way he touches me makes me feel more beautiful than I'll ever be in reality.

"Angela Kay Stoneking, are you ready?" His dark eyebrows raise up so far that they get lost under the loose curls hanging down his forehead.

"What if they don't like me?" I ask. It sounds silly, but what if it's true?

"They will love you." He says it in a way that lets me know he believes it even if I don't. I still haven't figured out Henry, the world behind his ocean eyes and how he's still seeing things inside of me that no one else does.

"Well, they have to say they love me. I'm their long-lost daughter." I'm trying to make a joke, but I mean every word.

"Angie, they will love you because you're their daughter, but they will also love you because you're you. You don't have to be perfect."

I bite my lip and start to shake my head but stop. I watched the Feely family for five years, and I thought they were perfect. In the past three months, I've gotten to know the real Feely family, and in their imperfection I've come to find that almost every family member is perfect for me in their own way, flaws and all.

"Do you think they can forgive me for taking so long? You know, for being such a coward?" It's my biggest fear, that they'll think I rejected them just like I thought for so many years they rejected me. Henry pulls me into his arms, and I rest my head in that special spot on his chest where I fit just perfectly.

"You are no coward, Angela. There is only one coward in this story, and she's in jail." He kisses my hair, and I want to tell him the words I've been storing up inside of me. I'll wait until I'm sure, but I think I'm right. I'm pretty sure I'm in love.

"Thank you." I rise up on my toes and give him a light kiss so I don't get lip gloss all over his face, but he doesn't seem to mind and pulls me in.

"Here they come. Here they come," Ryland chants, and Henry reluctantly lets me go. The TV host waves me forward, cameras rolling. I'm supposed to be the one to open the door and welcome my parents inside.

Through the front window I can see them approaching, Claire and Scott Stoneking, my real mother and father. Through the glass they look happier than they were at the police station. My mom is walking on her own without my dad keeping her steady, and my dad looks like he's grown half a foot now that his shoulders are straight and he's standing tall.

The doorbell rings, and I position myself behind the door, hand on the knob. I close my eyes and let out an unsteady breath, a million questions scrambling through my mind. Will this time be different? Can I love them? Did they miss me? Can we ever be a family again?

I open my eyes; I'm finally ready to meet my parents. I pull on the handle and yank hard, hoping for a dramatic swoosh, but instead the dead bolt thuds. It's locked.

A production assistant swears in the background and lunges forward to unlock the door, but I shoo him away with a wave and cover the lock with my hand. This piece of metal used to be the sentry of my private world, beautiful in its simplicity. It kept me inside and kept others out. But now, the cool metal warming against my touch is under my control.

It's time. My heart pounds, not just in my chest but in my ears and throat and shoulders, and I'm right on the edge of tears. I let them come—today I'm allowed to cry. I grasp the latch and twist. It scratches open, and I swing the door inward, finally ready to be seen.

ACKNOWLEDGMENTS

First, I'd like to thank all my readers for sticking with me, always asking, "When is your next book coming out?" and investing your time into reading my stories. You are my true inspiration. I never could've envisioned that so many "strangers" would touch my life, live inside of my imaginary worlds, and come to love the characters and stories that for so long had existed only inside of my mind.

And to my new extended family at Improv Playhouse—I started taking classes at iP to learn more about story and character as a writer and to step outside of my comfort zone as a human. But after a year of classes and another half a year performing with some truly talented improvisers, I've learned far more than I ever could've hoped when I started out. I'm so grateful for this little family. Funny family. Yeah—a really, really funny family.

My friend Joanne Osmond, thank you for being an inspiration and for being there for me always. But also thank you for letting me be there for you occasionally too. Your drive and endurance are a beautiful inspiration to me. I love you. I'm proud of you. I'm positive Bud is proud of you too. Let's keep doing the hard things, okay, friend?

Kelli Swofford Nielsen—you know what I love about you? You teach me to keep striving and to never laugh at the needs of my creative soul. You help me keep perspective, and somehow you always know just the right thing to say. I can say in all honesty that I would not be the author or woman I am today without you.

To my burgeoning writers' group, we are tiny but mighty. Your talent and passion fill me with so much anticipation for your ever-growing success and help me grow into a better writer with each meeting.

Sheila M. Lin—I adore your poet's heart, mind, and soul. Thank you for showing me how to write with stunning vulnerability and for sending me haikus via snail mail. ☺

Matt Hellyer—the depth you bring to your writing and feedback is a boon to our group and to me personally as a writer. Your passion for creativity and literature is contagious, and I hope you keep passing it on with the same speed and intensity as rats spread the black plague.

Keith Johns—you, sir, are a dang good writer (among a wealth of other talents). Thank you for sharing your experience and dreams. Most of all, thank you for sharing the rare commodity of positivity—it is a rising tide that lifts us all.

Chip Hosken—it's been so fascinating getting to know you as a friend and a writer. Thank you for taking risks, adulting like a pro, celebrating the sink empty of dishes as heartily as the met deadline, and sometimes just telling me to get to work.

Lorena Vazquez—woman, you not only tell me to do things that scare me but you show me how through your example. You are an incredibly talented human. It's almost not fair—nope, just checked—it is OFFICIALLY not fair. Keep doing all the scary things, and let's keep inviting each other to jump off life's cliffs. I'll be your safety net if you'll be mine. You're a good friend.

Speaking of good friends, my IGP friends who came up through the ranks with me—Nora Benjamin, Karen Schaffroth, and Lorena Vazquez—you've made my life full and been there for all my big moments. Thank you for brunches, walks, video chats, karaoke, improv, and too many orders of chips and salsa to count . . . oh . . . most importantly for always being my soft place to fall . . . you know . . . that little thing that changed my whole world. Wanna be BFFs? To that, I say—Yes, Please.

To my developmental editor extraordinaire, Tiffany Yates Martin, I joke that I want to start a fan club themed entirely around your awesomeness, but what you don't know is one already exists. Every author I've met who has worked with you sings your praises, and I know why— you rock. Obviously. Thank you for your honesty, guidance, and most of all patience. It is a joy working with you.

Chris Werner, I don't know if anyone has ever told you this, but you should be an editor or something . . . oh wait . . . Hey, I can't stop thanking you for signing on to this project and sticking with it even through illness and rewrites. I respect your feedback and feel creatively heard and understood by you, and that is an immense benefit to me as an author.

On that note, I have to say, I feel like Lake Union and the author team there is full of stellar people. I'd be remiss not to thank you all. When I became so, so ill last fall, you all met me with nothing but care, understanding, and a desire to help me through what would turn out to be one of the toughest times in my life. You were patient, kind, and thoughtful, and held on to some faith in me that I'd almost lost for myself. I'm stronger now, and with some time and distance from my trial, I can see the "helpers," and this team lands squarely on that list.

Another helper who is a constant in my life is my agent, Marlene Stringer. Marlene, you look out for me. I can sincerely say that I know you have my best interests at heart. I respect you professionally, but I also look up to you as an individual. Thank you for being such a great example and for putting in all the hard work that continues to make my dreams come true.

Mom and Dad—this sure was a crazy year, wasn't it? You are unfailingly there for me and my kids. Dad, thank you for spending ENDLESS HOURS on the phone with me and by my side as I went through hospital visits and surgery. I'm so glad my story had a happy ending this time, but knowing you were there for me helped me feel safe.

My sister, Elizabeth Sadler, you are one of the strongest women I know. You are making me so proud. Thank you for all your time and help and for pushing me to see myself the way you see me. I can't wait to find out what the future holds for you.

And my kids, who all asked to be named PERSONALLY (cough, cough—I'm doing it—cough, cough): Johnny, Brandon, Thomas, and Maddie—you are growing up so fast, insanely fast, and sometimes I want to tell you to slow down, but then I think about who you've grown into already. Every day you are becoming humans that I not only *love* ('cause I grew you and fed you and all that jazz) but also humans that I *like*—a lot. You are clever, kind, resilient, generous, and insightful. So, I guess instead of telling you to stop growing up, I'll say something more like—keep up the good work. I'm grateful for who you are and who you are growing into every single day. I love you, you four. You are my world.

ABOUT THE AUTHOR

Photo © 2019 Organic Headshots

Emily Bleeker is a former educator who learned to love writing while teaching a writers' workshop. After surviving a battle with a rare form of cancer, she finally found the courage to share her stories, starting with her debut novel, *Wreckage*, and followed by *When I'm Gone* (a *Wall Street Journal* bestseller), *Working Fire*, and *The Waiting Room*. Emily currently lives with her family in suburban Chicago. Connect with her or request a Skype visit with your book club at www.emilybleeker.com.